Much Ado About Dukes

USA TODAY BESTSELLING AUTHOR

EVA DEVON

Entangled Publishing, LLC
644 Shrewsbury Commons Ave., STE 181
Shrewsbury, PA 17361
Visit our website at www.entangledpublishing.com.

Amara is an imprint of Entangled Publishing, LLC.

Edited by Lydia Sharp
Cover art and design by Bree Archer
Photographer: Chris Cocozza
Stock Art Credit: bonetta/gettyimages
Interior design by Toni Kerr

Print ISBN 978-1-64937-140-9
ebook ISBN 978-1-64937-159-1

Manufactured in the United States of America

First Edition September 2022

AMARA

ALSO BY EVA DEVON

For Esaul, Ciaran, Declan, and Fionn.
In the storms of life, together we are a safe harbor.
I have so much love for you all,
no words will suffice.

CHAPTER ONE

Lady Beatrice Haven could not wait to give the Duke of Blackheath a devil of a time. Tonight, he would not be able to evade her, and she relished the possible adventure before her.

Even so, she was not particularly excited to call the man family. She *tsk*ed playfully and asked her dearest cousin, "Surely, *anyone* but him would be better?"

Him, in this particular case, was not the Duke of Blackheath but his younger brother. Blackheath was an elusive, infuriating person. It was the greatest of oddities that her cousin had thrown her lot in with his younger brother, Lord Christopher. Kit to his friends.

Of which Kit had many.

That was a shock, given what a frustrating fellow of a brother he had.

Margaret grinned, even as her blond brows rose at Beatrice's teasing but honest question. "Cousin, I'm in love with him. So, of course it must be *him*."

"But why?" Beatrice insisted, tugging at her long silk gloves. "Why fall in love with Lord Christopher? He is a fine man, but surely there are finer."

Margaret arched a tolerant brow. "It is not Lord Christopher you dislike."

Beatrice's cousin sat but a short distance away on the opposite bench of her uncle's well-appointed coach, with only the glow of moonlight to illuminate them. Her uncle was unusually quiet in his corner, but he watched with a loving expression as the two of them sallied.

Beatrice scowled, for her uncle was supremely happy about his daughter's match. Blackheath's family was one of the most powerful and wealthy in all the land.

He was a significant connection. Not one to be trifled with.

Even so, she sighed. "It is true that I find his brother to be arrogant. The duke does not deign to speak to mere mortals such as myself. This will be an impossible situation. I shall be *related* to *him*."

Beatrice shuddered. She'd never met the duke—but she did not need to see him in person to know he was a toad.

"Not related by blood," Maggie said, her blue eyes lilting with amusement. For she knew that Beatrice would never stand in the way of her happiness, even if her choice of husband was vexatious in the extreme.

Beatrice harrumphed and pushed her spectacles—which did not need pushing—up her nose. "It does not matter. I shall be forced to go to engagements and family arrangements with him." With exaggerated woe, she asked, "However shall I bear it?"

Maggie laughed deeply. "You shall bear, cousin, because you will hardly need to spend two minutes in his company if you so choose. We shall seat you at opposite ends of our table, so you shall never have to entertain him. But you must promise not to bite."

Beatrice grinned, for she enjoyed a good debate

and anticipated one this evening. "I cannot make such a promise. Though, the idea that I should act so irrationally—"

"And you shall bear it because you love me," cut in Maggie. "You know, I think that you like writing all those ferocious letters to His Grace."

Beatrice swept a nonexistent bit of fluff from her skirt. "How can you say such an atrocious thing? He is a duke."

Aside from that, what had frustrated her most were his terse replies that expressed thanks for her concern and an assurance that he had the matter of the *conditions of ladies* in hand.

Ha!

After throwing herself into the field of pamphlet writing, public speaking, and the joining of a blue-stocking league, the truth was Beatrice had grown to hate dukes. *All* dukes. Not just Blackheath, though he certainly deserved her particular attention with his arrogant dismissals.

Yes, all dukes were the very devil because they represented the thing she loathed with all her passion—the upholding of laws that kept her so wholly without rights.

Worse still, they so often upheld the trade which enslaved thousands in their territories in the West Indies. In her estimation, rights were for everyone. The world was full of injustice, and she couldn't stand idly by, sipping lemonade.

In fact, she had even followed Barbara Wilberforce's advice and stopped taking sugar altogether, for, like Mrs. Wilberforce, she could not forget the cruelty with which it was made.

Beatrice had a mission in this life, and that was to improve the fate of those trodden upon by the powerful, and dukes were always getting in the way, as far as she could tell. None of them did as they should—protest loudly and fully in Parliament that rights belonged to more than a few landed gentlemen.

Luckily, she had enough money on her own that she could make some protestations, and she had a seemingly indulgent uncle.

Even now, her uncle sat beside Maggie, his arms folded lightly over his strong chest. He had his silvery, shaggy brows raised in mock alarm.

"Beatrice," he warned gently. "You cannot have such an attitude in society."

"That is precisely why it is not a society I want to sustain," Beatrice said, a bit surprised by her uncle's comment, for he'd never suggested she contain herself to society's edicts before. She smiled at him, hoping to better his mood. "You are on my side, are you not?"

"Indeed, I am, Beatrice," he assured, though he seemed a bit strained. "But there comes a time in every lady's life when she must take up the yoke of matrimony."

"Yoke, indeed," she replied. "Do I look like an ox?"

"No," her uncle said. "You look like a lady, and ladies must marry."

"Do not *must* me. That is the most ridiculous drivel. I have the privilege of independence, and I shall not give a gentleman my property or my freedom," Beatrice retorted evenly. The truth was…she didn't hate marriage, exactly. It was more that she'd seen how much unhappiness it caused. Except in one case—her parents' marriage. They had loved each other so fully, with such loyalty, respect, and affinity, she'd never, ever be able to settle for anything less. As she'd grown older and become more aware of the harsh realities in this world, she realized her parents had been a veritable miracle. And because of the way they had treated each other, she'd accept nothing but the miraculous for herself.

A life of tolerance was one she could not...well, tolerate. And thankfully, unlike other young ladies, she did not have to.

"We all must do things and accept our roles, Beatrice. It is the way of the world," her uncle pointed out.

Such thinking, though she cared for her uncle, permitted the worst of things to continue unchallenged.

She eyed him carefully. "Are you about to tell me that I need to make a marriage, uncle?"

He was silent for a moment, and she felt a hint of dread.

Could he?

He'd always been incredibly supportive of the fact that she had no wish to marry, largely due to the fact that she had a private fortune from her parents, who had passed ten years ago. Her uncle had been an indulgent guardian and kind and given her much education and support in her endeavors. She had always appreciated him as a man of good sense. But now, as he sat beside her cousin, with Maggie's arm tucked in his, pleased as punch that his daughter was likely to marry the brother of a duke, Beatrice wondered...

No, no. She would not contemplate it.

"I, for one, am eager to marry," Maggie said, looking positively besotted. "I adore Kit. He is the most marvelous man in all of London."

"This cannot possibly be true," she replied flatly. "There is no marvelous man, save uncle here." She spotted the consternation worrying Maggie's brow and decided to relent. A bit. "But I will say that he is tolerable compared to his brother."

"His brother is not so very terrible," Maggie defended. "He does a great deal of good work."

"Indeed. On his terms, with no understanding or consultation of the people he deigns to assist. His arrogance is breathtaking," she returned.

"He is a duke," her uncle pointed out, as if it explained everything.

And largely, it did. She didn't have to like it, but neither did she have to leave it unchallenged—and challenge it she would, for she had the means and the ability. It was her duty to do better.

"Tonight, he shall not escape me," she said. "He cannot cast me aside as he did my letters. And he shall hear my case."

Both her uncle and Maggie let out simultaneous noises of alarm.

"Must you?" Maggie queried, her voice slightly strained.

"Indeed, I must," she affirmed. "For if no one else does, we shall be in a great deal of trouble and women shall continue to be shunted aside, mere codicils in the annals of history."

"Yes, yes," Maggie soothed. "We know, Beatrice. You are most articulate, and we appreciate your point of view. And I stand beside you, a sister in the bluestocking cause, yet I wish to marry. Can you not be happy for me?"

Beatrice stared at Maggie's beautiful visage for several moments, and her heart softened. "Of course, I'm happy for you," she said. "You are a wonderful friend, and I would never wish ill upon you."

Maggie nodded. "Thank you."

She shifted on her seat as the coach rolled up before the great house of the Duke of Blackheath. She stared up at the towering edifice that put to shame every other building in London.

It was going to be a long night.

Beatrice pulled her pamphlets from her reticule and clutched them. Her uncle rolled his eyes but made no protest.

She knew she was rather single-minded and that it could prove tiresome on occasion. But if no one was as tiresome as she was, nothing would get done.

Once the carriage stopped, she waited quietly for the footman to open the door.

Then it swung open, the coach step unfolded, and her cousin took the footman's gloved hand eagerly before she bounded out with great excitement.

Beatrice marched down after her, eager to enter the fray.

Adjusting her long silk skirts, she squared her shoulders. She adored the feel of the perfect gown swaying about her legs. It was a delicious feeling. For she did like a beautiful dress. It made her feel *more* powerful, not less. Though hers was not as bedecked

as some, she'd taken inspiration from the fiercest of
Grecian goddesses in the choosing of it.

At last, she bit back a small sigh of wonder. It really was one of the most magnificent houses in
England. Torches lined the walkway, casting a gold-
and-red glow along the pavement. Doric columns
soared into the air, supporting a portico that was
embossed with the most beautiful depiction of
Greek gods. The Blackheath ducal line knew art, and
they supported artists and intellectuals.

She couldn't hate the Duke of Blackheath. Not
entirely. Anyone who gave as much as he did to the
arts and published orations in the support of the
theater couldn't be wholly bad. But she did find him
to be incredibly frustrating.

One might argue it was through her frustrations
that her cousin Maggie had fallen in love with the
Duke of Blackheath's brother, Kit. A galling state of
affairs.

Beatrice had attempted to meet Blackheath so
many times and written him so many letters; then,
finally, one night when Kit asked Maggie to dance,
she had in turn asked if his brother, the duke, might
meet with Beatrice.

Kit had told Maggie that his brother would simply never meet with Beatrice.

He was far too *busy.*

She still didn't know how Maggie had fallen in
love with Kit after he said such a thing. But the
world was full of vagaries and mystery. There was no
getting around it. Maggie had lost her heart.

One would have thought that after weeks of his
brother courting her cousin, Beatrice would have

met Blackheath by now. Their families were almost certainly going to be united soon. It was likely that Kit would propose to her this very night.

One would have thought, indeed, that this would have ensured their paths would cross. But no, Blackheath proved ever elusive. He was always taken up with affairs of state, always doing something, always at work.

And apparently, he didn't like to attend parties, even though he had a reputation as an excellent host.

Suddenly, with furrowed brow, her uncle turned to her and said, "My dear, it's not such a very terrible thing. You might find yourself married before you know it."

Beatrice faced him and replied playfully, "Uncle, though doctors have called my sight in to question, I can see a church and a groom well in advance, and the moment I spot them, I shall hie myself hence." She shook her head, which caused her dark, curled hair to tease her neck. "I shall not find myself married any time soon."

Her uncle laughed, but it was a half groan. "Whatever you say, Beatrice. Whatever you say. I shall not argue. You would make an excellent lawyer."

"I would. If I were but allowed to study for the profession."

"Have done, love. Have done," her uncle urged before taking her hand in his and giving it a loving squeeze.

And then he followed the two women up the crowded set of stairs to the house.

The huge opening of the entryway glowed gold, and the sound of laughter and joy spilled out of the house. She thought it quite irritating that a man who refused to meet with her held such wonderful parties.

Everyone agreed the Duke of Blackheath gave the best parties, even if he frequently didn't attend them.

She allowed herself to listen for a moment and caught her heart swelling to the sounds.

The music floating toward them was sublime, for the Duke of Blackheath supported the arts. He liked all sorts of music, and he enthusiastically gave money to those who enjoyed playing. His generosity was widely known.

Surely, such a soul could be brought on side? For how could anyone so inclined toward assistance be willfully unhelpful? Surely, once he understood her, he would jump at the chance to aid her.

As they crossed over the threshold and handed aside their cloaks to a footman in emerald-and gold livery, Maggie turned to her. Her cobalt eyes rounded with alarm, and she pressed a gloved hand to her bosom. Her fingers brushed the silver ribbons woven through the fashionably low-cut, blue silk bodice. "Oh, dear. Beatrice, you have that look in your eyes."

"What look?" Beatrice asked innocently.

Maggie cocked her head to the side, and the diamond flower in her hair quivered. "The look of a bull about to charge."

"You know so very much about bulls?" she quipped.

Maggie grew resolute, a condition she did not often take up. "Now, listen here, Beatrice. Please do not cause a scene tonight. I beg of you. I want this to go well."

"A scene?" Beatrice gasped, blinking. "I am a well-mannered lady. I will simply blend in."

Maggie laughed, linking arms with her cousin's. "Oh, Beatrice, I love you. But do you think you might, well…do you need to show him your pamphlet this evening? Can it not wait?"

"I have waited for months," Beatrice replied evenly.

Maggie nodded, resigned, even as countless guests swarmed about them like busy, excited bees doing their work for their queen—or, in this case, their duke. "I suppose I understand your tenacity, but…"

And then Beatrice leaned forward and whispered firmly, "Maggie, I should never ruin your night, and I should never make things ill for you. I promise I shall be on my best behavior in public."

Maggie's eyes narrowed ever so slightly. "In public? What does that mean?"

"I shall not cause any gossip or difficulty for you," she vowed quite earnestly as they made their way through the crush of people. "This shall be a lovely night for you. I shall do everything that I can to support you, just as you have supported me, even if we have different ideas about love and matrimony."

Maggie beamed, and that smile was worth a thousand promises of goodwill. "Thank you, Beatrice. That's all I wished to hear."

And without ado, they were swept into the crowd of people entering into the ballroom. The music poured over them, and Beatrice girded her loins. Tonight, she would not be ignored.

CHAPTER TWO

William Leonidis Maximillian Easton, Duke of Blackheath, had a secret regarding Lady Beatrice. One he would never confess to anyone.

He admired her. Intensely. Too intensely, in his opinion.

For the one thing that Will forbade himself in any capacity was undue intensity. He already struggled mightily with a melancholic streak, and anything which caused him to feel too much? Well, it was to be avoided at all costs.

And Lady Beatrice's letters made him feel.

At first, he had not even known about the stack of increasingly passionate calls to action. But then he'd discovered that his secretary had taken it upon himself to "protect" Will from the "hysterical" young lady's letters. His secretary's words, not his.

Will had come to find out that his man of business had been keeping her letters from him, which was appalling. He needed protection from no one. Not even passionate bluestockings. He'd defended himself against French cavalry—he could defend himself, without aid, if necessary, from a lady.

But his secretary had intoned that letters from young ladies were a waste of time for the duke.

Will had fired the man on the spot.

Those letters… By God, they were the stuff of philosophers and held such sincere desire for justice that he had been awed. He had savored every word.

Every turn of phrase. Every resplendent, skewering argument.

Lady Beatrice Haven was a wonder. He had immediately liked her and liked her well. And so? He had avoided her at all costs.

Attachments, on his part, were simply not permissible. And he had felt the dangerous pull of her, from words scribed on the pages that he had held carefully in his hands.

Most would argue that a duke had no time to be reading little pamphlets and letters by such a person, who had no political position. He still had read them. Often late in the evening, after the rest of his work was done, over a snifter of brandy. He'd written her several assurances he would do his best for her.

This had not appeased her. In one regard, he was glad. She had kept writing.

Yes, he admired her spirit and dedication.

But passion blazed from her every sentence, and passion was not something in which he could indulge.

So, as he stood in the ballroom, knowing that he was likely going to come into contact with Lady Beatrice this evening, he drew in a deep breath and squared his shoulders.

He was a man of action.

He had seen war.

He would survive this night without turning into a besotted fool, and he certainly wouldn't yield to the amorous whispering that had bombarded him since he had first discovered those damned letters. His parents' marriage had taught him the importance of self-discipline and reserve.

Passion was not for him.

His brother, Kit, eyed him strangely and cocked his head to the side. "Are you about to suffer apoplexy, brother? You do look most perplexed."

"This cousin of your beloved…" He shook his head. "I do not know how I shall negotiate this evening."

Their younger brother, Ben, approached, a flute of champagne in his gloved hand. Benjamin had just been sent down from Oxford, a rake and a rogue. And with the budding skills of a spy, for he said boldly, "Her cousin is not so very bad."

"I quite like her," added Kit, clearly enjoying his older brother's discomfort.

"Do you, by God?" He cleared his throat, determined not to relay his actual feelings. "I have heard the worst possible tales."

Ben *tsk*ed, his dark eyes shining with mirth. "I never thought you were one to listen to gossip."

"Gossip?" Will echoed, recalling the various accounts he had heard and marveling at them. "These are testaments, not gossip."

He swallowed a laugh and arched his brow as he brought one particular account to mind. "She likes to go down to Parliament and holler at parliamentarians."

"That is not so very odd," returned Kit.

Ben took a long drink of champagne before pointing out, most annoyingly, "*You* like to holler at parliamentarians."

He narrowed his gaze at his brother, whom he loved well, and so replied, "That is different, puppy.

I'm a duke. I'm allowed to holler at parliamentarians. As a matter of fact, it's my job to do so."

Undeterred, Ben continued, "Yes, but I think she would like to do that as a profession."

"Ladies aren't allowed such a profession," Kit pointed out firmly.

Ben laughed. "I think she'd like to change that."

And then Kit shuddered. "Can you imagine? Ladies in Parliament?"

Actually, Will could.

He believed that ladies should have more possibilities in this life. He thought of his mother, who had bolted from their family home whilst he'd been a child. Ben had been in the nursery.

In the darkest, quietest moments of the night, he could still see her face leaning over his bed, tears in her eyes…

She'd fled to the continent because she could not bear the chains of motherhood and womanhood in England. Or at least, so their father had told him… when he'd spoken of her at all.

Thus, he could imagine why Lady Beatrice wished more for the fairer sex. And yet, he couldn't quite bear the idea of being alone with her. A woman like Beatrice? Her words had already ignited a fire within him. A fire he was determined to keep banked.

For he had seen the destruction that such fires could cause. He still tasted the ashes of it, alone in his chambers when the past came calling with bitter memories.

Still, tonight, for his brother, he would endure it. Dukes had to.

Suddenly, the names of Lady Beatrice, Lady Margaret, and her father were announced as they entered the ballroom. And much to his surprise, the crowd parted, allowing them entry with a sort of excited holding of breath. The entire company seemed delighted by the arrival of the earl and his daughter.

Was it because of the fact that Kit had paid Margaret so much attention?

Easily, he spotted Lady Margaret, Kit's future wife. Or at least, that was what his brother was telling him.

She was very pretty indeed. Perhaps a little on the short side, but her smile beamed, basking everyone about her in a golden glow. Everyone seemed to wish to be in the sun of that smile. Yes, she'd make an admirable wife and addition to the family.

And then, Will let his gaze trail slightly. He spotted the *other* one.

Beatrice.

And the world seemed to stop around him.

The buzz of conversation drifted away. Once he'd locked his gaze upon her, he was unable to look anywhere else.

"Is that her?" he rasped, his voice much lower than he'd intended, that banked fire already trying to escape its embers.

"Who?" Kit asked, his brows lifting as he smiled at his beloved across the room. "Margaret? Yes. That is definitely Margaret. Isn't she beautiful?"

"Yes. Yes, she's beautiful," he agreed, then corrected: "Not her, the other one."

"Oh?" Kit queried, eyes only for his love.

Ben leaned in and confirmed, "That, brother, is the lady you must bear. Lady Beatrice."

He could not draw breath nor blink as he took her in.

Lady Beatrice. Activist, bluestocking, woman extraordinaire. Harrier of politicians and a woman of letters.

There was only one word for her.

Magnificent.

He did not know what he had expected, but this was not it. She was a positive force of a woman, and he was…stunned.

She stood with her dark brown hair coiled upon her head, exposing a neck that begged one to kiss it. The candlelight glinted in those tresses, lacing them with a fiery hue.

Spectacles were perched on her nose. The thin gold rims sparkled like jewels when she eyed the company as if she were a queen in her own right.

He loved that she wore them. So many ladies disdained spectacles, even if they needed them in company and were constantly running into furniture. Not Lady Beatrice.

No. He couldn't see Beatrice being cowed by someone suggesting she might do better without them. In all his life, he'd never seen a lady so self-possessed. So assured. So…well, *magnificent*.

From the tilt of her pert nose and slightly pointed chin, she looked as if she was going to cause mischief wherever she went. Her shoulders were back, emphasizing her bosom, which was barely covered by a gown inspired by the present trend of Greeks frock. That ivory silk gown skimmed her shoulders and clung to her body with such perfection, his jaw nearly dropped.

He kept it closed with significant will.

This was whom he had so fiercely avoided and from whom his secretary had so nobly attempted to protect him?

This was *terrible*. He couldn't be tempted by his soon-to-be sister-in-law's cousin. Such a thing would be a damned coil. He, the Duke of Blackheath, was not the sort to be tempted.

He had a mastery of himself that his parents had not.

"You're sure you wish to marry Maggie?" he breathed.

For the life of him, he could not see how anyone could possibly look at Margaret when Beatrice was there beside her.

"Of course," Kit said brightly before he laughed. "You wouldn't suggest that I'd marry Beatrice? Can you imagine being married to someone so bad-tempered?"

Kit laughed again.

Will was tempted to find some dark corner to escape to. He'd have to wait for Gentleman Jackson's. "No, no, of course not," he agreed. "I cannot imagine it at all."

He had no intention of marrying—he was a confirmed bachelor. He might consider it when he was an old, crusty fellow beyond passion and the silliness of love that his brother had fallen victim to. The very idea of marrying sooner was absolutely appalling.

No, he would never fall in love. Love was the devil. Love was dangerous. Love was the road to hell as far as he could tell. It had certainly ruined his mother's life, and his father's, too.

He would not allow himself to imagine marrying Beatrice. Not even in jest.

And as he stood transfixed by Beatrice, he realized with a growing horror that she was striding his way.

Yes, *striding*.

There was no delicate traipsing for this young lady. No, she was crossing the room in fiery leaps and bounds. The way her silk gown skimmed her long, strong body was…captivating.

And he found himself filling not with horror but anticipation. *Good God*. Was this meeting going to be terrible — or absolutely wonderful? He wasn't certain. But she looked as if she was going to come over, grab him by the balls, and lead him in the most merry of dances.

He wasn't certain if he wished to linger or to run, but he was a good soldier. Retreat was not his line unless necessary.

And then… Then his reverie broke, for he took note of a pamphlet in her hand, held as a gentlemen might brace his hand upon his rapier.

"I can't," he groaned.

"She is a force to be reckoned with," Ben marveled, his lips twitching with amusement.

He'd never retreated before in his life. And he was not about to.

But bloody hell, all his prepared pleasantries vanished from his usually very organized brain at the sight of her blazing through his ballroom. He felt completely off foot. For she was inducing the strangest response in him. One he'd never felt in his entire life.

Will turned and faced his brothers, determined to collect himself and meet her with at least a tolerant smile. She was his guest, devil take it.

Bloody hell, he had been the leader of battalions in the face of the French. Where others faltered, he had raced ahead.

Surely, a lady should not give him such pause. And certainly not the cousin of the woman who would be his sister-in-law. He had to have a tolerable relationship with her.

His brothers were clearly choking back laughter at his dismay, and it was all he could do not to level them with crushing stares.

He was a duke. He was capable.

He would rise above their childish humor.

And just as he was about to turn and meet her with a perfectly appropriate greeting, he heard the most luxurious, deep, perfect voice call out his name.

CHAPTER THREE

Beatrice was aware that half the ballroom was staring at her. It mattered not.

All thoughts abandoned her except one. She had made good view of enough portraits to know that dukes were not supposed to look like the Duke of Blackheath.

Dukes were stodgy, respectable; capable, certainly; determined to uphold Rule Britannia and the status quo—but they were not beautiful.

She'd yet to see a portrait of a beautiful duke.

Yet if there was one thing that Blackheath was, it was *beautiful*.

She stared at him agog.

The man towered, positively *towered*. His shoulders were broad. The beautiful cut of his coat hugged them, only emphasizing the Herculean musculature of his body. His waistcoat framed a wasp waist that went into tight breeches, which were the fashion of the day. That fawn fabric clung to thighs worthy of, dare she say, a demigod?

She swallowed at the sight of those limbs that were quite unlike the limbs of most men of the *ton*. They were honed to perfection. As were his arms, which even the cut of his black coat could not hide.

Surely, a gentleman should not look so, well, ready for the sort of labors that Hercules had endured?

Blackheath did, and his dark, curling hair framed

his hard face, making him look strangely boyish. Yet when she looked into his eyes, something she could do now that she was but a few feet from him, there was nothing boyish in that steely glint.

Goodness, his eyes were the strangest color of blue. Not a sapphire at all, but rather an aquamarine—something icy which dared one to treat him lightly at one's peril.

The square cut of his jaw suggested that he was quite used to taking blows upon his chin and very capable of returning verbal remarks.

She wondered if he was as capable of wit and speech as he was of elegance and beauty. It was galling the way he made her feel.

Beatrice forced herself to step forward through the thick air of the ballroom, which suddenly felt much hotter, and before she could open her mouth to continue her greeting, he thrust out that beautiful hand of his and asked, "Dance?"

It was tempting to refuse, but how could she? With so many people watching, her cousin's happiness was at stake.

So, she lifted her chin, placed her hand in his, and replied, "With you, Your Grace? How could a lady say no?"

The moment their hands touched, electricity danced up her arm. She'd heard of electrical currents and their use in therapies before, but she'd never experienced it.

Now, she was a believer in its power.

And from the slight widening of his eyes, he had felt it, too.

His brothers stared at them, their mouths agape

as the duke led her onto the floor.

A waltz began to play.

A waltz! Why did it have to be a waltz?

Why could it not be a hopping reel where she barely need touch him at all?

Oh no.

The lilting tune began, and he stared down at her, daring her to retreat.

Clearly, he did not know the stuff she was made of.

She swept up her skirts in her free hand and waited for him to place his other hand just below her shoulder blade.

And when he did so…the feel of that hand…

She suppressed a gasp.

The hum and heat of his hand against her was impossible.

A muscle tightened ever so slightly in his jaw. She was not alone in her shock.

He rocked ever so slightly, his legs caressing her skirts.

She blinked, remembering to listen to the count of the music, and then they were off, sweeping across the floor.

What the blazes was happening to her? She was no silly schoolgirl to be overborne by a rake!

She gathered herself and said drily, "Afraid to face me in front of your brothers?"

"Face you?" he drawled.

His voice filled the air with a delicious, tempting timbre.

It all but caressed her skin. She was shocked at its headiness.

He cocked his head to the side, making good view of her. That gaze traveled over her with a languid heat that seemed to astonish them both. And as he lifted his eyes back to her face, he mocked ever so slightly, "I merely wished to avoid a battle, Lady Beatrice."

His lips tilted into an unwilling, slow smile. "And I thought perhaps you would not wish to bellow in public."

"*Bellow*, sir?" She jerked her chin back, quite surprised by his assessment of her future tone. "I do not bellow."

How did he know her so well already?

His eyes widened, those depths sparking with something she couldn't fathom before he declared, "I have heard tales of your rhetorical style, and I have heard that your volume is quite remarkable."

She nodded, annoyed that when she looked straight ahead, she saw only his snowy and perfectly pressed cravat. A ruby pin winked at her. "My reputation precedes me. Good."

"Indeed, it does," he assured, with a surprising note of approval as he took them about the ballroom so smoothly she felt as if they were flying.

Of course he was an excellent dancer. It was mostly annoying that she loved to dance. It would have been far easier if he'd been terrible.

He was not.

She cleared her throat. "As does yours."

"Does it?" he asked.

She gave a terse nod. "Indeed, as a rake and a rogue and a man of action."

"Thank you," he said before he turned them

quickly to avoid another couple.

For one brief moment, her breasts brushed his chest, and she felt his hand tighten ever so slightly about hers.

"It was not a compliment," she gritted.

Did he have to be so...so...infuriating?

She added, "Except perhaps the man of action part. I do admire that about a fellow. I don't like the gentlemen these days who sit about doing nothing. Life is for the bold."

Easily, he circled across the floor, his long, large steps taking up huge swaths of space. If he had not been so powerfully strong, it would have been unpleasant covering so much ground on the tips of her toes. But he easily supported her.

He frowned, clearly not believing her.

But it was true. She valued action and boldness.

Her own parents had died when she was small, and she was not going to waste one moment of her life in hesitation and waiting.

No, action needed to be taken, and so she required herself to take it.

"You have been avoiding me," she declared at last, grateful that the buzzing conversation around them and the loudness of the excellent orchestra allowed for private conversation.

"You are most blunt," he said.

She noted he did not actually reply to her statement.

"I am not," she protested, tilting her head back so she could more easily spy his visage. "And I have yet to say anything that might upset you."

"That is a matter of opinion," he returned. "I

have read your letters, all of them, and they speak volumes about your ability for bluntness."

"Your Grace," she scoffed. "Perhaps you find me blunt because everyone bows and scrapes before you. If you are unaware, as a duke, you are unlikely to be contradicted. But I cannot amend my speech for your benefit. And in this case, my speech is terse due to your lack of reply to my missives."

"That is not true," he countered, his gaze narrowing. "I have most definitely replied."

She snorted at his sheer audacity. "Yes, your letters have consisted of '*Thank you, Lady Beatrice, for your passionate entreaty. We will take such matters into consideration and do our best to support our constituents.*'" She scowled. "Your constituents are male, sir. And they own land."

He frowned.

After a long silence, he replied with more sincerity, "I never thought of it like that. I did not mean to make you feel so discounted."

She hesitated, hardly believing she had heard correctly. "I beg your pardon?"

He looked away for a moment, a clear indication he loathed being caught in the wrong. "I did not mean to make you feel discounted by stating I assist my constituents. It was rather ignorant of me." He blew out a breath and gazed down upon her. "To not think about the fact that you as a lady are not one of my constituents."

"That is correct," she agreed, uncertain exactly how to proceed now that he'd admitted his deficiency.

She bit her lower lip, tempted to keep up the

terse line of banter, but found herself admitting with unfettered passion, "I wrote to you as a concerned member of society. But male society is not interested in my concerns or my rights, unless it is to ensure I am denied them. If I marry, I would for all intents and purposes be the property of my husband."

He winced. "Yes."

That wince? It spoke volumes. For he had transformed, for an instant, from arrogant duke to horrified human. And then just as quickly, he was again the all-powerful, Herculean duke.

"Oh dear," she whispered, lowering her gaze as she made a startling realization.

"What?" he asked, the timbre of his voice deep.

This was not at all what she thought would occur. She was tempted to kick a rock, if there were one here to kick, because apparently, she had misjudged him. Not entirely, but certainly to a degree. "You are not against women."

"No," he replied, shocked by her words. "Not at all."

"Have you read *The Declaration of the Rights of Woman*?"

"Of course I have," he replied as if it was the gravest insult she could give to ask such a thing. "Do I look like a fool?"

She was silent. He did not. She did not think he could ever be a fool.

"Don't reply," he said. "I did not mean to give you such good fodder to feed upon."

"Fear not, Your Grace," she assured, feeling merry for the first time in several minutes. She couldn't help herself. He'd so thoroughly handed her a weapon against himself. "I never take up such easy stuff."

He nodded. "Noted. Very noble."

What the blazes was happening?

Where was the battle?

Surely, he would tell her to go to the devil at any moment? That he did not wish to hear the tiring tales of ladies who bemoaned their fates?

"Lady Beatrice," he began, "you and I are almost certainly going to be related and very soon, but I do not think we should be at odds. It is not good for my brother or for your cousin."

She hesitated. "I agree, but where does that leave us?"

"You clearly do not need to like me." He paused, then inclined his head. "We must be pleasant with each other in company."

"Must we?" She did not do pleasant particularly well. Niceties were her nemesis.

"We must, to come to terms," he affirmed in a tone that brooked no argument.

She sighed inwardly. He really was used to getting his way.

"Terms," she stated. "Would you care to elaborate?"

"Yes." He locked gazes with her for a moment, then turned her under his arm. "Despite what you seem to have concluded, I do not find you or your cause unimportant."

"Oh?" she queried, her breath catching in her throat at his artful maneuvering of her person.

"The rights of women—of all people—is an important thing. It's why I'm a firm supporter of the

Clapham Sect and their pursuits of abolition. Something you have clearly not heard about me, though you know my reputation. Society does prefer salacious gossip to quiet actions," he said firmly and without jest as he waltzed with ease. "But unfortunately, most of the men in this country do not agree with our shared idea."

She scowled, though she did not miss the words *our shared idea.* Did he truly mean that? She knew about the Clapham Sect and admired them greatly. She'd read all of Olaudah Equiano's writings and even once had the remarkable fortune of hearing the freed man speak.

"That doesn't make it right," she replied.

"Of course it does not," he agreed with alacrity. And then he hesitated as if he was about to say something he knew she would not like. "But one must proceed with caution."

"Caution," she mocked, her earlier anger at him returning. "Caution never got—"

"Lack of caution gets one dead, Lady Beatrice."

She clamped her jaw shut. She could not deny that.

"Do you know what happened to the author of *The Declaration of the Rights of Woman*?" he asked as he turned her again and set off in the opposite direction.

"Indeed, I do," she said, loathing that she had to trust him not to run her into anyone. And yet, in his arms, she surprisingly had no fear of collision.

He blew out a sigh, which suggested he, too, had given it a great deal of thought. "She met her end at the hands of Robespierre, did she not?"

"Yes," she confirmed before she bit the inside of her cheek. He *did* know about the bluestockings and the women who longed for better lives.

Olympe de Gouges, authoress of *The Declaration of the Rights of Woman*, had indeed met her end at the hands of Madame Guillotine and its prime operator, Robespierre.

It was a horrible thing to have to admit. That her hero had died in the pursuit of justice.

Was she willing to make such a sacrifice? She had no idea. She prayed England would have better judgment than France.

It was quite difficult to be an advocate for ladies' rights, but she would not give in. She had seen the difficulties far too often of what happened to ladies when they had no rights.

"I appreciate your point, Your Grace, but I cannot yield."

His gaze warmed with admiration and a hint of regret. "I admire your tenacity."

"Do you?" she piped.

"I do, Lady Beatrice." He drew in a breath, which expanded his broad chest against his coat and perfectly pressed cravat. The muscles in his throat moving with said breath were positively hypnotizing. "I admire your boldness, your tenacity, and your determination to make change, but you are not going about it in the correct way."

"Is there a *correct* way?" she challenged as a familiar dread took root in her belly.

Was he about to prove disappointing? Likely.

He frowned as if the weight of the world was on his shoulders, and perhaps it was. "You attract more bees with honey than vinegar, Lady Beatrice."

"I am tired of being honey for men to feed upon," she sighed, finding his reply to indeed be disappointing.

Concern tightened his visage, as well as confusion. "I don't quite follow. Have men fed upon you often?"

She looked away, hating to confess her trials. But perhaps he needed to understand them. "It feels as if they have, and it has not been pleasant. They expect me to be nice. They expect me to be kind. They expect me to fawn over them. All while they have things I can never hope to have."

His brows drew together, perplexed. "I don't expect you to fawn over me."

"Don't you?" she retorted. "I have been honest with you, and I have made my demands clear, and they have gotten me nowhere with you."

Again, he winced. He closed his eyes for a moment, considering. When he opened them again... there was sympathy. "Perhaps I am just as bad as the rest of them."

"I think you are worse," she said without mercy.

"How could I possibly be worse?" he exclaimed, clearly offended.

"The fact that you seem to understand that ladies should have rights but you do so little about it."

He stumbled ever so slightly, his perfectly fluid movement jerking.

She held on to him, righting him. It was an astonishing moment, but she easily balanced them, and he nodded his thanks. And in a moment, he again had them turning in graceful patterns.

Had she truly jarred him?

"Lady Beatrice," he began softly but with surprising determination, "you have no idea what I've done to advocate for ladies' rights, or the fact that I probably have as much motivation as you to advocate for them."

"That's impossible," she replied, though she found her breath growing short at his profession for her own cause.

"Why?" he ground out, clearly beside himself that they could not agree even when they seemingly agreed.

She wished he could understand. "Because I am actually a lady."

He drew in a breath to reply, then stopped.

He bit his lower lip, a shocking and surprising action.

It did the strangest things to her, his teeth on his sensual bottom lip.

"A fair point," he admitted. "I cannot argue it."

She allowed herself to smile up at him, though she was half certain she should frown at him for the rest of their acquaintance in retaliation for his honey nonsense. "I think it'd be very foolish of you to try."

"What are we to do, then?" he asked softly.

A breeze traveled through the crush of the ballroom from the open windows and sent the briefest hints of lemon and juniper over her. His scent.

She drank it in and dared herself to say, "You ought to take up my cause, and then all will be well."

His head lowered ever so slightly. "Are you blackmailing me?" And then he smiled, a beautiful, teasing, devastating sort of smile. "Are you going to make every family dinner a complete catastrophe until I agree?"

She cocked her head to the side. "Possibly."

That smile of his turned to something knowing, something hot as he gazed down at her. Mystified, it seemed, by her very presence, a sort of need filled his gaze.

"Why are you looking at me like that?" she asked, her own heart beginning to hammer.

"Because I'm trying to decide how to make peace between us and stop our war of words."

"It shall never cease."

"Why?" he blurted.

"Because you are a man." It was a simple sentence, and she knew it couldn't convey her reasoning truly. But as a man he could never understand all that he had. And all that she did not.

"Thank God." He laughed.

Those two words pounded through her, and all the heat and goodwill she'd felt vanished in an instant. "Exactly," she all but growled.

"I beg your pardon?"

It was tempting to yank her hands from his and hie off. But she couldn't do that to Margaret. And this fellow! He mightn't look like a toad, but he was no prince. "The fact that you thank God you're a man only proves my case."

"Lady Beatrice," he drawled with an infuriating dose of condescension. "You shall drive me mad."

"One can only hope," she gritted.

The music came to a stop, and she tugged her hands from his.

Instantly she felt the loss but shook the ridiculous sensation away.

"We have come back to the beginning of our argument, Your Grace, and since I am not one for torture, I shall take my leave."

And she did.

CHAPTER FOUR

A good ice bath normally set Will to rights when the dark hours of night sunk his spirits. And, much to his dismay, his spirits had, as they so often did, slipped into the murky depths of sorrow. Sometimes, there was no explaining it. The intense melancholy could hit him right after a night of revels.

And the power of it could feel like a full gale. The episodes had begun after his mother's departure, and he'd realized that he had his cocoon of safety and love brutally ripped away in one night. He had not realized how she had shielded her sons from the rather austere and cruel world of power...of men.

She had embraced them, sung to them, told them stories, read plays to them, and protected *him* from his father's barking and never-ending demands for perfection.

When she'd left, his father's expectations of a perfect heir had only increased, and Will had had no one to soften that intensity. He had learned to hide his emotions before his father could correct him for weakness.

Perfection was easier than shame.

He'd been alone ever since he'd made that realization, for at least if he remained alone he'd never have his world ripped asunder again.

But the ice bath did not jar him from his dark mood this morning, even as dawn's first rays trailed into his chamber. He sat in his large, specially made tub, waiting for the cold to have its effect.

The ice cubes bobbed. Mocking him.

He let out a hiss of breath through his teeth.

Usually, once he plunged into the shudder-inducing water and allowed all his thoughts to escape, he felt, if not at one with the world, at least release from the painful emotions he kept at bay.

But today, it wasn't just the melancholy that left him feeling…apprehensive, as if an army was threatening the fortress that he had so carefully built.

Today, at two-second intervals, that *woman* appeared in his thoughts. In all her infuriating glory.

It was absolutely…well, infuriating.

How could a single person drive him to such distraction? The therapy of his ice bath was meant to push away the deep sorrow that often plagued him. A sorrow he shielded his brothers from.

The jarring fact was she had disturbed the stoic facade that he had forged. This was exactly why he had not wished to meet her. Her letters… They were nothing compared to the sharp beauty of her mind combined with her presence. And now, he found himself unable to locate the tranquility that he usually did.

Because of her.

Blissful peace eluded him.

At least it wasn't the agonizing nightmares and resulting grief that wouldn't release their grip today. Or the deep longing for connection he could not allow himself to have.

It was the opposite—he was feeling connection. Connection to *her*. And it was damned alarming.

All he could see was her sparkling brown eyes,

her fiery cheeks, and the defiant tilt of her chin.

And there had been that moment when her breasts had brushed his chest…

He clenched his fists, unable to bear the cold this morning, because he kept thinking of her marching so soundly away from him on the dance floor. Hah.

And he couldn't quite shake how her gown had caressed her body so perfectly as she made her triumphant exit.

A note of sheer exasperation escaped his lips.

It wasn't working.

If anything, he was thinking of her *more*.

With thoughts of Beatrice glaring at him and flouncing away, he grabbed hold of the edges of his tub and thrust himself up from the bath. Today, he'd avoid his brothers. He never liked them to see him ill at ease. Anger was acceptable. Frustration was fine. But self-doubt or melancholy? They were not. He was his brothers' rock, and he wouldn't allow them to see him shaken.

Water sluiced down his hard frame, and he stepped out, grabbing a linen towel. He dried himself with far more vigor than necessary, drove a hand through his hair, and then hauled his riding clothes on, which had been set out by his man.

As soon as his coat was in place, he strode from his bedroom and roared down the long hall. He had so much to do today. He had reams of papers to go through. He had lists of laws to be considered. He had people to meet, and he had a country to govern. That, at least, would distract him.

If he did not find something to occupy his thoughts, he could spend the whole bloody day repeating that impossible exchange and leaving him fixated on her person.

How the devil had she done that?

He was going to shake her the next time he saw her and tell her that she would have to go and rail at some other duke to get her way.

And yet, he could not forget her passion.

She had made such a good argument.

Why could she not simply leave the matter for him to take care of? It's what he did, after all. Take care of things.

Now, he understood that she had felt discounted.

He could understand why women, and a great many men, might feel thus, since they had no voice in government.

But he was no mad King George or intractable House of Lords.

No. He was a man of reason. Of sense.

Good God, had she not heard a word he'd said?

A war would not gain women their voice in Parliament, and so he had to find a way to do it carefully.

But it was very clear that Beatrice was not going to trust him to do so, and the fact that she was going to be in his family soon made this all the more a coil, for he could not simply dismiss her.

Will stomped down the stairs, and into the breakfast room, where coffee and toast were laid out. He chose not to partake of the toast.

Coffee was what he needed.

He took up the engraved silver coffeepot and poured the black beverage into a painted blue teacup.

Will drank the stuff down as if it was a lifeline. Indeed, it was. The beverage immediately had a positive impact upon him. Or so he convinced himself.

He ground his teeth.

Perhaps a ride in the park was just the thing before his rounds at his boxing club. Eyeing the silver pot, he decided he needed another. He'd barely slept. His sheets had been a blasted tangle after a night with Beatrice on the brain.

He would not recall some of those thoughts. He wouldn't allow them to be repeated. He could not.

And so, he downed another cup of coffee, headed out the door, and called for his hat and coat. His butler, Greaves, came apace, items in hand.

Will always marveled at the efficiency of his butler, who seemed to know exactly what he needed before he did. He took the items, thanked his butler, and headed out the door and onto the street to find his stallion, Pericles, waiting, reins in the hands of one of his many capable grooms.

With a nod, he took the leather reins easily and swung up onto the animal, who nickered happily at the prospect of exercise.

Luckily, his forebears had planned well when choosing their London seat. His home was adjacent to St. James's Park.

He adored it.

He also loved the ride down St. James's Park to Hyde Park. He quickly passed Speaker's Corner, lest more thoughts of Beatrice descend. It was far too easy to consider her pontificating to a rapt crowd.

As he raced across the green, toward the

Serpentine, he drew in long breaths. The trees in London always had a good effect upon him. The city could occasionally work upon his brain, and getting out into the fresh air performed wonders.

Yes, this was exactly what he needed. He drew in breath after breath, attempting to feel the calm that those breaths brought.

Indeed, he must forget that maddening woman. Each thunder of his horse's hooves calmed him, and he allowed his nerves to relax.

He loathed the fact that his nerves had been irritated at all. He usually thought of himself as a stoic individual unaffected by anything particularly difficult. He had spent most of his life curating such an approach. He'd seen what happened when he was a victim to feeling.

Yet *she*…she unlocked something with him. It was most aggravating.

He took Rotten Row, glad that few people were riding upon it, though several people were walking on the park side. The water glimmered in the early light, and at last he allowed himself a smile.

This was what would drive her out of his head, and just as he was about to let out a pleased laugh—

He heard his name…upon those dratted, perfect lips. *Again.*

CHAPTER FIVE

Will had never been unseated. Not in the entirety of his life. But Beatrice, it seemed, was bringing a myriad of firsts into his existence.

For as he turned to catch sight of the owner of that voice, his thoughts and hands went in two entirely different directions.

And poor Pericles, who was galloping apace, came to a sudden halt.

The force and gravity were such that he found himself soaring through the air with a predictable downward trajectory.

Thoughts too terrible to be given breath passed through his head as he rushed toward the dubious water. Ducks quacked in alarm and took flight, a feat he wished he could manage at this moment.

Alas, he could not, and so, he crashed through the surface and wondered, yet again, how the hell Beatrice had managed such a thing.

As he flailed for a moment in the disturbed water, he knew there was only one answer.

She had bewitched his horse.

It was the only logical conclusion. For surely, he could not have been so struck at the surprising sight of her that he had allowed himself to be flung from his saddle?

He could hear exclamations of horror and a far more forceful voice giving instruction.

He knew exactly whose voice it was.

Lady Beatrice would never exclaim in horror.

Oh no. Through the water clogging his ears, he could hear her ordering him to put his feet down.

He was tempted not to in a pique of defiance.

But gentlemen, especially dukes, did not give in to fits of pique.

He did as bid and stood.

For the second time in the span of an hour, cold water sluiced down his frame. Only this time it soaked his clothes to his skin.

With a barely muted curse, he stood for a moment, then wiped the water from his eyes in one swipe and drove his hand through his hair, shoving it back.

When he was able to focus, he spotted Lady Beatrice.

Her eyes were wide, and her mouth was ever so slightly open.

The morning light caught her dark brown hair, casting it with golden highlights.

Though he should have reached forward a few feet and dragged her in with him for startling him so, he could only gaze upon her, all reasonable thoughts vanishing, much like his horse.

She looked positively sublime.

Some people looked quite terrible in the morning, but not Beatrice.

She looked fresh, alive, and ready to meet the world with the power of an army. Yes, it was really the only way to describe her. A glorious being ready to wage battle on anyone that came into her presence.

He could not see himself as Theseus to her Hippolyta. Though there was a war between them, it seemed, he would never conquer her. He did not wish it. Taming? It was not for the likes of a creature such as Beatrice. He was loath that any man should try such a thing with any woman.

He admired her wildness far too much—though it drove him senseless—to try to take it from her.

Besides, she might win.

"Your Grace," she at last ventured. "Would you like assistance in extricating yourself?"

He trudged forward two steps and up onto the bank.

"Ah. I see you are most capable."

"I am impervious to wind and water, Lady Beatrice." He towered over her, water dripping. "And ladies who shout at me in the park."

She cleared her throat, and for a single moment had the good grace to look flummoxed. "Forgive me. I had no idea my salutation would result in such surprise ablutions."

Ablutions. Now, that was a word for it. "Your apology is noted."

Her face did the strangest thing, as if she longed to make comment but thought better of it. And he found himself liking her for that play of emotions and her self-control as well as her amusement. She was a merry creature. And life was full enough of sorrow. Yes...he admired her. Far more than he wanted to admit.

• • •

"It is most early for a walk, ladies."

Beatrice cleared her throat, pleased and surprised the duke was laughing and not thundering about with indignation as she'd expected of him. "We like a good walk."

Margaret's lips twitched. "Are you hurt, Your Grace?"

"I am made of a mettle stronger than earth, Lady Margaret." The duke then did something else Beatrice had not expected: he *winked*. "No harm done except to my reputation as a rider. And since no one is about but you two, I needn't fear. Need I? You won't tell anyone?"

Lady Beatrice grinned, again surprised by his joviality. Where was the crusty, implacable, impervious duke she'd built up in her imagination? Gone. Almost everything she'd imagined, except his power and avoidance of working with her on her cause, was gone. "In this, your secret is safe. And you see, I was most amazed that you were awake at all, Your Grace. I would have thought you were still lounging about in your bed. That is how I imagined you spending your mornings."

A mischievous look danced across his face, and for a single moment, there was a spark in his gaze. "You imagine me in my bed, Lady Beatrice?" he teased.

She arched a brow, tempted to cut him down with a scathing reply, but then much to her horror...she suddenly did envision him in bed. His long limbs sprawled out over tousled linen sheets.

She swallowed and blinked. Chagrined, she found herself thinking of dry political texts opposing the so-called "wandering uterus" to drive the extremely invigorating image from her brain.

Even so, she couldn't quite stop the burning of

her cheeks as she choked out her reply. "Not at all, sir, but I do imagine that you sleep a good deal."

"You'd be surprised," he said, peeling off his coat. "I sleep but little and rise from my bed early."

"As do I," she replied, skeptical. Surely, a man so handsome, so wealthy, and so used to being fawned over lounged about?

For the first time in his presence, she felt off foot. Because her gaze kept wandering to his wet linen shirt plastered to his chest.

The magnificent sight was doing the most irritating things to her usually highly rational thought process.

"Do you?" he asked. "That does not surprise me. You seem to have the constitution of a general."

She narrowed her eyes, and Margaret coughed.

"Was that meant to be a compliment or an insult?"

"A compliment, Lady Beatrice, a compliment," he assured quickly. "I think if we did send you abroad, you should have the whole world sorted in but a moment."

She did not feel convinced that he wasn't subtly mocking her.

Their gazes held for a long moment, and then he abruptly looked away.

She, too, suddenly felt as if she needed to look anywhere but at his entrancing form. For her mind was wandering back to that exceptionally unruly thought of him sprawled in his bed.

Her body heated despite the crisp morning air.

He, too, seemed…odd. His languid, arrogant stance appeared somewhat tense as his gaze lit with unknown emotions.

He cleared his throat and bowed. "Forgive me for my abruptness. I have an appointment at Gentlemen Jackson's."

She cocked her head to the side. "Boxing?"

"Indeed," he replied.

"Of course." She nodded, relieved to be on a subject about which she could argue. "Men do seem to like to bash one another about, rather than have it out in a good discussion."

His lips twitched as if he was tempted to rise to her bait, but instead he tried another tactic. "You are correct, of course; gentlemen do like to box."

"I will never understand it," she said, shrugging her shoulders, which caused her green pelisse to tighten slightly, and, quite ungentlemanly, his eyes dropped to her breasts.

His mouth tightened ever so slightly before he yanked his gaze back to her face.

What the blazes had passed through his mind just then? Whatever it was, it had caused the strangest sensation to dance across her skin.

"That is because you do not box," he pointed out, trying to discreetly coil his hand into a fist, but she spotted it.

"Women are not allowed," she pointed out, her breath doing the oddest things as she attempted to regulate it. For goodness' sake, they were in the park. Margaret was present. She was not attracted to the arrogant lout.

She wasn't!

Oh dear heavens…

She was, and it was most impossible. She'd have

to nip that in the proverbial bud. Such things were not for her. No, she'd never risk temptation. Not when she had so very much to accomplish with her life.

Her parents' great love affair made anything less a very unappealing prospect, too.

Yes. He was unappealing.

"That's not true," he replied, his gaze changing from one of strain to delight.

"I beg your pardon?" she queried.

"Women most definitely box," he stated, all but beaming now as he informed her of something she did not know.

It was most irritating, that look. And yet...his news was too fascinating to dismiss.

"They do?" she said, trying not to sound astounded. "Surely not."

"Oh yes," he affirmed, appearing most pleased that he had shocked her.

Beatrice tapped her chin as an idea occurred to her. And before she could think twice, she blurted, "Would you teach me, then, if you like it so well? Since we are to be family. You seem a logical choice."

He coughed. "I beg your pardon?"

"Teach me to box," she carried on, refusing to back down now. And frankly, the idea was quite thrilling. Ladies were so limited in what they were generally allowed that she was going to leap at this. "So that I might understand why gentlemen like it so well. You seem to think it merely for lack of education that women do not care for boxing. And it could prove very useful if ever I'm in a difficult spot."

He blanched. "I hate the idea of you in a difficult spot."

"Hate it as you will, but it is the lot of a lady," she stated.

His face darkened, and he swung his gaze to Margaret and then back to Beatrice. "But...surely your guardian protects you—"

"I did not take you for naive, Your Grace," mused Beatrice. "How interesting."

"I?" he echoed. "Naive? Hardly."

"Ah, but you don't realize how many ladies have had to issue a good stomp to keep a gentleman's hand from wandering too far *south*."

"And that is but one instance, and one rather easily dealt with," Margaret confessed.

A muscle tightened in his jaw. "You both seem so..."

"Resigned?" Beatrice prompted.

He gave a terse nod.

She shrugged again. "As said, it is the lot of ladies. Gentlemen are ever doing what they wish, despite what we wish."

A look of grim fury overtook him, and he blew out a breath. "I appreciate your education of my naïveté. But I'm not certain I can do as you ask."

"Of course not," she replied. "How predictable."

His grim look turned to one of strange contradiction as something clearly warred within him. It would have been comical if not for the fact that there was a genuine serious point to the conversation.

"It is not suitable for me to teach you to box," he replied, his voice rougher, with more emotion than she'd ever heard from him.

"Why not?" she queried innocently.

A look of sheer torture crossed his face. "Because ladies don't…"

She gave him a knowing smile.

And then he stopped himself. "You've admirably maneuvered me into a corner, Lady Beatrice. If you so wish it, I shall happily teach you to box, but I'm not sure that Gentlemen Jackson shall allow you to enter."

"Of course not," she said, surprisingly cheerful as she helped him see just how ignorant he was to the lives of her sisterhood. "Ladies are not allowed. We are not allowed in many of the hallowed realms gentlemen fill."

Her mocking tone seemed to strike him.

"You are ever correct," he stated without rancor.

"Which must be most difficult for you, since, no doubt," she replied, "you are accustomed to being the one in that position."

Another strange look passed over his visage, but then he let out a sigh.

"Surely you can teach me in my home?" she offered, wondering if he would renege.

But he was caught. Well and truly. "I'd be delighted."

"Good. It is a beginning," she stated, triumphant.

"Yes," he agreed. "A beginning. And I have a feeling you shall lay me out upon the floor. For you have the wily mind of a boxer."

It was perhaps the greatest compliment she'd ever received from a man.

He gave her a tight smile. "Now, if you'll forgive

me, I must go and ensure my horse is not halfway to Cornwall before I meet my brothers."

He gave them both a bow and turned. As he strode away with as much dignity as he could muster with clothes soaking and boots creaking, Lady Beatrice found herself alarmed. There was something about Blackheath. All her life, she'd known she'd never be intrigued by a man. Not when she'd had such an example of perfect marriage before her. Not when the world could steal everything from her if she miscalculated.

But without question, Beatrice was intrigued. And that was most alarming.

As her heart hammered and breath tightened at the sight of him walking away, she blew out a frustrated sound.

"Are we to live out our lives in the hands of dukes?" she exclaimed before she turned and started heading down the Serpentine in the direction of Kensington Palace.

Margaret hastened her step to keep up, her pink parasol bobbing. "Indeed! For it is the way of the world."

The way of the world, ha! She stalked along the gravel path. How the devil had he made her feel so awoken by him and yet flummoxed all at once?

Did she truly have to rely on a duke to teach her? To help her? Why did ladies need gentlemen to protect them from other gentlemen? Absurd. That's what it was.

They were past the Age of Enlightenment. They had passed the age of Rousseau, passed Montaigne and Thomas Paine. Had they not had Newton,

Descartes, and Burke?

Had not great women, too, made their mark, such as Aphra Behn, Elizabeth Montagu, the Duchess of Devonshire, and Mary Wollstonecraft?

Were women still to be relegated to bed and board? And being protected?

Not if she had a say.

There was promise of change upon the horizon. And though the duke was like many men in his lack of understanding of the state of women's lives, she wanted to make him see. To make him help her on simply more than a boxing match. If she did not, and if England did not embrace change, they would go the way of France. And that would be utter catastrophe!

The French had almost gotten it right. Life, liberty, and all that for men and for a brief, shining moment! Vive la France!

And then it had all gone horribly wrong.

But surely it couldn't be like that forever?

The longing for more was so intense it was a physical pain. She thought of her mother and father, who had loved and respected each other in a way she'd not seen again.

Sometimes…if she admitted it to herself, she was lonely.

And the way the duke made her body feel as if it was awakening from a long sleep… And caused her mind to crackle in debate…

Could a man and a woman truly align? Could she be tempted by the duke and pursue her cause at once? Her mind rioted at the confusion. From her experience, the answer was no. She'd not met a single man who would see her as a true equal and love her, too. Men did not generally love. They worshipped. A very different thing, indeed.

Could the Duke of Blackheath ever see her as an actual person with passion, desires, dreams, thoughts, and rights equal to his own?

All evidence told her no.

Yet to her utter annoyance, the tiniest spark had been lit, daring to think of him in carnal terms.

But humans were ever a disappointment. And she couldn't bear to be disappointed.

"If you think any harder," Maggie warned, "your hair shall burst into flame."

She looked back at her cousin, who was almost laughing. But only just.

"Do not laugh!" she exclaimed, her lips twitching at her cousin's own bemused expression.

"I would never do such a thing," Margaret said with exaggerated seriousness. "But I can see the feelings are positively radiating off you."

It was true that sometimes she did grow so impassioned that the only thing Margaret could do was nod and murmur at her. Still. Was it wrong to be angered for every woman and for every person who was the subject of the current system? *No.*

Was it wrong to long for more and settle for nothing less?

It was an impossible system, allowing only a few men to make the decisions for all. Allowing women to be put on pedestals but never be seen for who they were.

Who truly had thought that was a good idea?

Well, she knew: men. A few men, that was.

"Few people have any rights to make any decisions at all, Margaret. It's preposterous!"

Margaret's eyes widened, and she nodded dutifully.

Beatrice groaned. "I'm lecturing, aren't I?"

"A bit," confessed Maggie. "But I adore your lectures."

"Do you?" she asked, trying not to feel downcast.

"Most definitely," Maggie said honestly, patting Beatrice's hand atop her forearm. "Few have the courage to live with as much passion as you."

"That's one way to put it." She sighed.

Beatrice was deeply grateful for the fashion of the era, for she could take great strides across the path along the Serpentine. But a few years ago, women were veritable prisoners in massive underskirts and contraptions, massive wigs, and gowns cut in such a way a lady couldn't even raise her arms above her shoulders.

Why had they tolerated such things?

But in this new, promising era, her stays were light, and her skirts were voluminous but free-flowing from the belt under her bosom. She felt far freer now than she had when as a child she'd been forced to wear mini versions of the costumes ladies had worn.

She drew in a fortifying breath as she rushed along the shining waters of the Serpentine. She was most glad that so many had decided parks were a vital part of London life. She did not know what she'd do without trees. They were like wise old friends. Especially in London's bustle.

She gave her affable cousin a grateful smile. Margaret always brought sound judgment and good advice. She was truly grateful that her cousin was so staid, though sometimes she wished she was a bit more passionate about the current state of the world.

But if she was honest, such passion did come at a cost. While many people enjoyed Beatrice's antics, if she truly allowed herself to speak her mind, they often gave her looks as if she had grown another head or turned into a veritable Medusa. She was most decidedly not Medusa. And she'd found one gentleman's comparison to that Greek terror quite offensive. She could not turn men to stone with a single glance.

Though such a thing could have proven most useful on several occasions.

She smiled to herself, thinking of Blackheath. He did not seem intimidated or offended by her passion. Still, he was typical of politicians who insisted they were changing things—as they did nothing.

She groaned. He was so promising—but that promise was frightening. She'd been disappointed so many times.

And he had a strange air of perfection about him, as if he was untouchable, as if he would never allow anyone past his carefully crafted facade of the ideal duke. She wondered at that need to appear so…well, perfect. It seemed exhausting. And she wondered if anyone knew who the real man behind the duke was at all.

"I cannot believe you are marrying into that family of obtuse men," she burst out.

"My dear," Maggie chided gently as she turned her pretty face to the sun. "All men are obtuse to some degree, and one must simply get on with it and find ways around it."

"That sounds most tiring," Beatrice replied.

"Are you not tired of all your railing at the state of the world?" Margaret asked without judgment.

"I do not rail." She paused. "Well, perhaps I do a bit."

Maggie laughed gently. "Indeed, you do, cousin, and I adore you for it. But no matter which track we choose, it will be full of challenges. I hope you will allow me to choose mine without too much difficulty."

She let out a large huff of a breath, frustrated now with herself. She had no wish for Maggie to feel judged. "Of course I shall," she assured sincerely. "I believe that we should all have the ability to make the choices we so desire, and I would never stand in your way."

She swallowed, drawing herself up, knowing what she needed to say. "Kit is very handsome and very intelligent."

Maggie beamed. "Indeed, he is! We shall go through this life together hand in hand."

"As long as you walk by his side and not two paces behind him"—she squeezed her cousin's hand—"I shall have no trouble at all."

"Can you imagine that as soon as the banns are read, we shall marry?" Maggie's eyes lit with anticipation. "That is but four weeks!"

Beatrice could imagine, and she had some trepidation, but she could not speak of it to her cousin. So instead, she said, "I shall sing praises to you lovebirds at all hours if that is what you desire, for, cousin, I do not wish to cause you anything but joy."

"Thank you, Beatrice," Margaret replied. And then she gushed, "It shall be a grand wedding, I think. All of London will be there."

"Is that what you want?" Beatrice asked, surprised. "For all of London to be there?"

If she ever wed—which, of course, she never would—she would want a small ceremony in some little church where only the people who loved her could bear witness to her vows.

"I think so," Margaret ventured before she nibbled her lip, a very old habit. "I'd love everyone to feel as happy as me, including you, Beatrice. Don't you think there's someone that you could possibly ever—"

"No," Beatrice cut in, alarmed at that line of thought. "I shall never marry."

A bell-like laugh bounced from Maggie's lips. "But haven't you ever longed to kiss someone?"

It made her furious that young ladies were so limited, as opposed to their male counterparts, who seemed to kiss anything that moved.

Ladies could only ever kiss one man; or at least that's what they were meant to do.

Suddenly, the idea of kissing Blackheath danced through her head. Worse, he was in his bed, and her legs were wound with his in the sheets.

It was the most terrifying thought.

Because as it took root, she realized…she liked the idea. Very much indeed. For surely, such a beautiful fellow would be a wonderful kisser.

She shook the thought away and focused on her cousin.

"Margaret," she said, "whatever shall I do when you go away from me?"

"I shan't go away from you," Maggie protested. "We will be but a few streets apart."

"Those streets already feel like a thousand miles," Beatrice lamented. "You and I have slept in the same room since we were almost children."

"It shall be quite different," agreed Maggie, solemn for the first time that morning. "But you'll always be beside me. Shall you not continue to offer assistance and guidance?"

Beatrice stared at her cousin, astonished. "I do not think I can be able to guide you at all. I know nothing of being a wife, and I never shall. No, I'll be an old lady who will happily be auntie to all your dozen children."

"A dozen?" Margaret choked.

"Certainly." She waggled her brows. "I have seen the way you two look at each other."

Maggie looked quite perplexed. And so Beatrice rushed, "I know that you'll be happy. For that is your destiny in life. A star smiled the day you were born, Margaret, and it shall smile every day of your life. Of that I am certain."

Tears shone in Maggie's eyes. She did not blink them away but rather smiled through them. "That is the kindest thing you have ever said, Beatrice."

"It is true."

"And you," Margaret sallied, "did no star shine the day you were born?"

"It did not," Beatrice countered. "A star laughed and made me difficult and at odds with everyone. And yet I enjoy it. It is a merry war that I make. For

I am ever the optimist despite all odds."

Though, in her heart of hearts, she knew that was not true. For love? Love was almost always a myth, a song, a poem spun by bards to make the long days of life seem bearable.

CHAPTER SIX

"You look as if you've been in the wars, old man."

Will glared at his brother Ben and drawled, "I don't wish to discuss it, puppy."

Ben's eyes widened with a mixture of amusement and surprise. Quickly, he pulled his purple brocade waistcoat off and threw it. The garment landed on the bench at the side of the large room full of gentlemen happily pummeling each other. "Indeed?" he queried.

"Indeed," Will replied, not wishing to think about his near battle with ducks who had been most offended by his intrusion into their placid home.

He'd gone home, changed quickly—for there was no way he could go about London like a drowned rat—and was relieved to find that Pericles had indeed found his way home. Intelligent horse that he was, if traitorous in his upheaval, he'd wandered back to the source of his favorite thing aside from a good jaunt.

Food.

"We thought you'd never arrive," Kit observed as he untied his starched cravat. "What the devil happened to you?"

Will glared at Kit. He was not about to admit that he'd been downed by Lady Beatrice. His morale couldn't take it.

"None of your bloody business," he stated, unwinding his own cravat. Besides, his brothers were not supposed to have been at the boxing club so early. They'd both had a late night, but his expectation of being able to avoid them whilst in such an odd state was proving impossible. An unacceptable state of affairs.

Ben swept his slightly flopping hair back from his forehead. "Hmm, given your agitation, a lady must be involved. We all know how you feel about love."

"Ha. Think what you please," he replied tersely, even though his brother's thinking was completely on the mark.

He wasn't about to confirm that. Ben thought well enough of himself without getting the better of his elder at this moment.

After shrugging off his tailored dark blue coat and unbuttoning his simple ivory waistcoat, he placed the two down beside his brothers' items with slightly more care.

Will faced the boxing arena—and could not wait to get into it. The best thing about this club was that no one paid attention to anyone else. Gentlemen came here to stay in form, to exercise their bodies and minds. And unlike their clubs, they didn't sit about and gossip.

No, a man could be left to it. So, as he climbed through the ropes, he felt respite, knowing that he and his brothers did not need to worry about the men working at the end of the long, cavern-like hall.

Immediately, he began bouncing on the balls of his toes, moving his arms, and loosening his muscles by rolling his head to stretch his neck.

"My goodness, you are on edge," Ben observed.

"Fewer words; more action," he replied, focusing

straight ahead, throwing a jab. "Who's first?"

"Oh, you wish to face us one after the other?" Kit asked, his arms folded over his wide chest as he assessed his brother.

"Indeed, I do," he informed, waggling his brows at his brothers, daring one of them to go first.

He needed this.

"Then we must do it by birth," Ben said firmly, plunking himself down on the bench happily. "Kit, you're up first."

"Hell's bells, Ben," Kit lamented with faux horror. "That means I'm going to get the worst of him."

Ben laughed and stretched out his feet before him, hooking one boot over the other. "I shall enjoy being the referee to this merry row."

Kit sighed and climbed into the ring.

They began circling each other, eyeing where they could each make a good landing.

Will could not stop thinking about *her* again. It was the most infuriating thing, for he'd come here to cease thinking about her. He had gone on his ride to cease thinking about her. But wherever he went and whatever he did, Beatrice was still on his mind.

"Come on, then. Come at me," he urged, dancing back.

Kit arched his brow and grinned. "Whatever you command, old man."

Picking up the banter that he and his brothers so enjoyed, he returned, "Come on, then, puppy."

Kit darted in and swung a right hook at him.

Will darted to the side and just out of reach. He only just managed to escape. But then, Kit swiftly advanced and landed a quick blow to his nose.

Pain lanced through his face, but it was not so hellish he couldn't spot an in as he twisted to recover. He punched and hit Kit with a solid blow to his lower back.

Kit almost fell to one knee and groaned. "Not playing today, now, are we, dearest brother?"

"Always playing," he replied. For he would never truly hurt one of his brothers. But today, he wanted Kit to give as hard as he could. And Kit could lay waste to professional fighters if he chose.

They all had reputations as excellent boxers, though none of them fought for money. They fought for pleasure. After all, when three brothers were raised together, one often found that scrapping was a common occurrence.

Even among the nobility.

Sometimes it was even encouraged. The three of them, all capable of discourse in Latin, Greek, French, Spanish, and Italian, enjoyed sometimes sorting out their problems with their fists.

They were a bane to their tutors, who were ever clasping hands trained to hold hallowed volumes rather than fight.

Yes, he and his brothers enjoyed a good row.

In that, Beatrice was not mistaken.

Kit readjusted his stance. "Right. I see what you're hoping for. Pity the lady who loves your face, for I am about to rearrange it."

He winked and drawled, "So you say."

He was in a foul mood and desperately trying to hide it from his younger brothers. Brothers he'd attempted to protect from the vagaries of this world since he became the eldest.

He knew Ben and Kit would have shared his troubles if he but allowed them.

But he couldn't explain to them that he *liked* Beatrice. He liked her too well. She did things to him that no woman had ever done before. It was damned impossible, and as he and Kit circled, he prayed his brother would shake her from his head.

As Kit gave him a cocky smile, he rolled up his sleeves to his forearms, readjusted his stance, then danced on the balls of his booted toes. They each made attempts, neither of them landing anything.

The exertion of the circling and darting was causing his lungs to burn beautifully, and Kit's brow furrowed, jokes dimming now.

He was praying that Kit would get in a good blow, and soon. Because he kept seeing Beatrice's perfect lips castigating him.

As if making his wish come true, Kit darted in, and even though he attempted to swing out of the way quickly, Kit's right jab came forward and cracked him on the jaw.

His head blew back, and the world went dark for a moment.

Yes, this was exactly what he needed.

He could think of nothing but the ringing sound of his ears and the disappearing of the room. He had to keep moving or Kit would slam him again in another blow, and indeed he did. It came out of nowhere, right on the chin, whipping his head to the side.

He did not recover quickly enough, because so much of his brain was *still* trying to think of Beatrice.

But finally, as Kit pummeled him with a left hook

to his rib cage, survival kicked in.

Air *whooshed* out of his lungs, and he began to circle fast, blinking the sweat from his eyes.

"Off your game, old boy?" Ben called from the side, grinning.

"You got in a good shot there," Kit said, "but your age must be catching up to you. You just don't have the legs to keep up with me."

Will snorted and wiped blood from his lip. He darted to the left and then to the right, but Kit danced around him, circling him.

Letting out a slow breath, Will allowed himself to calm, to focus, to not let frustration rule him and chose to spar rather than to battle. "Now, Kit, I'm being kind. We can't have you black and blue for your wedding."

Kit's eyes lit with love. "Margaret would marry me anyway."

Will only just refrained from rolling his eyes. He was damn irritating, his younger brother, for the man was too happy. He was glad, of course, that Kit was making such a good marriage, and Margaret was lovely.

But she was no Beatrice, and that was the truth of it.

As he realized that thought, he began to feel a certain sense of dread. He liked Beatrice. He admired Beatrice. And Beatrice would make an excellent companion for someone. But not him.

Not *him*.

That was absolutely certain. He wondered who might make Beatrice a good husband. His insides twisted at the nausea-inducing idea.

And before he could think another thing, Kit circled round and slammed his fist into his lower back. Will dropped to one knee and gasped, the pain astonishing.

Kit frowned and hesitated before his eyes filled with understanding. And he let out a stunned laugh. "You're thinking about her, aren't you?"

Ben clapped his hands together and laughed in agreement. "Of course! He's thinking of Lady Beatrice. I will never forget the look on her face last night, when she left you on the dance floor."

"That's enough. I am the elder," he intoned in his most serious duke voice, "and I shall have none of this mockery from you young things."

Truthfully, they all loved this game. It kept them close when so many brothers drifted apart in the *ton*.

"You're not *that* old," Ben teased relentlessly. "You still have all your hair."

"Indeed I do," he drawled. "But you two are trying to drive me into an early dotage. No doubt she will aid you."

Ben wiped a nonexistent tear from his brown eyes. "She *did* get the best of you. It was a beautiful thing to watch. And now Kit is getting the best of you, too. Dear God, brother. Are you about to dodder into your dotage?"

"I certainly shall before a lady gets the best of me."

Except she did keep getting the best of him, and he rather enjoyed it.

And with that realization, he pulled himself to his feet, and he and Kit began again. This time, they circled each other wordlessly. Sweat flew from their brows as they each came in for blow after blow, each giving as good as they got. It was wonderful. It was exactly what he'd hoped for, and he loved every bit of it.

"Are you going to marry her?" Kit asked abruptly in the lowest of blows.

Marry…

He stared at his brother for an instant too long, and of course, Kit drove his fist into his stomach. Air whooshed out of him yet again, and he jolted back.

"That was against every code known to man," he said drily. "I ought to murder you."

"That's not allowed in boxing!" Ben pointed out merrily from his bench.

And he swung his brother a dagger glare. "Come on up here now. It's your turn."

Kit laughed as he staggered to the ropes. "Oh, thank the heavens. A break from your moody besotted self is most welcome."

Will couldn't stop himself. He *blushed.*

"I am *not* besotted, nor am I in a mood."

Kit just chortled as he jumped down out of the ring. "Of course not, elder. You're the pinnacle of Stoicism at present."

He sensed the sarcasm, but the truth was, he had always tried to protect his brothers from his melancholia. "Even the Stoics had moods," he pointed out.

"And you always overcome them," Ben said merrily. "Come. All will be well. You always rise above any difficulty. And your mood shall pass as quickly as the sun on an English summer day."

Ben said that line with such an air of earnestness that Will hesitated. He tried to read his brother and immediately understood what his brother was doing. He blew out a breath. "Ben, you can keep giving me hell; you needn't make me feel better."

"Of course I do. That's my job."

"What do you mean?"

As the words slipped past his lips, he realized something.

"Oh God..." He groaned, closing his eyes, then opened them again and swung his gaze from brother to brother.

"What?" Kit asked.

He wiped a hand over his face. "You're doing what she said everyone does."

Ben sat up. "What?"

"You're bowing and scraping." He locked his gaze with Ben, then Kit. "You're my brothers. You're not supposed to do that."

Kit and Ben exchanged a quick glance before they both shifted uncomfortably.

"You're a duke," Ben pointed out with a shrug. "Even though you're our brother, we still have to bow and scrape a bit. We wouldn't want you to grow totally despondent. You have important work to do."

"Damnation," he groaned, realizing just how right she was, and it was worse than getting popped on the jaw. "Please, God, don't make that woman right *again*."

Both of his brothers broke out laughing, a deep, booming sound.

"Lady Beatrice is a force to be reckoned with; there's no question," Ben proclaimed happily. "We think you should just yield to her right away."

He jerked his chin back, astonished at this suggestion. "Dukes do not yield."

"I have a handkerchief," Ben declared, reaching into his coat beside him. "You could wave the white flag at her on your next meeting."

"I already met her today," he finally confessed, leaning against the ropes of the ring. "And I have no intention of admitting defeat."

He'd promised her a boxing lesson, of course, but that didn't have to be for the next few days.

He needed time away from her to gather himself, to fortify himself, to make sure he did not fall victim to her prowess in verbal battle again. No, when he saw her next, he'd be prepared. He would not fall under the mercy of her delicious argument, because that's exactly what it was. *Delicious*.

Bloody hell, she loved to argue, and it was an incredible thing to behold.

He had not been lying yesterday when he'd said that she would make a wonderful lawyer. She would have been an excellent parliamentarian, too, if only she'd been born a man.

But she had not. And that was a great loss to them all.

"Oh my God," Ben breathed.

Kit nodded, his brow furrowing with dramatic horror. "I see it, too."

"See what?" Will demanded.

"You are besotted with Lady Beatrice," Ben announced.

"I am not," he said. "I will never fall in love. I will not be ruled by emotion."

"Emotion is not bad, brother; it's part of human nature," Ben said earnestly.

He blew out a derisive sound. "I do not give in to human nature."

He'd spent years ensuring it to be so. He couldn't make the same mistakes his parents had made.

"You're not a Stoic, no matter what you say," Kit added. "You cannot convince me that you are a modern Cato."

"I am." In fact, his admiration of the Stoics was one of the reasons he rose so early, took cold baths, and worked so hard. Detachment from emotion was the only way to live. Otherwise...one was merely twisting in the wind.

Ben stood and *tsk*ed as he picked up his cravat, clearly deciding to give boxing a miss. "No matter how many cold baths you take, you have the soul of a lover."

"A lover? No. A man of action," he countered.

"Yes, you are indeed a man who makes the world turn," Kit agreed. "But you are passionate, too."

As if warming to this and loving his own current state of bliss, Kit continued on in the arrogance only a man in love could have. "And you shall fall to Beatrice. Make no mistake. I see it in your future. She shall conquer you, and you shall have to surrender to her and get down on one knee and—"

"Kit!" he said. "I should hate to make Margaret a widow before a wife, if only because Lady Beatrice would likely turn my guts into garters."

"You must marry eventually," Ben stated factually.

He did not meet his brothers' gazes as he vaulted over the ropes and queried, "Must I?"

"Indeed," Kit proclaimed cheekily as he pulled

his waistcoat on, wincing slightly. "For you must people the world with a little duke and as many lords and ladies as possible to ensure our line stretches on to infinity."

"Why do you say that I must?" he cut in, gesturing to them. "I have brothers; you could do that for me."

Both Kit and Ben rolled their eyes.

"Neither of us want to be the duke," Kit pointed out, "or to have the necessity of siring one. That's your job."

It was interesting that he was really just a stud, ensuring the continuation of the Blackheath dynasty. But he wasn't truly surprised to hear his brothers speak thus. Everyone loved being near dukes, but no one actually wanted to be one. Not in reality. Not with the weight and responsibilities that kept him up most nights.

He would likely have to marry. One day. Far in the future, and he would choose a lady very carefully. A lady who expected only the luxury and importance of being a duchess. A lady who lived by her sense of duty and family obligation without a need for love or grand passion.

Love and grand passion were the devil.

"Exactly," Ben continued easily. "I have no desire to have your responsibility. I am much happier swanning about London, gambling your money."

He let out a long sigh. "We should discuss that."

Ben sighed, too, as he tugged his coat on, his emerald pin winking in the morning light. "Must we?"

He leveled his brother with as sober a stare as he could manage. "You were sent down from Oxford.

We have to have a conversation about your behavior."

Ben let out a sound of elaborate indignation. "My behavior is perfectly exemplary." He scowled. "Those old dons are absolute devils."

He laughed, recalling his own time there. "Yes, some of them were," he said. "I am glad we've abandoned discussing my love life. We can get on to realistic matters."

"You don't have a love life," Ben pointed out.

"Exactly," Kit agreed. "You go from opera dancer to singer to artist to authoress, but you never have a love affair. You leave them too soon to love them."

"I do that on purpose," he said, stunned at Kit's vehemence. Wasn't that what most gentlemen did? If not, they should. It was best to make certain no one got hurt in such things.

"Of course you do," Kit said, clapping his hand on his back. "Because you are absolutely terrified."

"Terrified?" he echoed, snorting. "I do not know the meaning of the word terror."

Kit nodded woefully. "Indeed you do. You quiver in your boots at the very idea of love."

"I do not," he protested. "I am merely a sensible fellow who understands that love often puts a person in a very dangerous situation."

"I'm in love with Margaret," Kit confessed.

"I know." Will sighed. "And I worry about you."

"Why?" Kit's face transformed in rapturous expectation. "Margaret is an angel."

"She is an angel," he affirmed.

Although he didn't necessarily think Margaret would like being described so. She was a woman, whole and full. Yes, she was good-tempered and kind, but he could tell that she had a mischievous spirit about her. And he was looking forward to seeing more of that in his sister-in-law. He was glad that she was a woman of parts and not just a pretty piece.

Kit needed someone like that.

"I shall wish you both happy," Will said, clapping his brother back on his shoulder. "I could never do otherwise, but I worry about the way sometimes love can inflame people and cause them to do things they regret."

"I am not Papa." Kit grew serious. Earnest. "Nor am I Mother," he added. "I have been raised by you, and I am careful, and I shall not make the mistake of falling prey to my own emotions."

"I'm glad to hear it," he said, his voice gruff. Not with emotion. Certainly not. But with the events of the day. Being thrown into the Serpentine couldn't be good for his voice.

And he *had* raised his brothers over the last decade. It had been a difficult thing, for not only had their mother abandoned them, dying on the continent, but their father, too, had died when they were all young.

It had been a brutal childhood.

None of them had truly recovered from the wounds of their father dying far too young and the fact that their mother had bolted.

They had all felt it. And he had sworn, as he protected his brothers and did his best to keep them safe from the cruel gossip of the world, that he would never, ever succumb to love as their mother had done.

For love had driven their mother to ruin all of their lives.

There was silence for a long moment, before Ben stood up suddenly and clapped his hands together.

"A drink! A drink!" he said firmly. "Let us go to the tavern. It is the only thing for our present mood."

"That is not at all the thing for one who is in a state—"

"Devil take it," Kit ground out. "You are an old man."

"I am only thirty," he reminded them.

"An old man in spirit, then," Ben lamented, hanging his head.

"All right, then. I shall go to a tavern with you, just to prove that I am not so entirely old and rigid."

"Wonderful." Kit winked at Ben. "And you must come to the play."

"What play?" he asked, shaking his head.

"Ben and I are going to go see *Much Ado About Nothing* in seven days' time." Kit gave him a wily smile. "And you will come with us. For we must pass the long weeks until my wedding!"

"Your wedding is in a month. And I don't have time to go to the theater," he said flatly.

Ben and Kit leveled him with a look that only younger brothers could give when determined to get their way.

"*Much Ado About Nothing*, is it?" he relented on a sigh.

"Yes," said Kit, smiling, a strange gleam in his eyes. "I think you shall enjoy it very much."

"I doubt that, but I'll go anyway," he said.

"Good," Ben said. "Now, to the East of London! Let us revel and make merry!"

Will rolled his eyes. The entire day was going to waste. Well, not to total waste. It had already been an adventure, and he needed an escape. Since the boxing hadn't worked, perhaps gin would.

CHAPTER SEVEN

Beatrice loved Shakespeare. In fact, she knew many of his plays by heart, and all the sonnets.

With a name like Beatrice, how could she not? Much to her good fortune, she was named after one of the greatest characters in the canon. And now she sat in her uncle's glittering, red velvet box, awaiting the beginning of the play she adored.

She and Margaret sat side by side in their beautiful evening gowns. Her cousin's pink gown was quite nice, but she loved hers. It was not the typical shade of a lady who had yet to marry. The soft green did wonders for her complexion and the fiery notes in her hair.

She absolutely adored green, and, though she was a young lady, she'd managed to convince her modiste to make the beautiful gown embroidered with golden leaves.

She positively loved the way it looked in the light dancing from the chandelier. She could feel the hum of the audience down below, the excitement of the people who had come to witness the Bard's work come alive.

As anticipation filled the air, everyone in the boxes lining the balcony leaned together, waving their fans, gossiping, anxious for the performance to start. Some looked about with delicate binoculars, elaborate telescopes, and monocles.

Whilst they'd all come to a play, that was not the

only thing occurring tonight.

The audience's performance was just as elaborate as the performance onstage.

The lords and ladies could not stop talking about what everyone was wearing, who was sitting with whom, and what everyone was potentially doing after the performance.

No doubt, affairs were being arranged. Oh yes, she knew about those, because she was a well-read lady.

Politics were being discussed, and debates were being held over who had the best seat and who would win the majority in government in the upcoming election.

One did not come to the theater just to watch the stage, but to be seen.

Though she knew it was the objective of many of her set, it was not hers. For whilst she adored a good gossip, she truly did love a good play. It was one of the highlights of the Season, and she was very fortunate that her uncle encouraged them to attend, for some did not believe that the theater was truly suitable for a young lady.

For they were exposed to actresses.

What horror! She longed to laugh at the silly, prudish people who feared the great artists who'd lived a life too large for them to understand.

The simple fact was the opera and the theater were sparkling, thrilling things to bring a bit of wonder to their lives.

Beatrice dearly loved the opera, and she knew many people thought it superior. But if she were to be honest, she far preferred the plays of William

Shakespeare and Sheridan. She loved a good laugh and a good cry. But these days, she found that a good laugh was exactly what her soul needed, since she felt rather melancholy about the whole idea of Margaret leaving her and going on to greener pastures.

She only hoped those grasses stayed verdant.

"I do hope Beatrice and Benedick are good," Margaret said, leaning her arm against the gilded edge of their box.

"Oh, I'm sure they shall be," she assured, waving her painted ivory fan. "They can never be too terrible. The lines are written too well."

"Too true, cousin," Margaret enthused.

For they both did love reading *Much Ado About Nothing* out loud to each other. The witty banter between Benedick and Beatrice always had them in fits of laughter, though the subplot wherein the poor cousin, Hero, was maligned by Don John was simply too much to bear.

Surely even Shakespeare realized that such a thing could never happen in real life.

Margaret stood, closing her fan. "I am going to find Papa and perhaps make a quick venture to the cloak room. Do you wish to accompany me?"

"I shall wait here," she replied with an easy smile.

Margaret headed out of their box and into the busy hall, as people still had several minutes to find their seats. She found her gaze wandering over the crowd, for Kit and his brother Ben were meant to attend.

Much to their good fortune and surprising convenience, they were next to the Blackheath box. She hated that she found herself shifting in her seat anxiously.

But she knew exactly why she was nervous.

She was wondering if the duke would come tonight.

Of course he would not.

He did not usually attend the theater. She had heard about the legendary private Shakespeare performances put on by himself, his brothers, and their friends at his house. They were apparently quite fun and not for young debutantes. Which didn't mean they were particularly scandalous, though Shakespeare was very naughty indeed.

But alas, unmarried ladies were forbidden many delightful things.

She'd never seen him in the box next to theirs, which seemed rather odd, for he was reputed to be a patron of the theater. He gave a great deal of money to actors and playwrights, which was another remarkable thing about him.

She could not understand why he proved so difficult so often. Anyone who loved music and the theater couldn't be wholly bad.

And she couldn't forget he'd agreed to give her boxing lessons, except he had yet to make good. True, it had only been a week. But she had heard nothing from him in that time.

It seemed to be a line with him. The promise of taking care of something and the failure to make good on said promise. Yes, he was like all men, disappointing in the end.

Yet, much to her consternation, she could not stop watching the door of his box, waiting to see if the curtain would sway and herald his entrance.

She waved her fan slowly before her face, determined not to let her absurd obsession show. It was hot, of course, given the crush of bodies and the number of lit candles illuminating the space.

She reached forward to the small table beside her and took a sip of wine. She allowed the refreshing beverage to coat her tongue. And just when she was about to give up all hope that the duke or even his brothers were coming, for no doubt they all thought they had better things to do, she heard footsteps behind her. Then a voice.

"Lady Beatrice. A pleasure to see you at the theater."

Her breath paused in her throat, and a positive thrill raced through her. It was highly irritating, but she couldn't deny it. There was no one else quite like him, and she found herself now looking forward to their verbal exchanges.

She turned in her seat, glancing back.

He stood in the curtained arch of the box, shadows playing over his strong face.

"I had no idea that my presence caused you pleasure," she replied, looking up at him. "I rather thought it was pain; after all, I did nearly cause your drowning last time."

He took a step closer, lingering beside her chair.

In the golden candle glow of the theater, he was as beautiful as ever.

"A man cannot drown in but a few feet of water," he assured.

"Too true," she agreed, snapping her fan shut, "but it was a very near thing, and I still have yet to forgive myself for the ruin of your shirt."

He laughed.

The inescapable and terrible truth was that the image of his shirt plastered to his immaculately sculpted chest had yet to leave her mind.

As a matter of fact, it had given her many sleepless nights. She'd never lost sleep over a gentleman before.

But to be fair, there were no other men like Blackheath.

Even so, she attempted to give her brain a good talking-to about behaving itself when the candles had all been snuffed out.

But the duke had indeed invaded her dreams.

Night after night this past week, she had lain awake in her bed, her light chemise skimming her body. She'd attempted to convince herself that the heat she'd felt as she'd wondered what his muscles felt like beneath that shirt was due to the hot summer weather.

Alas, she had not been able to fool herself. For no summer air had made her body feel so alive before. So wild. So hungry for something it did not know and had never had.

Even now, gazing at him clothed from the top of his cravat-adorned neck to the tips of his polished boots, she struggled to banish the memory of how his wet linen had clung to him and become nearly translucent so that she could see almost every angle and nook of him.

She swallowed and forced herself to give him an enigmatic smile. She did not wish him to know she was considering what his lips might feel like upon hers.

Her imagination had become absolutely scandal-ous!

She could not stand him. Truly. Even if he was a witty sparring partner.

Why would she wish to kiss him?

It was absurd.

No doubt it was merely the frustration and hot temper that he induced in her. For such passions were often known to cause the blood to boil. Whole books had been written upon the subject.

Everyone said hot blood caused amorous thoughts to rise. She would have to go for several weeks eating no meat whatsoever and eschewing red wine to help cool her temperament, and then she would be back to rights. Not a single thought of his lips on hers or his hands upon—

"Have your wits gone wandering, Lady Beatrice?" He took another step into the box so he was but a few feet away from her. "That is not at all like you." He cocked his head to the side. "Whatever are you thinking on? Your cheeks have gone bright red."

"They have not," she countered firmly. But they were burning. *Oh dear*. Denial would seem most foolish. She cleared her throat and rushed, "Or if they have, it is merely because of the heat of the evening." She waved at the audience with her closed fan. "It is a terrible crush here tonight."

"Yes," he agreed, seeming rather pleased. "Every seat is filled. It's a good thing to see. I do dearly enjoy that everyone loves Shakespeare."

"And as I understand, you love it quite well, too?" she replied. "Yet I have never seen you at a play before this night."

He folded his hands behind his back, and his gaze lowered to her lips for a brief moment before he snapped it back up to her eyes. He cleared his throat. "In general, I do not have time to go to the theater. You see, I am usually otherwise engaged."

She raised a brow at him. "Otherwise engaged?" She gave him a wicked smile. "Perhaps with an actress?"

"You may not say such things to me, Lady Beatrice," he exclaimed sotto voce.

"Why not?" she asked, shrugging. "We are to be family. Why should we pretend that dukes do not have friendships with actresses?"

He choked. "You are verging on a scandal."

"Oh dear." She nipped at her lower lip. Was he truly shocked? He hadn't seemed as if he'd be. "I must not do that, for I would not wish you to tell your brother that a marriage to my cousin is out of the question."

He shook his head. "Such a thing is not possible, Lady Beatrice. My brother has agreed to marry her publicly, and to call it off could cause legal difficulties."

"Oh," she said. "Of course." She beamed at him. "How marvelous. I can say anything that I wish to you and not have to worry."

"I wouldn't go that far," he warned softly, then eyed the stage. "And are you named after the character we shall see onstage this night?"

"You have the right of it, Your Grace."

"Aha." He bowed. "My Lady Disdain," he said grandly. "How fascinating."

She laughed, not at all insulted, for he had aptly quoted Benedick. "If I could prove but as witty and wise as Beatrice, I should be pleased."

"Benedick asks her lover to kill his best friend," he pointed out.

Her mouth dropped open, and then she snorted. "For good reason."

"Yes," he agreed. "I always liked Benedick. Very wise fellow. Until he fell in love, that is."

"You are terrible," she replied. "But I cannot disagree with you. I shall not marry as Beatrice did in the end. Just as you shall not. We shall both choose freedom."

He bowed. "A life well lived."

"I think so." She loved that he did not try to convince her that all ladies should marry and crave babies.

Children were all well and good. And perhaps she'd like being a mother, but the price seemed terribly steep. No. She'd stay as she was.

"Perhaps we have more in common than we thought," he said softly.

"The horror," she teased before she inclined her head. "Who'd have thought it?"

"I should have guessed. You are as feisty as her. I'm a ruff, doublet, and hose away from being the Bard himself."

Then she looked at him and swung her gaze to his box, which was now occupied by his brothers, Kit and Benjamin.

She gasped. "Your names."

His lips twitched. "Yes?"

"You're all named after Elizabethan playwrights."

"Aha. Clever, Lady Beatrice." His gaze sparked with admiration.

"William Shakespeare, Christopher Marlowe," she listed. "And Ben Jonson."

He lifted his strong, gloved hands and applauded. "Well spotted. Which playwright is your favorite?"

"You, of course." She cleared her throat as his brows rose ever so slightly. "I mean William Shakespeare."

"Mine too," he rumbled, his voice so low, so delicious, that it did the strangest things to her limbs. Warming them in a way the heat of the theater never could.

"Who chose those names?" she asked, desperate to avoid the strange sensations he was evoking in her.

A sad smile curved his lips. His brow crooked with a bittersweet memory. "My mother. She loved plays. She'd read them to us every night. I could recite *Henry V* to you by heart. Or *Twelfth Night*. Or the sonnets."

"More and more in common, Your Grace," she breathed. "My parents read them to me, too."

His lips parted as if he was about to pursue this intimate history, but the curtains of the box swished open, and the duke stepped farther into the box.

"Are you to sit with us, then, Your Grace," her uncle asked as he and Margaret strode in, "or shall you sit with your brothers?"

The duke bowed to Margaret, then contemplated her father, who was not a small man. "I do not see how we could all fit in your box," he said.

"You are rather large," Beatrice agreed.

The duke's eyes bulged with surprise.

"You have a great many muscles underneath all of those clothes, have you not?" she said, gesturing with her fan at his person.

"Beatrice." Her uncle groaned. "That is a shocking question from a young lady."

"Is it, uncle?" she queried, her eyes merry. "I had no idea. I thought it was merely an anatomical inquiry regarding the physics of our seating arrangement."

The duke's lips twitched as he was barely suppressing a smile.

Her uncle shook his head. "Margaret and I shall greet Lord Christopher, then return. Beatrice, do not let your repartee insult the duke."

"I find your niece refreshing," Blackheath assured.

Her uncle gave a relieved sigh before he and Margaret turned and headed back into the hall.

For once, she did not mind the last ten minutes before the performance. She found their conversation to be most curious, and she wished to know more about him.

"To answer your question, I do have a vast many muscles, Lady Beatrice," he informed. "The better for me to do my work. If I am in good condition, I need less sleep and I am able to stand for hours. And I often do stand for hours whilst I argue with old fools in the Lords."

"So, you do not believe men to be bastions of superiority?"

He cocked his head to the side and frowned. "Surely you know I do not."

She *tsk*ed with exaggerated woe. "And yet we cannot find ourselves allies."

"So it seems," he said, his voice intoxicating.

Silence stretched between them, and it was hard to know what to say. The air fairly crackled. Was he to be trusted?

She gestured to the empty chair near her, and, as invited, he sat. His long legs stretched out, and his polished boot nearly touched the hem of her gown.

Beatrice pulled at her gloves, looking away, quite aware that their conversation needed to attract no undue attention. "You are remiss, sir."

"Am I?" he asked, blinking, apparently surprised by her sudden change in conversation.

She shook her head and wagged a finger at him. "You promise to give me a boxing lesson, and yet you have failed to do so."

"Forgive me," he allowed, looking contrite, even though it was slightly exaggerated—as much a performance as the actors would soon give upon the stage. "A most lamentable failure on my part, to disappoint a lady." He placed a hand on his heart and inclined his head, which caused shadows to fall over the hard planes of his face. "I should have sent you a note explaining my absence. But I have been much taken up with important affairs of state and some of the charities that I run. I do hope you shall not cast me from your good graces forever."

She smiled at him, then pressed her lips together. Studying her fan, she replied, "How could I not forgive a man so engaged in important work, so far above the ways of women?"

"Blast, Lady Beatrice, not again," he insisted.

"You know that's not what I meant."

She snapped her fan open and laughed behind it ever so slightly. She couldn't help herself. He was so easy to enrage.

"Of course not," she said honestly. "I'm glad that you do such good work. You must think me terribly idle, engaged in naught but eating bonbons and embroidering cushions all day."

He narrowed his eyes. "I could never think such a thing of you. Remember, I did research. Now, if you enjoy embroidery, Lady Beatrice, I would never think less of you. For it's just a skill like any other that requires great attention and practice. But I cannot imagine you sitting about, eating bonbons, staring at your ceiling, contemplating nothing but the next hat of the season."

"Hats are wonderful things," she exclaimed defensively. "Why should I not contemplate them? They are made with great skill and labor. And fashion is important."

"Fashion is important?" he echoed, clearly astonished by her sudden passion for clothes. "I am surprised to hear you say so."

"Fashion is exceptionally important, Your Grace," she explained, sitting a little straighter. "For what a lady wears dictates what she's able to do."

He studied her. "I don't follow."

"Of course you don't," she said without rancor. She was ready to shrug off his ignorance, but then she realized what a loss of opportunity that would be. She wanted him to understand how clothes changed a woman's life. "Have you given any thought to the fashions of the previous century versus the fashions of now?"

He shrugged his immaculately clad shoulders. "Not particularly, if you must know."

She refrained from rolling her eyes at his cavalier attitude—an attitude he was not alone in. "Are you opposed to bright color?" she asked, genuinely curious. So many men now valued themselves by the cut of their plain breeches and the austerity of their coat.

"No, not at all," he admitted easily. "I recall men applying makeup, donning elaborate wigs, and enjoying a good red heel. I don't mind if my fellow men are happy to do so, but I do not think that I should look particularly well in pale paint and rouged lips. And I loathe wigs." He frowned. "Terribly itchy."

She laughed, pleased that he was far more open than most. "I have to say, I do think the new fashion suits you very well. The truth of it is, the dress of fifteen years ago was not very functional. While I do wish gentlemen were allowed to wear far more color than is fashionable at present, I think the idea of being able to stride about in Hessians must feel very nice. I have no idea what that feels like."

She sighed, considering the bliss of pantaloons, an item of clothing denied her.

"You wish to stride about in Hessians?" he asked as he started to laugh, caught her gaze, then coughed.

"Whyever not?" she demanded, determined. She'd often wondered what it was like. "I can only imagine what it should feel like to be in breeches." She nodded toward the stage. "Actresses occasionally get to wear them, and I do envy that greatly. For instance,

Viola, in her pants role in *Twelfth Night,* spends most of the play in men's clothes."

It was extremely irritating that her stride would always be confined to the width of her skirts. "I can only imagine how delightful it must be to scamper about, and climb, and go anywhere that one might wish and not have to worry about their skirts getting caught up or even fitting through a door."

His eyes widened. "How true. I recall from my childhood the way ladies had to turn sideways to achieve entry to a room."

"Because you're a man," she intoned. "Think of all those ladies in a room, trying to get about, turning this way and that, and ensuring their wigs did not land upon the floor like a furry little friend."

"You do profess the truth with humor, Lady Beatrice."

"The truth is often humorous and horrifying," she replied without irony.

He hesitated, then said, "Perhaps one day you'll get to wear breeches after all. My estate is vast. You could don breeches if you wish when you go riding. No one would see you, except perhaps some of my tenants. And you will visit, since your cousin shall be my sister-in-law."

She eyed him carefully, suspicious of a trap. "Are you quite serious?" she asked, barely daring to believe such an offer.

Even her uncle had never suggested she be allowed to go about in breeches and a shirt.

"I don't see why not," he said, his brow furrowing.

"I cannot believe I am saying this, but you've surprised me," she admitted.

"Have I?" he asked, looking rather pleased.

"Truly, I don't know what to make of you," she whispered.

And just as he leaned in toward her and said, "I promise that I will come tomorrow for our lesson," her uncle came up behind them and clapped the duke on the shoulder in a jovial moment.

"Your Grace, Your Grace, I think it would be most wonderful if you kept Lady Beatrice company throughout the play." Her uncle beamed hopefully at the duke, his silver hair shining in the golden light. "You two seem to be getting along as well as two peas in a pod, and I should hate to see that interrupted. Besides, I have some questions for Lord Benjamin about Oxford and all that."

The duke seemed to tense, and she wondered if he was actually horrified by the idea of having to sit by her for the rest of the play.

Did he dislike her company so very much?

He hadn't seemed to. He actually seemed to have been enjoying it.

She all but held her breath, waiting to see what he would do.

"Of course I shall keep Lady Beatrice company," the duke announced, resuming a dignified stance, head high, hands folded behind his back. "No doubt it will be most amusing."

"But we agreed you are rather large," she drawled.

He shot her a mischievous look. "I shall fit just fine if your uncle goes and sits with Benjamin. If Kit and Margaret sit just there"—he pointed to the two red-and-gold chairs to his right—"we shall all cram in like sardines together."

"That is a most interesting thought," she replied but found herself far too happy that he had decided to stay with her.

Which was quite a surprise in itself. When had she begun to wish for his company?

Her uncle inclined his head, all but bouncing with his pleasure at the outcome. He backed out of the box again and into the hall.

Beatrice considered how it would feel to sit with the duke in the dark.

Nearly touching, their bodies close as they both sighed and gasped and watched the actors upon the stage as antics ensued. She felt her blood warm, and not as a result of the crowded theater.

Suddenly, she wondered if it was such a very good idea at all.

Would she even watch the play with him nearby? Would she be able to think of anything else but him? And the dream of his lips upon hers?

CHAPTER EIGHT

He had no idea how he'd been maneuvered into sitting next to Lady Beatrice for a play that lasted two and a half hours. It was wonderful and awful.

It was like having a cake put in front of him that was the most delicious, wonderful thing in the whole world. And yet he was not able to eat it.

And bloody hell, he wanted to devour her. She was a temptation to his mind, his soul, his body.

His entire frame felt on edge, and it was all he could do not to positively vibrate next to her like a piano string that had been struck.

Deliberately, he drew in slow, deep breaths to keep himself from fidgeting like an overzealous school boy next to his first experience of carnal admiration.

But here, in the box, he was sitting so close to her that his boot brushed the hem of her silk skirt. His thigh nearly skimmed hers.

His chair was but a relegated few inches away from hers, and she was leaning slightly toward him, and he toward her.

He did not know why. Were their bodies unwittingly drawn to each other?

It was true, he was a large man. There was no denying it. He did take up a great deal of space. As he was doing now.

And in the sensual hush of the darkened theater, the lights fading so that the audience could focus upon the stage…he felt drunk with her nearness.

Lady Beatrice was no petite creature herself. And because of that? The possibility they might touch substantially increased with every moment that passed.

He swallowed and stared at the stage as musicians began to play. As the jolly tune filled the air and the singer bade the audience to not sigh for lovers due to men's inconstancy, he felt himself drifting away, unable to listen to the ensuing witty banter of the characters below, though he dearly adored *Much Ado About Nothing*.

It was a great play. One of his favorites.

It was a powerful tale of jealousy, friendship, misunderstandings, and ultimately love in the most unexpected of places.

He enjoyed reading it to himself at night by the fire when he had a few moments. His father and mother had loved it, too.

It was why he still would turn to the pages, reading it time and time again. In those words, he was filled with nostalgia for a happier time.

But sometimes it was also was painful.

And perhaps that was why he didn't go to the theater as often as he would have liked. For both his father and his mother had been great patrons of it when they had been much in love and happy. They'd attended at least once a week and invited playwrights and actors into their salons almost nightly.

He shook the painful memory away.

Beatrice laughed, a rich, bell-like sound, and he smiled to himself.

He daren't look at Lady Beatrice. Bloody hell, he

was there to watch the actors. And yet he kept trying to sneak glances at her from the corner of his eye.

Her sensual yet witty lips were parted in a smile, her eyes wide, and her whole face glowing, rapt with happiness as she watched the antics below.

Could anyone love anything so well as Beatrice seemed to love the goings-on onstage?

Did she truly love the theater that much?

Perhaps she loved the freedom that the theater brought. Actors could play many parts. One day a king, a queen, a warrior, a lover, and sometimes men pretended to be women and women pretended to be men.

One could be whomever they wished to be.

And given Lady Beatrice and her longings for a more just world, it was not surprising that she would adore a medium that allowed her to see people transform from mere actors to heroes and heroines.

He thought of her impassioned longing for breeches.

What in God's name had possessed him to invite her to his estate to wear breeches? What the devil had he been thinking? What drivel had come out of his mouth?

It wasn't drivel, though, really. He had understood her. She longed to climb mountains but was relegated to rooms.

It wasn't because he was opposed to the idea of Lady Beatrice in breeches that he was suddenly re-criminating himself. No, now that she had made him aware, he could completely understand why she might wish to experience such a thing so completely out of her sphere.

But as uncomfortable as it made him feel, the idea of seeing her in breeches and a linen shirt, without the armament of the female costume…well, he did not know what he'd do with himself.

He would have to go to the farthest reaches of his house, or go down to the lake and take a bath in it, and hope that the cooling water would work this time, though it had not before.

Seeing her in such garments would be a torment. For as strange as it was, he found himself longing to see the curve of her calf and the length of her thigh leading to her hips.

He placed his hands on his knees and tried to relax, but as he did so, he realized that his hand was exceptionally close to Lady Beatrice's.

She leaned forward, peering at the stage as she joined the riotous laughter of the audience. They all marveled at the witty quips between the enemies to lovers below them.

He marveled at her and the play of the candlelight on her face, her breasts, the golden leaves embroidered into her gown.

If he moved just a breadth to his right, his hand would touch hers. For her hand, too, was resting on her knee. Did he dare? Would she think that he'd done it on purpose, or could he perhaps…

Before he could stop himself, he angled himself so little that it was a feather's breadth of movement. The edge of his hand touched hers ever so slightly. So slightly that it might have been but an illusion.

She did not seem to notice, and he felt a wave of ridiculous disappointment. Of course she hadn't noticed. What a ludicrous fool he was.

Lady Beatrice felt nothing for him except disdain and a fleeting amusement, just like the Beatrice in the play did for Benedick.

Beatrice. It truly was an apt name for her. She was so wonderful and intelligent and capable. She went slipper to boot with him without flinching. And in a world that kept her from being her full self, she seemed determined to keep trying.

Despite all odds.

How could he not admire her?

How could he not wish to take her hand in his and do everything that he could to help her?

And as he sat there, he realized that's exactly what he had to do. He had to do everything he could to help her, and he would. He would stop being so stubborn and so caught up in all his rules and engagements. He would listen to her, and he would do as she asked, and then she would feel as if he truly was her ally.

Instead of doing it *his* way, he would try doing it hers.

And then, much to his amazement, her hand moved, and her fingers brushed the top of his.

For one brief moment, her hand rested atop his, and the weight of it, the softness, the power of that touch nearly undid him. And he could scarce believe that something so small could feel so great.

CHAPTER NINE

Will had not felt like a schoolboy since, well, he was a schoolboy.

But Lady Beatrice had invigorated his view of life in a way that he absolutely relished.

He ran up the granite steps of her uncle's well-appointed townhouse, rapped the gold-painted knocker, and before he could wait two seconds—something uncommon for a duke—the door swung open.

Will crossed the threshold and stepped onto the black-and-white floor without waiting to be invited in.

As he did this and then stopped in the center of the room, with its curving stair and high-domed ceiling spilling sunlight through its glass windows, he reflected for a moment on Lady Beatrice's words about bowing and scraping.

Bloody hell. Was his life full of small moments in which he did not even realize how privileged he was?

Yes. The simple answer was unequivocal.

Will paused, then turned toward the butler, with his perfectly pomaded silver hair and pressed blue livery. "Do forgive me. I gained admittance without waiting for you to even greet me."

"Oh, Your Grace," replied the butler swiftly, his voice deep with obeisance, "you are always allowed to enter into this home. You need not wait for invitation."

"Perhaps I do not need to," Will allowed, smiling pleasantly at the older man, "but I *wish* to. And that is a world of difference. It is very easy for me to go about doing whatever I please, but I should not." He took a step toward the butler. "Your name?"

The man's brows rose, and his mouth dropped before he rushed, "Heaton, Your Grace."

He nodded. "Heaton. A pleasure to meet you."

"And you, Your Grace," the butler replied, his voice reedy in his disbelief.

Heaton said nothing else, as a good butler should not.

No doubt Heaton was quite surprised that a duke should wish to respect him so entirely. And he did. How could he not? The truth was he felt great respect for all the servants that he met, the hardworking people of London and those who kept the country running. He thought they deserved a great deal more respect and a great many more resources than they were given. He did not approve of the hoarding of land, wealth, and power that his class maintained. And even dignity.

With Lady Beatrice's well-put castigation still rattling around his brain, he knew that he had to do better to make people *realize* that he respected them. One could not just think things. One had to *act* upon them.

"Thank you, Heaton," he said at last, looking about. "Will you take me in to Lady Beatrice? I do believe she's expecting me this morning."

Heaton nodded, jolted into action from his stunned state. "Yes, Your Grace. Indeed she is."

Will clapped his hands together in anticipation, because he could not wait to see her. It was almost unfathomable.

His mind had raced with intensity and possibility. He had been thinking all the waking hours of the night about the theater and their impending boxing lesson. In general, he slept but little. He could usually not turn his mind off and needed but five hours of repose, which meant he went through a great many candles and all the books he could devour.

Heaton led him through the light and airy house, refurbished into the height of fashion.

The butler stopped before a white door edged with gilding.

He nodded at Heaton.

As soon as Heaton opened the door, he stepped through, knowing that in this case etiquette did not need him to wait.

He was expected.

The small salon was beautifully appointed with bright blue silk walls and the most stunning white stucco ceiling depicting Diana at the hunt. Elaborate stucco foliage trailed over the ceiling and lined the walls in balanced proportion.

The chairs were delicate and beautiful, and the French writing desk in the corner was covered in books and papers.

He smiled at that. It looked nothing like his own, upon which all documents were squared. Hers were positively exploding as if they were as full of passion as their owner.

And much like Diana above them, Beatrice filled

the room with her formidable presence as she paced before the tall windows overlooking the park.

It was not at all how he'd expected to find her. She was whispering aloud, gesturing as if speaking to several people.

It reminded him of his rehearsals for when he spoke in Parliament.

It suddenly dawned on him that while he was expected, she was not sitting around *waiting* for him.

He couldn't describe the emotion that overtook him at the realization. It was more than relief. It was pleasure.

So often it seemed as if people had arranged themselves into their seating positions or poses a good fifteen minutes before he arrived anywhere. And when they spoke? He often felt certain that whomever he was speaking with had rehearsed everything they were going to say to him before they'd even met.

Not Lady Beatrice.

It was almost as if she did not care that he was going to arrive, which was startling in itself. But oh, he loved the fact that she was so transfixed in her work she seemed wholly unaware that he was there.

It was impossible to pretend ignorance of how intimidated people often were in his presence, and her complete lack of diffidence thrilled him.

He cleared his throat, and Heaton left the door ever so slightly ajar behind them.

Beatrice turned to him and nearly jumped. "Goodness," she said, "you're here." She pressed a hand to her middle, laughing in her surprise. "I did not think you were coming until ten o'clock."

He smiled at her. "It *is* ten o'clock, Lady Beatrice."

She swung her gaze to the French clock on the marble mantel. "Oh dear," she said, blowing out a breath. "I had no idea so much time had passed since six."

"Have you been in here since six o'clock?" he queried, unable to stop his brows from rising.

"Indeed I have," she replied easily. "I took my coffee in here this morning and have been at work ever since."

"What occupies you?" The intensity of her interest and work reminded him of his own dedication. What could so captivate her?

"You are not interested," she said with a shake of her head.

"Of course I am," he protested, shocked she would suggest otherwise. Still, he knew humor worked best with her, and so he winked. "I am interested in all the things that take up your time so that you may cause trouble in the world."

She gave him a wry look before she propped a hand on her hip, which caused her pale yellow gown to swing about her long legs. "I'm working on a new pamphlet and a speech that I will deliver to the Ladies' League of Rights."

"Indeed?" he said, impressed by her tenacity. "Will you allow me to hear it?"

"I will not," she replied, narrowing her gaze, though she didn't appear actually angry. "You have had the opportunity to read all of my pamphlets, sir, and responded meaningfully to none of them. If you ever wish to hear one again, you will have to earn the right to do so."

God, she was something. He loved how she stood up to him. It was true… If she had been born a man? She would no doubt have been at the front of rule.

As it was, she had to do whatever she could to make change at all.

That sort of determination and strength was no small endeavor. For one had to overcome disappointment after disappointment.

No doubt *he* had been a recurring disappointment. Which was quite frustrating, given the depth of his love for those pamphlets. A fact he wouldn't confess. He could scarce admit to himself the way her words affected him. The way they shook him from his stoic anchor and urged him to throw off all he had worked for and give in to the delicious things he felt when reading her passionate petitions.

The painful reality, given his promises to himself and the brutality of society, was that she wished things from him he couldn't give. She longed for freedom for all women, and whilst he supported that, he doubted even his power to change Parliament, society, and a thousand years of male rule.

But he would do what he could to at least make her seen and heard.

"Fair play, Lady Beatrice," he said with an elaborate bow and twirl of his wrist. "Shall I grovel? Would that work? I've never done it so will likely do it poorly, but I've heard groveling can—"

"Now, do not mock me, sir," she warned.

"I would never do such a thing," he said

earnestly. "My respect for your mousetrap of a mind is too great."

She pursed her lips. "Is that a compliment or an insult?"

"You will forever wonder if I am complimenting or insulting you, but I promise you this, Lady Beatrice: I never insult you," he said with honesty and no subterfuge. "I have a great admiration for you, even if you do not believe it yourself."

She eyed him carefully. "I think that you do in the way that you can."

"In the way that I can?" He felt as if he was about to have his guts handed to him on a silver platter yet again—and he was growing to like it. It was such a pity he couldn't have more of her.

Because his body ached for her. Ached like a parched man for cool springs. But since he'd never marry her, he couldn't have her. No, he couldn't stretch her out on his bed, as he had in his dreams. He couldn't strip her stockings from her limbs. Kiss his way up her thighs and give her pleasure whilst slaking his thirst for her.

He curled his hand into a fist behind his back, willing the thoughts of her naked under him out of his disobedient brain. But he'd never wanted a woman he couldn't have. Surely he could fulfill his promises to her without succumbing to her worst suspicions about men and their desire to assist women?

Yes. He could. He was determined.

He could never love her. He'd never be so irresponsible. But he also knew that to keep himself in check, the only thing he'd ever be able to give a woman like Beatrice was power and distance.

It suddenly occurred to him, much to his horror, that he had just contemplated taking her to wife.

To be his duchess. The mother of his heirs. But he could never offer such cold fare to a woman of such passion. It would ruin her life. And he would be the worst thing for her.

"I know that those words are not a compliment," he replied at last. "You are always giving me set downs."

"Because you are a duke, you always need them," she replied merrily.

He rolled his eyes and laughed, savoring the humor that dissipated the tension in his body built up from that damned desire in which he couldn't indulge. "I suppose it is good to have a critic," he said. "So few people, except my enemies, will choose to point out my errors."

"I shall happily continue to do so," she assured.

"But are you my enemy?" he sallied. "You keep insisting we are not friends."

"Indeed, I am *not* your enemy," she declared, dropping her hand to her side. "Since I am going to be your family. That would be bad form."

"Indeed." She had a strong sense of noblesse oblige. More than most gentleman, he'd wager. He drew in a breath and said softly, "So you shall tell me when I am going amiss so I can know it before my enemies do?"

She laughed, a rueful tone. "Would you give me such an important role?"

"I would," he replied, taking a step forward, wishing he could close the distance between them entirely. "For I think very few could handle the laying out of my sins with the intelligence, the alacrity, and the wit that you do." He grinned. "At least sometimes you make me laugh when you point out my flaws."

"Ha! I have yet to see you laugh when I do so."

"Inside, Lady Beatrice," he teased. "I laugh on the inside. Indeed, when you bring me low, I cry there as well."

"How very terrible for you," she observed. "One should cry when they feel like crying, and one should laugh when they feel like laughing."

"Do you?" he queried, not believing for a moment that Lady Beatrice was an open book of feeling. Of wit and anger and merriment, yes. The rest? He was not so certain.

"Of course I do," she retorted. But then she paused, her brows drawing together. "Except I don't seem to cry. I don't cry particularly well in front of people. I haven't since my parents died. I cried all my tears then, and I have not permitted myself since. It is a rather impossible circumstance of our English existence, is it not?"

He'd lost both of his parents at a fairly young age, but he had not felt an accord with them. Beatrice? When she spoke of her parents? Her eyes lit with admiration and a hint of sadness.

They must have been wonderful. He found himself glad that she had not known the cruelties of his own childhood. Cruelties that would deny him love for the rest of his life.

"True," he rushed, desperate to shove unpleasant memories aside. He thought of Admiral Nelson. "But ten years ago, men used to cry quite happily in public, carrying about handkerchiefs, pressing them to the tears on their face. Kissing their friends without accusations of foppishness, and, of course, they recited poetry and wrote long, emotive letters."

She nodded. "Yes, it is a sad thing lost, but along with the colorful clothes of the era, it does seem to be no longer the fashion for men to be emotional. Ladies, either, really. We're all meant to go about being stoic and great wits, are we not? Though most of us haven't the wit to please ourselves, let alone a dinner companion." Beatrice sighed, genuinely at a loss. "I am so sorry. I hope it does not affect you too greatly."

He stared at her for a long moment.

He didn't really know how to reply to that.

In many ways, he was glad that he did not have to air his emotions and that he could keep them inside. There had been so many painful ones about his parents' situation. He did not know if he could ever let them out, for if he did, he wasn't entirely certain he could ever put them back in.

And it wasn't always easy to keep himself in line. But he did. With a hard hand. He'd never forget the night his mother slipped away…leaving him.

For love.

His mother had run away for love, abandoning him and his brothers. And whatever gentleness his father had had was broken.

Love was the devil. And he was glad he'd never feel it.

It was so strange to him that a lady as sensible as Beatrice did not seem as against love as he was. Will was tempted to ask, but it seemed a dangerous road.

It was enough to know she had no wish to marry. She loved her independence, and that would keep them each on their own paths...

She gazed at him strangely, a depth and contemplation to her that had not been there a moment before.

They had wandered onto potentially dangerous ground. "I am not here for such considerations," he said lightly. "I shall never know if burying our emotions behind our wit is folly." He upturned his lips into a slow smile. "But I do have the knowledge of a boxer. Did you wish to begin your lessons today?"

Her gaze lit with excitement. "Indeed, Your Grace. How could I not wish a bout of fisticuffs with you? We have bantered so often with words that I think it most suitable we should now use our fists."

"Lady Beatrice, you and I shall never truly fight with fists."

"Why?" she asked before she waggled her brows at him. "Do you think you shall overpower me?"

"No, no. I have already considered more than once that you could easily turn out the victor, for you are so determined," he assured happily. "And as they say, it does not matter the size of the dog in the fight, Lady Beatrice."

She arched a sardonic brow. "I beg your pardon?"

He asserted, "It matters the size of the fight in said dog."

"That is the most...well, accurate statement I think I've ever heard, even if it is terribly unpoetic."

He laughed. "I am not a poet, even if I admire poets. I'm glad you find the idea apt."

"And I am glad that you admire poets, even if you are not quoting them as gentlemen did before." She let out a wistful sigh. "I think that reading poetry is one of the best ways to sharpen our minds."

"As do I," he agreed easily. He'd read so much of the stuff it was a miracle he did not speak in verse or iambic pentameter by default.

"Do you really?" she queried, her cheeks flushed pink with pleasure.

He quite liked that look on her face… Would she look thus after a kiss? Eyes sparkling, skin aglow…

He cleared his throat. "I spend hours reading. It is one of the great pleasures of my life. I stay up every night reading after I finish my work. You know, I did read all your pamphlets," he said.

"Did you, by God?" she blurted before folding her arms just under her breasts, which plumped them against the line of her bodice. "I was certain that you threw them all in the fire."

"No," he said. "I would never burn words. The very idea! That is the most horrific accusation you have yet made at me."

She smiled, relenting. "Forgive me. I realize that truly was beyond the pale."

"Indeed it was," he said with great seriousness before grinning again.

How was it he smiled so much in her presence?

She hesitated—an oddity for her—then rushed, "What did you think of my pamphlets? Not much, clearly."

He groaned inwardly. She'd never let him live down his short replies to her petitions.

"I think they are all passionate," he said

truthfully, "and all make good points. You are correct; you need someone to give them…"

"What?" she challenged, readying herself for battle.

He drew in a fortifying breath. Her anger was spectacular, and he loved sparring with her, but this was important, and he didn't wish to offend.

"You're going to be angry with me if I say it."

"I am almost always angry with you, Your Grace. How would that change things?" she drawled.

He leveled her with a determined stare. "You need legitimacy. You need someone to lend your organization and your words authority."

"Yes," she countered, throwing her hands up. "I know. Why would you think that would make me angry? Why do you think that I have written to you so many times?"

"Forgive me for taking so long to understand. That's why I assumed you'd be angry. Because I finally do understand."

"Oh," she replied, as if she was glad that he had reached this conclusion that she had no doubt formed long ago.

He cleared his throat and stated, "I would very much like to be the patron of the Ladies' League of Rights, if you will allow me to be."

She stared at him for a long moment, her jaw all but dropping to the green-and-white Aubusson rug. "You cannot possibly mean it."

"Indeed I do," he assured. "I only regret that I did not offer it to you sooner."

She gasped with apparent relief, but then she stared at him with suspicion. "What has made this change?"

"You," he said honestly.

"You like me, and so you'll help me?" she exclaimed. "Just like a—"

"No," he cut in. "I only like you a little, anyway."

She scowled at him. "Come, now; out with it. What has caused the change?"

He was still for a moment, then replied, "It was something that you said to me."

"Something I said?" she echoed, her shoulders relaxing as she looked mystified.

He nodded. "You told me that everyone always bows and scrapes and tells me what I want to hear and that you would not do that with me. And ever since, I have noticed when people bow and scrape. I always knew that they did, but I just assumed I was supposed to accept that. After all, I'm the duke."

He shook his head and looked to the windows. "I never wanted to be, you know. No one actually *wants* to be a duke, but when you are the duke, you become accustomed to it, and you think it is your due."

He swung his gaze back to her, astonished to see how serious she had grown. "You reminded me that I am just a human being, even if I do have the title, and I should question when people bow and scrape, and I should question my own response to it. It has been a revelation in the way I view the world, and I am deeply grateful to you because it has given me a feeling as if I am more in the world than out of it."

"Did you ever feel out of the world?" she said softly, her eyes widening with sympathy.

"When one is a duke," he explained, not allowing himself to indulge in self-pity, "one is always a little removed. We are not like others."

"Is this arrogance speaking?" she asked carefully.

"No, it is a fact," he stated with a shrug. "We must always be isolated, because the truth is, people never want us for ourselves. They always want us for what we can give them. Did you truly ever wish to know *me*?" he asked. "You never wrote me a letter asking me about myself, did you?"

"No," she allowed quietly. "I never did. Nor did I particularly have any interest in knowing you, Your Grace."

"William," he returned gently. "That is my name. And I am named after William Shakespeare because my mother and father loved his plays so well. That is who I truly am." He locked gazes with her and stated, "The rest, well, it's just ornament."

"Ornament often tricks us," she pointed out.

Was that it? The only thing she had to say after his confession? His spirits sank.

But then she held out her hand. "I am grateful to meet you, William," she said brightly. "It shall be a pleasure having a lesson from you today."

He stared at that hand a moment. It felt so different than nearly any other greeting that he'd had since becoming Duke of Blackheath. It was earnest. Sincere. As if she was seeing *him* and not his title.

He had not felt that in years, and it felt…so *good*. He could not describe it. And as he reached out his hand and took hers, the world spun about him. Their palms clasped, warm, electric.

He swallowed and felt his heart hammer. Then he looked at her, not with the power and authority of a duke but as a man who was so very happy to be seen for just himself.

That? That jarred him in a way he'd not expected. And as he let his hand slip away, he knew he was going to have to be damned certain that *liking* never turned to *love*.

CHAPTER TEN

Beatrice did not know entirely what was happening, but whatever it was, it had completely shaken her. She had assumed the duke was coming here for a boxing lesson, not for a revelation.

No. Not the duke.

William.

And it was indeed a revelation, for not only was he about to give his support to the Ladies' League of Rights—and who knew what else—she had just discovered him as a *person*, not only a duke.

As William, she could not hold him to quite such disdain as perhaps she might've in the past. Oh, she'd still be able to criticize him as the duke for certain, but now, she felt as if she was seeing a window into his life and his feelings, and there was not that wall, that guard, that had been there just a moment before.

How could something so small do such a thing?

Could her blunt honesty have allowed it?

It *had*.

Or so he said.

She gazed at him for a moment, her hand still warm with his touch. The feeling was exquisite, perfect, strange.

'Twas as if she was meeting her best friend.

All her life, she'd had love. First from her wonderful parents. Then, after their tragic deaths, from Margaret and her uncle. She'd had friendly acquaintances from many people.

But so often, she'd felt alone because her ideas about the world were so different than so many others'. Her passions often drove people away, though she did not mean them to. She was too blunt. Too fierce. Too much.

While people enjoyed her company over tea, they often could not meet her in her deep need to make changes in an unjust world.

But standing here in silence, she felt William truly was her friend and someone who perhaps understood her in a way that no one else did. For he, too, felt passionately about the world and thought on the way he could change it.

She blinked quickly, the reverie breaking. She could not allow herself to linger too long in such thoughts, thoughts that might lead to silliness, and silliness was not for them.

A man like William? He could never give her the great love her father had given her mother. It required too much sacrifice. Too much fearlessness.

And much to her amazement, she knew without a doubt his heart was locked up so entirely, the key could never be found.

She wouldn't be fool enough to try to find it.

"So," she said quickly, "my lesson. Shall we proceed forthwith?"

He inclined his head. "Forthwith, indeed, Lady Beatrice."

She folded her hands before her. "You must not call me Lady Beatrice if I am to call you William. Please call me Beatrice."

"As you wish…Beatrice," he said.

That voice. It caressed and coaxed and tempted.

"Now," he said, taking on the role of instructor, "we cannot go into this abruptly. We must loosen ourselves up a bit, or else we risk injury."

"Risk injury?" she repeated. "Without being punched?"

"Have you not engaged in anything that has potential to cause you damage without letting your body warm up a bit?"

"I have not," she answered. She wagged her finger at him. "Remember, ladies are not encouraged to be engaged in particularly strenuous endeavors. Walking and riding at most. Oh, and dancing, of course. All meant to show one off to the best advantage to get a husband."

"It is strange," he mused with a touch of horror. "I think so little about what ladies are not allowed to do that I do appreciate these moments with you. You show me what I need to see, and that allows me to do better."

"I'm glad you think so," she said, stunned again. Where was the arrogant duke who had not even wished to meet her? "When we first met, I was fairly certain you hated those moments."

"I do hate them," he said. "They make me feel uncomfortable. But that doesn't mean they're not valuable to me. I am so used to being right that it's very difficult to be told when I'm wrong. Still, I do not need to be right all the time. Such a thing is impossible anyway."

"Do my ears deceive me?" she teased. "Does the duke admit he can be wrong on occasion?"

"More than 'on occasion,' but promise not to tell anyone."

She made the motion of buttoning her lips. "I shall keep your secrets if you keep mine."

His eyes darkened at that comment.

She had no idea why.

Darkened not with anger but with something else. Something exciting.

"So, what shall I do?" she said, not quite sure what to make of the sudden warmth traveling through her veins. "I am your pupil. I offer myself up to your tutelage."

"Let's bounce a bit." True to statement, he began to bounce on his toes.

She started to laugh. "Are we to dance? Is this a reel or a jig?"

"No," he replied. "There shall be neither reel nor jig, though both dances could be argued as eminently helpful in the avoiding of one's opponent."

She frowned. "I thought one just merely stood there and punched at the other person."

"If you stand still, you will be hit and hit good," he pointed out, sliding his coat off his broad shoulders.

Her breath caught in her throat as he turned to face her in his green brocade waistcoat, which hugged his torso in a way that made her wish to discover what lay beneath the layers.

"Oh, dear," she said. "So I must dodge about."

"If you wish to be the victor, yes." William untied his cuffs, then slowly rolled the linen shirt up his forearms. "Being still is quite dangerous."

She found the process of revealing his lower arms to be…fascinating. The sinew and skin over bone…

Suddenly, she couldn't breathe as adequately as

she liked, and they had not even begun.

"That's interesting," she forced herself to reply, trying not to fixate on how he was revealing more and more of himself. "Being still in life is quite dangerous, too."

"Whatever do you mean?" he asked, crossing to her.

She licked her lips, rather disappointed he did not need to remove anything else. "Well, if you stand still, you don't grow and you don't change. Of course, it's good for a moment's tranquility, but to remain still for too long, well, that's death of opportunity."

"You have the mind of a philosopher," he observed.

She rolled her eyes. "I suppose that's one way of putting it. Others have put it in a less flattering light."

"Others," he said firmly, "are fools."

Those words—those affirming words that she was in the right, not everyone else—sent a wave of sheer happiness through her, and she couldn't stop the smile that tilted her lips.

So filled with joy at his response, she began bouncing.

He, too, took up the action directly in front of her. "Follow me," he urged.

She nodded and bounced on her toes back and forth, mirroring his movements.

Their bodies began to move in harmony, though they touched not at all.

Her limbs warmed; her breathing came faster. Their gazes held.

It was so remarkable to see him doing something,

well, so unduke-like.

She had thought this would be full of aggression and domination and determination, but that was not the case. He was light and fluid and strong as he bounced about on his legs.

"Bend your knees," he suggested. He crossed to her and showed her how his own long limbs were loose, ready. His hand came to her hip, then to her thigh.

His hand lingered just above the fabric of her gown. "The angle of your thigh allows you to support your body but be ready to move away quickly."

Flicking her gaze rapidly away from his hand hovering just over her body, she bent her knees and followed his movement.

Her skirts began to swing, and she felt them brush his hand.

As if shocked, he pulled his arm up, and a muscle tightened in his jaw.

"Good," he said firmly.

But with every bounce beside him, her full skirts swung about her legs and the hem cascaded over his boots.

She said nothing but reveled in the fact that he was so close. But this felt different. As their bodies synced, the air seemed to charge, to heat.

Though both were at ease in the lesson, she could not stop thinking about the way his body moved so breathtakingly beside her own.

A tension took hold of him as he abruptly moved away from her, and she realized he'd felt it, too. That symmetry and charge.

"Now we're going to practice your guard, for

while it is more fun to strike, it is incredibly important to avoid being hit."

"Very good advice," she said, watching his strong hands fold into fists.

He glanced to her hands. "Now you must put your guard up."

"How do I do that?" She laughed, loving feeling something so unknown. Surely it was simply the boxing that caused her to feel thus?

It wasn't his body moving with hers, mirroring hers, was it?

"You take your arms," he began, bringing both of his forearms up. He tucked his elbows in toward his body and kept his fists just at his jawline. "And place them so."

She looked at him, studied his stance, and did as he did.

"You are a very good student," he stated, and as he turned, his waistcoat shone in the light spilling through the windows.

"Thank you," she said, stunned that she liked his praise.

"Now let me help you to make small adjustments," he warned. He studied her frame. It was assessing, but something else flickered in his observation. Something heady. "Because if you stand that way, you will be knocked over easily."

"I will not," she scoffed, doing her best to ignore the hypnotic pull toward him that was taking root in her center. "I may not be a man, but I am of stern stuff."

Then without a word, he reached over and slightly pushed her shoulder.

She very nearly toppled over.

A peal of laughter erupted from her.

But then...then she felt it. The power of his touch on her shoulder. The way their bodies connected and how she stumbled back, lost balance, overcorrected, and fell through the air toward him. Just as if gravity conspired to make them one.

He caught her, his arm swooping around her waist.

The length of his body stroked hers as she slid against him. Her skirts enveloped his legs, and she grabbed onto his shoulders. Her breasts pressed into his hard chest, and his scent surrounded her. It was a terrifying heaven, for there was nothing formal about this hold.

A long pulse of need traveled through her. She did not know what to do, it so overtook her.

His hands froze on her body as he clasped her to him. For one agonizing moment, he angled his head toward her, his dark hair dancing against his cheeks. His palms pressed into her side, holding her tightly to him as if he did not wish to ever let her go.

And then he abruptly set her to rights and stepped back, his chest expanding in a deep breath.

"My goodness," she confessed, brushing her hands down her skirts, desperate to put her rioting thoughts in place. "You were not mistaken."

"If you do not have your balance right," he replied, his voice lower and rougher than before, "you shall keel over faster than a drunk after a long tipple."

"How very vivid," she replied, still feeling his arm about her middle. She'd liked the feel of it. Yes, she'd liked it far too well, for she could still feel the strong sinew of his forearm pressed to her side.

"Keep your knees bent," he said simply. "Adjust your step. Your feet must not be parallel. If you have one slightly in front of the other, you will have a better purchase."

She did as instructed, her insides aflutter at his nearness as he continued.

"Good. Very nice. Now—"

"Yes?" she prompted, meeting his gaze, which sparked as it took in her stance.

"Here. I shall show you," he said, quickly crossing to her side and facing the windows as she did.

He brought his guard up, and she almost laughed, for his fists were above her head.

"Why are you laughing?" he asked.

"You are so very tall," she observed honestly, craning her neck to make good view of him. "I shall get quite a crick if I have to continue in this."

"A seeming difficulty," he admitted, his lips tilting with amusement. "But height is not necessarily an advantage."

"Is it not?" she asked, hardly believing it. He all but towered over her, despite the fact she was no waif. "I would have thought being the biggest and the strongest was the best advantage."

"It is a good advantage," he agreed. "But it is not necessary to win. Sometimes, to be the smallest and the fastest is the best."

"Why?" she queried, suspicious that he was merely placating her. "Couldn't you knock me flat with your fist?"

He cringed at the very idea, apparently. "Yes," he

concurred. "I could knock someone of your size into next week if I wished."

She marveled at the idea of his power, but she was also glad to know that he would never do such a thing to her. Will was a man of honor. That was very clear.

She did not envy his brothers and the men who came into play with those fists for entertainment. How anyone could wish to be entertained by having their head struck, she did not know.

Men truly were odd.

"If you are fast and nimble," he pointed out easily, "you can outmaneuver me and you can tire me out so that I don't even get a blow in." He gazed down at her. "You see, my reach is longer—"

She shook her head, confused. "What do you mean by reach?"

Slowly, he stretched out his arm and placed it on her shoulder. "Do you see?"

She studied that arm, swallowing. Indeed, she could see how long and muscled it was through the thin linen. And she felt the power and energy of him through his palm resting on her capped sleeve.

Unable to reply, she nodded.

"That is the reach that I have. Now you try to reach," he urged.

She guffawed. "I think I can guess that mine is shorter."

"Do it anyway," he prompted.

Since he was giving the lesson and she wished to be a good sport, she humored him. Beatrice stretched out her arm.

Her hand was a few inches from his chest.

"So you observe," he said gently. "My reach exceeds yours, but that is not the end of the story."

All she could think of was the feel of his hand upon her shoulder and the fact that their bodies were but feet away from each other.

"Now I could easily land a good blow from this standpoint," he continued as if her body wasn't suddenly on fire at the mere touch of his hand. "But you are so nimble and quick that it might be difficult for me to catch hold of you or land a blow."

"Oh, I see," she breathed, liking this bit of information very much. Life always seemed to be in favor of the big and powerful. It was nice to know there were advantages to the other side. "Who knew I was a veritable David to your Goliath?"

William choked out a laugh. "You shall never bore me."

"One does hate to be bored," she replied, feeling merrier by the moment.

"Yes, one does," he admitted.

It was something that they both seemed to share. Neither of them could be too still or alone with their thoughts too long. They both seemed to find it imperative to keep moving, to keep acting, to keep changing the world.

"We shall begin slowly circling each other," he said, stepping to his left.

"You're not teaching me how to punch," she pointed out, rather liking the idea of hitting something. Ladies were not allowed to express their anger or frustrations physically. And while she did not plan on boxing with someone truly, she liked the idea of at least having the option of punching the devil out of a pillow.

"Not yet," he said. "Right now, I just wish you to circle and copy my movement."

They began rotating. Twin points, moving back and forth, slowly round and round. It was hypnotic the way they balanced each other's every move.

She locked gazes with him, and he with her.

Everything about this moment was captivating. It deviated from the formality of the waltz they had shared, and there was an inescapable fluidity to their exchange.

But William was coiled. Ready for action.

Even in this practice setting, he seemed completely at ease in his body, as if it was the perfect home for him. She marveled at the way he embodied his physique and the way he so easily and kindly instructed her.

She followed him about the room, then her slipper caught in the hem of her gown. "Blazes," she blurted as she nearly went down but staggered back into circling.

He moved toward her, but she waved him off.

"Oh, dear," she said lightly. "This gown is a definite hazard."

He gave a rueful grin. "I confess I don't ever have to worry about such things."

"Another thing that gentlemen do not have to worry about." She sighed playfully.

"We shall have to make a list."

"It will not be a list," she said honestly. "It shall be a three-volume tome."

"Devilish pain," he replied sympathetically. "It's most unjust, a damn nuisance."

"To say the least," she agreed.

As they circled again, this time a little bit more slowly, she found her balance. It was very easy to do on the balls of her feet.

"Right. Very nice." He stopped and waggled his brows. "Now, time for the punch you're so curious about. We will start with a right jab."

All her life she'd largely been a pacifist, not necessarily out of principle but for the simple fact that ladies were not allowed to be warlike. She was rather looking forward to this bit.

He nodded to her right hand still held up, guarding her face. "Now, you're to jab at my palm."

It felt quite odd, but she eyed his opened palm and its map of lines.

It was beautiful. And for a moment, she wondered what it would be like to feel that palm on her bare skin.

Before she could think a far wickeder thought, she shot her fist out at it.

He caught her fist easily, his fingers warm about her hand. "Very good effort." His thumb caressed her knuckles. "Now, use your body to create momentum. Pull your fist into your body, then launch it forward. Imagine how charged you felt the night we met, and rotate your body toward me. Hit me like I just insulted your pamphlet."

She started to laugh. William gave her a most serious stare, and she worked to eradicate her grin. It was no easy thing.

Her lips twitched, but she focused and did it exactly as he bid.

She envisioned him making his most arrogant

face and using his most sardonic droll. Instantly, she felt the power of her punch.

So much so that she went off-balance and launched toward his chest.

He caught her in his arms, quite pleased. "Very powerful!"

But once she was wrapped in his arms, to her horror, she did not wish to retreat.

And to her amazement, he did not immediately let her go.

Quite the contrary.

They lingered like that.

A strange war danced across his face like he was having an argument worthy of the House of Lords in his head.

Until suddenly he growled softly. The connection between them and the intensity of the hunger between their bodies clearly had caught him off guard. "I cannot explain it, Beatrice, but despite the strangeness of such a thought, I long to kiss you. Nor can I pretend any longer. It is a terrible idea, but it is the truth."

Standing in his arms, her body pressed to his so tightly that not even a ray of daylight could pass between them, she wished for it, too. Had dreamt about it now for days and spent far too many waking hours imagining it.

He would never love her. She knew it in her bones. He wouldn't be her grand passion. And yet, she couldn't deny that he evoked something in her that demanded answer. All logic seemed to abandon her. There was only one thing guiding her now... She needed to discover if reality was as desirable as her imaginings.

She tilted her head up, stunned that this was happening but not wishing for it to be any other way. "I don't mind a bit of strangeness."

And before either of them could say another word, Beatrice, much to her own astonishment, reached up, took his waistcoat in her hands, and pressed her lips to his.

CHAPTER ELEVEN

Unlike some libertines of his class, William was not in the habit of risking the ruin of young ladies. As a matter of fact, kissing a young lady such as Beatrice was so entirely foreign to him, he might as well have been in the Antipodes.

The *last* woman he was supposed to be kissing was Lady Beatrice. He couldn't give her anything but his political aid and perhaps a few lessons in bobbing and weaving.

He'd warned her that he wanted to kiss her, knowing he needed to make a fast retreat. That's what it was. He knew now. A warning. Perhaps it was for himself.

His damned brain had been trying to send up the alarm.

Because his passion for her was so entire that the arguments that had kept him on the straight and narrow his whole life could not be heard above the cacophony of his need for her.

Bloody hell, he did not know what the devil he was doing, but her mouth—it was perfection under his; the way they seemed to meld and meet defied all expectation. Each breath, each kiss, each touch of lips tossed him higher and higher toward some fiery passion that he'd never experienced before.

The kiss burned through him, turning him to a positive cinder. Except it didn't leave him in ashes. No, it sparked something in him, which then grew and blazed.

Beatrice's own passion seemed to be just as fiery as his until, kiss for kiss, they were consuming each other.

They clung to each other like two souls lost upon the sea, and the only salvation lay in their bodies entwined together.

Her hands slid up to his jaw and then into his thick hair.

He marveled at the feel of something so intimate and so passionate at once. He found himself wrapping his arms around her back, pulling her into him until they both arced, as if somehow they could become one with this kiss.

The feel of her body against his was sheer perfection, her breasts pressed into his hard chest, a contrast to her softness, and he savored the feel of her hips cradled just below his.

Breath for breath, gasp for gasp, touch for touch, the kiss built. Driving further and further down a path he could not understand.

He had to have her. In all his life, he'd never desired anyone so much.

As if she was equally astonished, her lips parted, and he found himself unable to resist touching her tongue with his. The kiss turned wild, as if they had both been starving for years and finally found exactly what they needed to fulfill their hunger.

He let out a soft moan of appreciation as he caressed her tongue with his, and she let out a sigh of bliss as she relaxed into him.

"Ahem!" a voice called from the door.

They both tensed, then jolted back from each

other, as if their touching was as dangerous as being struck by lightning.

"I did not mean to intrude," Lady Margaret ventured, her eyes wide but not with judgment. He fancied fascination and delight danced there. "But Father is asking for Beatrice. We have an appointment this afternoon."

"Lady Margaret," he said and gave her a quick bow. She stared at them as if they had been replaced by complete strangers.

"It is a good thing that it was me who found you two," she piped.

"I hope you did not watch much," he replied.

"Indeed, no," she assured as she swung her gaze from Beatrice to him. "Just enough…" Margaret cleared her throat.

Beatrice's eyes were wide with horror. "Can you imagine if my uncle caught us? You would be trapped. I would be trapped. *We* would be trapped."

The real horror of it hit him at her words. What the bloody hell had he been thinking?

"You were most lucky," put in Margaret, who still seemed amazed. "Are you two getting married?"

"No!" roared Beatrice.

"Absolutely not," he stated. "I was giving her a boxing lesson."

"A boxing lesson," repeated Margaret.

He frowned. "Yes."

"I see. Who knew one needed to stand so close?" Margaret coughed.

"I tripped," blurted Beatrice.

Margaret nodded and said rather enthusiastically, "Of course you did. Very common in a boxing lesson, no doubt."

He planned on remaining a bachelor for a very long time. And the idea of having to marry someone like Lady Beatrice, well, it was positively horrifying, wasn't it? Of course it was.

He'd spent his whole life shoring himself up against the possibility of the sort of pain his parents had endured. The sort of abandonment he had experienced as a child. He would not fall short now.

He clapped his hands together. "Well, we can be grateful that it was Margaret who caught us in such an embrace. Anyone else would have thought we were about to cause a scandal. Forgive us, Lady Margaret."

She beamed at them. "Oh, not at all. You both looked most happy, and I shall never need apologies when witnessing…such happiness."

Beatrice groaned. "We best go. I don't wish Uncle barging in."

She turned to him.

And for one brief moment his world hung in the balance. Had this ruined their friendship? He might not be able to bear it if it had.

Beatrice gave a quick curtsy. "Until our next lesson…William."

With that, she bustled toward Margaret, her pale yellow skirts swooshing playfully about her slippered feet.

The ladies rushed through the door and left him standing there, relieved and agog.

Beatrice was, without question, the most interesting person he'd met in his entire life.

He found himself wondering what else he could

do to assist Lady Beatrice in her pursuits. Surely there was something more a duke like himself could do than just lend his name?

A young lady of such determination should be rewarded for her desire to change the world.

He turned and headed for the hall, then to the foyer. Heaton gave him a nod, which he returned, and a bow as William exited to the pavement.

He stopped, London rushing by him.

And a thought struck him. One that went into his heart and hit home so hard he almost couldn't breathe.

He desperately wished someone had been around years ago to assist his mother in her endeavors. No one had, not even his father, who should have been the first person to support her.

The Bolter.

That was how she'd be forever remembered.

The scandalous lady who had left her marriage and bolted for the continent.

He sucked in a ragged breath as a wave of melancholy crashed over him. Every day, he carried the memory of that loss with him. The darkness of it. The suffering of finding oneself alone. It was as if she had died, and none of them had been allowed to grieve her. He'd done everything he could to be strong for his brothers, to not show them the extent of his pain.

Yes, he would assist Beatrice in her cause. And he would use all his skills and his power to lead the way.

CHAPTER TWELVE

Every week, as another set of banns was read, Margaret all but bounded about the breakfast room, unable to sit still to eat her toast.

Beatrice could understand her cousin's enthusiasm.

For whilst she had no intention of marrying, she, too, had trouble keeping herself still over the rasher of bacon and pots of steeping hot tea at breakfast.

After all, Beatrice could not shake the memory of the kiss that had happened a few days before.

She had not seen William since, but he had written her several—*several*—detailed letters on how he believed he could help the Ladies' League of Rights and also involve himself with some of her other endeavors, such as funds for women without homes in the East End, homes for women and their babies where they could be safe together, and schools so that ladies might learn viable occupations that were not just in service, where they would not be able to keep their children.

William was a whirlwind of energy, ready to dictate the projects. He was certainly thorough with lists of estimated costs and the amounts he would allocate.

The letters filled her with so much hope, even if he was moving at such speed he wasn't consulting the women he hoped to help. She would make him see that would backfire in the end. She could see he wanted to be successful, but men hardly knew anything about the trials of women. If he did not seek out the testimonies of those he wished to help, much of it would be for naught. But she believed with a little correction, he would adapt.

After all, she'd done more research and discovered the extent of support he'd lent the endeavors of the Clapham Sect. The amount of funds he'd donated toward the printing of antislavery pamphlets was astonishing.

And if she was honest, she could not forget how not only their minds had met...but their bodies, too. That kiss...

How could she not keep recalling the way that she had kissed William and how he had kissed her back?

It had been a shocking moment. Though she'd dreamed of it, she'd never expected it to come to pass.

The kiss had been, well, nothing short of meteoric for her. In all her life, she'd never felt so entirely alive, so entirely lost in the moment as she had while kissing him.

It had been so...*wild*.

All her life was driven by her need to seek rights for her sex. Better lives for people. And so she had not spent much time at all on pleasure.

It had been both intense pleasure and extremely sensual all at once.

It was a miracle she could think at all, that kiss had caused her mind to riot so.

Beatrice took a fortifying sip of tea as Margaret trilled about her wedding gown, the guests who would attend her wedding breakfast, and how tall her cake would be.

Beatrice did her absolute best to nod her support as she sipped her tea and then turned her face to the news sheet. She read it every day, front to back, so that she could understand the current events of the world.

There was a great deal of gossip and hyperbolic ranting in it. Still, she enjoyed cursing at the writers who clearly were mistaken in their interpretations of events.

France was in a right state.

It was terrible.

William had not been mistaken in his point that Olympe de Gouge had essentially been murdered by the very party she had helped put in power.

It was most upsetting.

One moment Madame de Gouge had been at the height of her power, reveling in the future of the French people, and then she had been killed...for asking the French Assembly for equal rights for women.

She did not like to think the same thing could happen here in England, but one never knew.

Perhaps William was correct on one point. Perhaps arguing too fiercely and being completely unyielding was a mistake. Perhaps she would try to argue with more finesse. It was not easy. She preferred to argue fiercely, but he was a powerful man, and she had managed to change his mind by being blunt and honest, but she had not railed at him.

It was worth considering.

She turned the page and spotted an article on

Lord Byron. Dear God, what was that nincompoop up to now? Was he going to insist he ate naught but potatoes and vinegar?

She'd wager he went home every night after the balls he attended and stuffed himself with steak or cake.

Her uncle took a step into the room, then paused.

She heard the creak of the floor, or else she wouldn't have looked up. She caught the sight of her uncle's pale face and flinched. Quite unusually, he was still in his dark green banyan. A cup of coffee was clutched in his hand.

It shook slightly.

Her cousin stopped her chatter and smiled at her father. "Good morning, Papa."

"Good morning, my darling," he replied, though his smile seemed forced today.

And without another word, her uncle whipped around and headed down the hall in the direction of his study.

Beatrice found his behavior most odd. Her uncle was usually a kind, jovial fellow.

Margaret was consumed with dress plates as she sipped her tea and apparently had not noticed.

Considering that his only daughter had made a very advantageous marriage, Beatrice felt a wave of concern. Carefully, she folded her paper and pushed her chair back.

Margaret paid no attention as she pored over her potential choices of costume.

Taking her tea with her, Beatrice followed her uncle down the hall and into his study.

He stood staring out the window, coffee cup held

midair as if he was in a trance.

She looked about the room filled with books and globes and all sorts of fascinating objects that he had collected in his travels as a young man, unsure exactly how to begin.

He seemed oblivious to her presence, which wasn't like him at all. Her uncle was usually an attentive and caring person.

"Uncle," she ventured. "Are you unwell? You seem— Well, you do not seem yourself."

She crossed toward him but stopped just short, feeling he might not wish her in his presence.

He drove a hand through his usually immaculately groomed silver hair. She was suddenly uncertain when he had washed it last.

In fact, everything about him looked quite...disheveled.

And it was then that she realized the slight scent in the air was not his cologne but brandy.

That was not coffee in his cup, and a wave of dread washed over her. What would drive him to imbibe so early?

Her uncle met her gaze with watery blue eyes. He sucked in a shaking breath, then rasped, "I am in a difficulty, Beatrice."

"Unburden yourself," she urged, even as her own heart squeezed with growing concern.

"I suppose I can tell you. Now that Margaret is safe. Lord Christopher cannot abandon her now. Not with the engagement public."

Beatrice's stomach tightened as her ill ease increased dramatically. "Uncle, I do not understand what you are trying to tell me."

His brow furrowed, and in an instant his whole face seemed to buckle with emotion. "Beatrice," he said in a broken whisper, "you're a very sensible young lady, and I know that I can be plain with you in a way that I perhaps cannot be with Margaret."

"Uncle, you are making this worse with prevaricating," she said gently but firmly. "Please, out with it. None of these niceties or warnings."

He nodded and looked away as if he could not bear to see her reaction. "I have lost my fortune, Beatrice."

She blinked, taking those words in but not comprehending them. How could she? Such a thing wasn't possible. Was it?

"I don't understand," she said flatly.

He drank deeply from his coffee cup, then blurted, "I invested heavily in some new ventures, and they have proved at fault." A wild laugh that turned into a sob erupted from his throat. "I have lost my fortune."

Her uncle clapped a wrinkled hand over his mouth, stifling the sob. He shook his head, his silver hair flying about his worn face. He laughed again, a dark, almost frightening sound.

"Uncle," she breathed as his words finally hit her with their severity. "I am so terribly sorry."

"I am, too," he gritted. He slurped from his cup. "I am only glad that I have managed to secure Margaret a good match so that she will be kept and treated well."

Her uncle stared into the lowering contents of his cup as though it was tea leaves bearing their fortune. "But I have more news for you, Beatrice."

She stilled, dread pooling inside her once again. "Yes?"

Her uncle pressed his lips together as he stared at her. 'Twas as if he was waging a war with himself in what he could say or could not say to her. "I know that you insist on not marrying, but I must tell you something that could change that. And I pray to God you shall not hate me for it."

"Hate you?" she asked, even as the room began to spin and she felt a wave of growing nausea. "How could I hate you?"

He began to tremble, his face racked with pain as he confessed, "Your fortune is gone, too."

Her body went numb. She stared at him, unable to fathom his terrible words.

"How?" she demanded, her throat tight.

He looked away again and staggered back to the window, leaning on the sill. "I am your guardian, and I was given the task of managing your fortune for you…until you came of age. And I thought to increase it for you so that you would never have to worry another day about having to do things you did not wish. With it increased, you should have been able to continue on in the way that you have been doing until old age."

Her parents had left her secure. And she'd always felt certain she'd never have to worry about funds. It had always been such a relief. Her funds had enabled her to help so many people. Not just herself.

"I am so very sorry," he whispered. "But I have lost it. I hate myself for it, Beatrice."

He looked back to her, awaiting her condemnation. Tears filled his gaze.

"Uncle," she urged, hastening toward him. "I can never hate you. I love you."

The words spilled out of her even as these horrific new circumstances began to dawn on her.

But her uncle had looked after her since she was a girl and had done everything he could to raise her well and give her the freedoms that most men never would a young lady. She could not hate him, but there was no question her world was whipping around and around at the most sickening speed.

For she did not know what to do next.

"Uncle, I find that I am at sea."

"I am so sorry, Beatrice," he rushed, his voice full of self-loathing. "I am terribly sorry, but we are going to lose everything."

How could one go from complete astonishment to doom in a single moment? How could one be independent, wealthy, full of privilege and possibility, then in the gravest of circumstances in an instant?

And how did one navigate such wild thoughts and feelings?

She gazed about them, at the books, the pictures, the artifacts. She thought of all the beautiful things in the house. Their coach. Their clothes. The money she gave away.

His words took effect, and she struggled to breathe.

No doubt the house would go with everything in it, and the horses, and the fine clothes, and the coach, and the country estate.

It would all go.

As would her future and her freedom.

For she was no fool. A woman without a fortune

was in great danger of the whims of society.

"Well," she said softly, determined not to break down, "at least, as you say, Margaret is taken care of."

Her uncle nodded. "Perhaps I should have told you sooner so that you could find a husband right away."

"Do not be ridiculous, Uncle," she countered. "Why would I change…"

But even as she said it, her words died in her throat. For how could she boldly declare her determination now? It was very different to be a wealthy spinster than a poor one.

"Beatrice," he said, his voice finally firm, "I think you should. I think you should try to find a match almost immediately."

She widened her eyes. "This cannot be occurring."

All her life, she'd been determined to never have to put her fate in the hands of a man—especially one she did not love. Not realizing her future already was in the hands of a man—her uncle. And now it was all going terribly wrong.

"You know the fate of impoverished women, Beatrice," he whispered. "It is not pretty."

It was not. She was not such a fool as to be noble about it. "Uncle, I cannot. I cannot do it."

He swallowed, then took her hand in his. "You must. We can keep this private for a bit longer. Last night, I could not sleep, and so I composed a list with several candidates for you to consider. Any one of them would be willing to take you up if they believed…"

"That I had a dowry?" she ground out, yanking her hand from his grasp.

"Indeed," he replied, lifting his gaze to hers at last. There was a steely determination there. A willingness to do whatever it took to see her secure in a marriage with money so that she never faced poverty.

"Let me understand." Her stomach roiled as his meaning dawned on her. "You wish me to trick a man into marrying me?"

He drank his cup to the dregs, then declared passionately, "I wish you to find safety and security, Beatrice. This world is not kind to people without money."

She knew it. She'd seen it.

She'd gone to the East End herself on many occasions and seen the poverty there. The children playing in veritable cesspits. Children who likely would not pass their fifth birthday.

Ladies who would not survive thirty. Dying of disease, living in filth…

Fear swept over her, stealing away her calm for a single moment, for she knew unequivocally how difficult it was for the lives of even the intellectual classes, the artists. Most of them lived in fear of debtors' prison.

So many of the people she admired barely clung to stability, and they had the skills to manage and survive such conditions. She'd never been taught to do such a thing.

She could learn, of course. But it would be no small thing. She'd be a fool to think it would.

Whatever was she to do?

"Oh, Uncle," she lamented, blinking her burning eyes. "This is terrible. I do not see how I can will myself to the fate to which you've resigned me."

She placed a hand to her middle, determined to not be overborne.

"I am so sorry," he said again, as if somehow his regret could change their circumstance. *Her* circumstance.

Her fate had been put into the hands of a man, of a guardian, and it had been his duty to ensure her safety—and he had *failed*.

The cruelty of it, the absurdity of it filled her until finally she stepped forward, took her uncle's hand in hers, and said, "I shall always love you for the care you have given me, and I can never be angry with you or hate you, but I do find that I need a moment alone."

"Of course you do, Beatrice," he murmured, squeezing her hand.

"Uncle, I will always forgive you," she said firmly. "But this…this is most difficult indeed."

And with that, she turned and strode out of the room.

Marriage? *Marriage?*

All her jokes and teasing, all her protestations about how she'd never wed…how she would be no man's fool. They flooded back to her, taunting her.

She couldn't. She could not choose marriage. Her parents' faces, so full of love as they gazed at each other, seized her thoughts. Beatrice bit down on her lip, the pain of the news so intense she longed to curl into a ball and sob.

Marriage without love?

All her happiness seeped out of her in that instant. How could she do something so traitorous to her parents' memories? To herself?

She couldn't.

As she entered the hall, she felt as if she was drowning in a vast sea and could not get air. Just as she was about to run to her own room so she could gather herself and decide what to do next, Heaton turned the corner and met her.

"Lady Beatrice, the Duke of Blackheath is here to see you."

She blinked. William? She had not been expecting him this morning.

"He is waiting in the drawing room."

Her throat tightened. "Tell him I am not available at the moment."

"He seems most determined, and I am not certain how to tell a duke that you are not home when he knows that you are."

She let out a long sigh, not wishing to put Heaton into such a difficult position.

It was another reason she loathed dukes. They were always accustomed to getting their way. Though William wasn't quite so bad—she knew that now.

Even so. She wasn't prepared to see him. How would she manage? She'd simply have to tell him she was unwell… But. She was no coward, and she would not begin acting like one. Even if her circumstances had taken an abrupt reversal.

She was still her strong-willed self. Even if she had no money.

CHAPTER THIRTEEN

Will had absolutely no idea what he was doing.

Which was not his typical state of affairs.

He shouldn't be striding up to Lady Beatrice's townhouse. Not after their kiss. He should be avoiding her at all costs—but he was no coward. And they were going to have to sort the situation before Kit and Margaret married.

They had to come to some sort of terms that would keep them both on their very separate yet amicable paths. Paths that wouldn't allow for the sort of fiery embrace that had stolen his mind, his wits, and his ability to sleep. For if he did close his eyes, his dreams were fixated by her and her form and every possible pleasure he could give her between his linen sheets.

Usually, he was in complete command of his decision-making rationality. He prided himself on being a man of reason, a man of boldness, and a man of action. After all, his entire life had put him in such a position; when some men faltered, he went forward.

It had been his strong suit in Parliament and the halls of power. When some men heard the shouting and manipulations of the opposing party and turned to retreat, Will thrived. He turned their arguments, their pettiness, and drove his own cause home. And his boldness moved those who were uncertain to boldness.

The arguments he'd had with prime ministers and the king's own advisors were legend.

Yet, the strange turn his life was taking was completely different than the dangerous games played at the center of English power. And he was relieved. Everything was falling into place.

Beatrice was a marvel. A friend in a world where dukes did not have friends. Not truly. But the kiss... It had made their friendship...different.

And he needed to speak with her about it.

He had not felt so strange since the day he'd learned he was to be the duke. He'd not truly been ready, though his father had been unrelenting in Will's preparation to take up the family's power. Will had simply thought he'd have more time to himself to learn and find some joy, despite the loss of his mother, before he was saddled with such a monumental job.

His father never should have died so young.

And from something so silly as a dip in the water.

They all loved to winter swim in lakes and rivers. Their father had encouraged such endeavors to build mental and physical strength. And his father had done it every day of his life since boyhood.

It should have been just another day when they all took the icy plane. And yet, his father had developed a chill after their frigid outing.

He'd been forced to his bed, another odd thing for their father, who considered himself above illness.

He'd never risen.

It had shaken Will to his very core.

Perhaps some might have responded to such a

thing by becoming cautious. Instead, it seemed that he and his brothers had responded in quite the opposite fashion.

No, they damn well wanted to honor their father's life by living. To the full.

They all acted as if this was perhaps their last day. Not in wild debauchery but in purpose and intensity. One never knew if one would be struck down by illness or step into the road and be killed by a coach.

He had been a hard and demanding man, but he had still been their father.

This life was a most strange thing.

And so, to honor his father, he had tried to live dedicated to the good that a duke could do. Yes, his father had never chosen the easy or cautious path.

He wondered if his father would approve of his support of Beatrice.

He did not know. His father had taken a fairly narrow view of ladies, what he believed their limitations to be, and their role in society.

If he was honest, he didn't think his father would have liked or approved of Beatrice. But deep down, Will knew his father's one fault was in his view of women.

And he would never be the same.

The sound of footsteps thundered toward the door. He knew at once, that step. Lady Beatrice.

She threw the doors open and crossed the threshold. As always, she was a force to be reckoned with. He found himself eager to begin to set things to rights. She seemed most upset, no doubt with him and the position he'd put her in, and he was eager to put her mind at ease.

But bloody hell, standing before her, he couldn't deny that she made him feel vital as no one else could.

Not many ladies gave themselves the permission to live so fully. He loved that she did, but her countenance did not reflect the joviality or passion of the day before.

Even her typical mischievous wit seemed absent from her visage.

Was she so out of sorts with him?

There was genuine distress on her features, and he found himself alarmed.

"Lady Beatrice, are you unwell?" he asked, preparing himself for her rightful recriminations.

"I am most well," she said, though the flatness of her voice belied the claim. "I am as healthy as a horse."

"I'm glad to hear it," he ventured, studying her warily.

Her glasses were pushed up high on her nose, and she looked pale.

"But I am most busy today. Please forgive me, but I would prefer if you departed and came back at another time."

He stilled. "Forgive me. I've behaved abominably, but surely we can—"

Her eyes sparked with passion. "You are a duke, and so your comment is perfectly natural, but not everything is about you, Will."

He blinked, reconciling the abrupt entry to her townhome. Her displeasure was not about him at all. He felt an initial wave of relief, and foolishness for making the assumption that their kiss was so profound, but then a growing tide of concern swept over him. Beatrice was no silly miss to be upset easily.

It had to be something significant. She was so completely at odds with her usual self.

"I will of course go," he assured, hoping to offer her a rock in her storm, "if you'd like me to, but you seem distressed, and I would far prefer to offer my aid to you. As your friend."

She stared at him, the battle inside her evident in the stormy darkening of her gaze. She bit her lower lip as if she was holding back a surge of words.

"Truly," he urged, "let me assist you. What else is a duke for?"

"I cannot," she insisted, wiping a hand over her strained face. "It is not right that I should share my difficulty with you."

"Who, if not your friend?" he replied, his heart hammering at her genuine state of emotion.

They were friends. They had to be. It was the only thing that explained his sudden desire to lay waste to whomever had hurt her.

What could shake his Beatrice?

"It is… It is a matter of practicality, and yet so much more."

He nodded, hoping his silence would induce her to fill it.

"Oh, William," she rushed, leading them into the small parlor they had kissed in, as if she could not hold back the tide of misfortune. "I am a pauper."

"But you have a fortune," he protested, crossing over the Aubusson to her.

She let out a horrified laugh. "I *was* a woman of

fortune, but this morning I find that I awake penniless."

"How has it come to pass?" he asked calmly, determined to be steady for her. To allow her to crash upon him like a storm upon the shore should she so need.

"My uncle, alas." Her eyes shone with tears that refused to slip free. "Poor man. Poorer investments."

He winced.

If her uncle had lost everything, including her fortune, there would be a scandal.

He might be able to mitigate it, but it would not be easy.

"This shan't affect Margaret and Kit's wedding," he assured. "Kit has more than enough money and doesn't require Margaret's dowry."

"I'm glad," she rushed. "I should hate to think that you would withdraw your support if you found out that one of the parties was destitute."

"I would prefer there not to be a financial disaster," he said honestly, "but sometimes these things happen. Margaret is worth far more than a dowry."

He loathed seeing her in so much pain. He had spent all his life ensuring he felt nothing akin to such agony. And here she was in the depths of it. Yet she fought her tears, which only added to the tension gripping her body.

"I don't know what I'm going to do," she whispered, her voice breaking. "My uncle has advised me to marry as a way out of my problems. Otherwise, I suppose I must find work. And I do not know what I am capable of doing that will gain me adequate funds to ensure that I do not live in poverty for the rest of my life." She sucked in a shuddering breath. "I have no skills, William. Not any that would do me good."

Some people — those who did not know better — might boldly declare that they were going to go out and live as a pauper to keep their principles.

He was glad she was not so naive.

She let out a horrible sound of pain, and he found his own soul breaking, because he suddenly understood what it meant to be a lady who could not be self-sufficient, especially a lady like Lady Beatrice.

"I am so very sorry," he said. "Surely we can find a solution to your problem."

She shook her head. "My uncle says it is marriage, society says that it is marriage, and yet I have sworn to myself that I would never marry without…" She swallowed as if she was about to admit something she preferred not to, then continued. "That I would have my independence, that I would continue to do my work and to help all the causes…"

And then her face went positively pale. "Oh dear God," she cried.

"What is it?" he asked, taking her hands into his.

"I supply so many funds to so many organizations that care for vulnerable women and children," she raced, clearly panicked. "Food, blankets, shoes for those who've known naught but the frigid cobbles and mud, educations… Can I be so selfish to choose poverty over marriage and allow all those I've helped to suffer anew?"

And then she pulled her hands from his, turned

to the fire, and buried her face in her palms.

For one moment, he found himself completely at a loss in the face of her agony.

Her entire life and purpose were escaping her. All the power she had was tied up in her financial independence, and without money, her power was slipping away like sand through an hourglass.

She was not mistaken. She was capable, intelligent, and passionate, but she had no skills that would find a woman work. If she'd been a man? It would have been different. He would have set her up immediately as a clerk or found her an apprenticeship that would lead to a good wage.

Perhaps she could acquire a position as a governess. Or a dressmaker might give her work. But both were doubtful.

She'd not worked a day in her life. Not by the standards of a profession.

His thoughts whirled about his head like the hurricanes he had read about that took place across the Atlantic.

He crossed quickly to her, searching for reasonable advice. "Marry me," he blurted, and before he could finish his sentence, he recoiled at his own rash proclamation.

What had he just said? Could he take it back? Surely she'd refuse him; she was so opposed to marriage.

What the devil had possessed him? For that was not his own sensible self asking such a thing.

How had those words escaped his lips?

She swung her gaze to him and looked as if he had completely lost his wits.

"Marry you?" she demanded.

He swallowed. Then froze. What the hell had he done?

"Will, you have no wish to marry…at least, you do not wish to marry now."

"No, I don't," he agreed.

Only an hour before, he would have laughed at anyone who said he'd propose to a lady that day, let alone that year.

But then he began to allow himself to contemplate Beatrice by his side as his duchess. And in his bed. He'd asked her… What if he didn't take it back?

What if she said yes?

He cleared his throat. "You don't wish to wed me, either."

"No," she agreed.

"Marry me anyway," he said, apparently casting all logic away. Because he could not allow his Beatrice to fall to further harm in a world that would misuse her, eat her up, and work her until she was naught but a shadow of the magnificent woman he knew.

"What? Have you thought this through?"

"Perhaps not," he whispered. "But we have a choice before us."

She eyed him carefully.

"I know you're not afraid of being poor or finding a thankless position," he began. "But if we unite, you will do far more good than you ever could have on your own. You're no fool. Imagine the power at your fingertips as my duchess."

"We face the prospect of misery," she said flatly.

"Not if we are logical," he found himself arguing.

What the bloody hell was he still doing? Surely he should be convincing her that he could set her up with a pension.

But one day he was going to marry. Sire an heir. And why not her? She was going to be miserable in poverty. He could ensure her independence and spirit were fanned, not extinguished.

"I don't follow," she said, folding her hands across her bosom.

He nodded, warming to the idea. "You're a logical woman and will never expect foolish, romantic drivel from me. And I can give you a family name that will gain you entry into politics."

"Allies?" she whispered as the idea clearly began to make some sense to her.

He could see her mind going over the dangers and the benefits.

"Allies," he agreed. "And nothing more. We shall never have to worry about being typical husband and wife. You and I? We are above that drivel that so many long for."

"Drivel?" she echoed.

"Love," he explained. "We share a cause instead. And that's what matters most. Truly, I am the answer. And I think you can be mine."

CHAPTER FOURTEEN

Once a duke, always a duke, it seemed.

Good God, William did act as if he knew all and could fix all. His attempts at perfection could be most difficult.

If he was like this all of the time, she could not have borne his presence, and yet she knew, ultimately, he was trying to do good.

It was always the case with William. He tried to do good. And he was trying to do good in this moment. She knew he'd never had any intention to marry in the near future, and yet here he was offering to take her out of a very difficult position.

But she couldn't possibly say yes.

Could she?

She had proclaimed her determination not to marry so often she'd feel a fool if she did. And the one condition she'd told herself would make it possible was a remarkable love.

He was telling her now that he would never love her.

She swallowed at her circumstance. It was bitter.

Because now, she understood how foolish she'd truly been to be so insistent. She could be so determined because of her own wealth.

She wasn't wealthy now. And any woman with sense understood the terror of an impoverished life stretching out into old age. Smaller and smaller rooms; colder, too; and little food awaited her.

There'd be no doctors if she was ill. For she'd have no money to pay them. There'd be no comfortable bed or chair for her aging limbs.

Her gowns would be turned year after year until they could be worn no longer.

Impoverished, she faced a long, cruel fate in which she could help no one, let alone herself.

She had no trade. No farm. No house. Nothing. She had only her wit and her will.

What would she do if she did not marry him? At least she knew William to be a good man of noble intention, if occasionally insufferable in his ducal arrogance.

She could do far, far worse, which was why he was so sure he was the solution.

They were friends, after all.

True friends. It had happened so rapidly, it was hard to give it credence. But they had crossed a line somewhere, allowing each to see into their true selves.

Deep in her bones, she knew they had an affinity for each other that could not be denied. But this was not how she'd imagined their relationship to go.

It all seemed moot now. For she had not money to provide for those causes.

She bit down on the inside of her cheek as another wave of despair crashed over her. She paid so many salaries. Kept so many organizations helping people in need afloat. How could she let them down?

William took her hand in his, trying to catch her gaze. "Darling friend, you must not allow this to bring you low. I promise I shall not make the demands that most men do. We can be different. We already are different. Choose business."

There was a terror in his own eyes even as he spoke confidently. As if he couldn't quite believe what he was saying. "Choose friendship," he urged, his voice low.

She paused, and she gazed up at him, studying his face, which was not as unflappable as usual. "This is a veritable night terror for both of us. Why are you doing this?"

He was quiet for a long moment, then said very seriously, "Because I can."

It should have sounded far too cocky. It did not. It was his admission that he could help her as no one else could, and he was willing and wanting to do so.

"But William," she protested, "I never wanted to be a duchess. I do not want to be your duchess."

A look of relief eased his strong features. "I see."

Much to her horror, she felt disappointment. Disappointment that he was happy she was turning his offer aside. But after all she'd said, how could she say yes?

"Then we are agreed," she stated. "I shall not marry you."

He cocked his head to the side. "I never took you for a fool."

"I beg your pardon?" she ground out. "I can see your relief."

He was silent for a long moment. "It is not what you think. I'm terrified, Beatrice. You make me feel things I swore I never would. If I leave you to the wolves—and that's what I'd be doing—yes, I might feel a moment's relief that I avoided marriage to you. But I would never sleep again. I would lie awake night after night until I die, hating myself. Hating that I let you go into the wild world to face it without me there. Please... Please, let us not be fools."

She flinched, and her heart? Her blasted heart, it fairly ripped open at his declaration, which sounded so close to love she could hardly bear it.

He took her hand in his. "I will have to marry one day. You're the perfect candidate for a duchess. You shall be able to do far more than most ladies ever could. You already have a politically astute mind. You understand society, and you know how to run organizations. You are everything that I require."

He gave her that slow, wolfish smile of his, which did the most delicious things to her insides. "You will no doubt be so good at the job that I might actually be able to sleep an extra hour every night."

She laughed, feeling shaky but also realizing he meant the words he said. "You think so highly of me?"

His sharp gaze wandered over her face, drinking in the details, studying them, memorizing them. "I do, Beatrice. And I cannot bear to see you in distress. I despise the idea of you marrying some man who doesn't value you, but being forced into poverty is unacceptable. Neither is an option to be considered."

William reached forward and stroked an errant lock of hair behind her ear before trailing his knuckles gently along her jaw. "Do not risk it. Marry me. You need never love me or fawn over me. Just do your duty as a duchess *and* pursue your dreams."

She swallowed. She believed he would not desire the sort of wife that other men wanted.

Dear God, it was tempting to tilt her face into his touch. To allow his caress to be a healing balm. But first…she had to be reasonable.

"I want it in writing," she said, locking gazes with him. "If… If you and I agree to the disagreeable, I want it in writing that you will allow me autonomy and freedom. That whilst you own me, you give me free rein with the funds you name in the contract. That you will not dictate my behavior or my actions."

He looked taken aback for a moment that she'd even think him capable of treating her poorly, but then he nodded. "Such wisdom. I expect nothing less from you."

"Thank you…" Her throat tightened with the tears she had not shed, with the fear that still shook through her. Fear at betraying herself and choosing a loveless marriage. "William."

He cupped her cheek, tilting her head back. "Beatrice, we shall make London quake underneath our polished boots, for you and I can make the world sit up and take notice. Nothing will ever be the same."

How right he surely was.

CHAPTER FIFTEEN

"I beg your pardon, you're getting what now?" Ben drawled over his gin.

"Married," Will repeated, this time so loudly that half of the Cock's Comb Tavern turned in his direction.

The already raucous, hard-drinking group lifted their chargers and glasses and shouted, "Eh!!! Cheers to the toff getting married!!!!"

There was a great deal of applause and more, and the fiddle began to play "For He's a Jolly Good Fellow."

Will longed to crawl under the table, but such a thing would be immensely foolish, given the company.

Besides. He was getting married. And to a remarkable woman.

So, he raised his own glass of gin high and called, "A round for all, my dear friends!"

And the entire tavern erupted in hollers of triumph, whistles, applause, and felicitations on the future happy event. Ben and Kit were hiding laughter but failing as they leaned back on the rough-hewn wood benches.

Will looked upon them as if they were mere toddlers guffawing at a silly joke.

After all, they were but boys when compared to him, and they had the most ridiculous ideas about how adults should run their lives.

Even Kit, who was getting married in little more than two weeks' time.

"Married," Kit repeated, shaking his head in disbelief.

"To whom?" Ben asked before he leaned forward and begged, "Please say her."

"Her," breathed Kit with delight. "It has to be Lady Beatrice."

His brothers both leaned forward in a parody of breathless anticipation.

"He's in love with her, after all," Ben said out of the side of his mouth to Kit.

Will's neck burned with a blush.

"I am not in love with Beatrice," he roared before clearing his throat and adding calmly, "That is the furthest thing from the truth. We are friends."

"Friends," Ben repeated. He nodded. "Oh, yes."

Kit pursed his lips, nodding, too. "Certainly. Friends."

He leveled them both with a ball-crushing stare. "We have an affinity for each other. What is so strange about that?"

"Nothing," Ben said. He took a long drink of gin, his face contorting as he struggled not to show his amusement.

Will blew out a breath, rolling his eyes at their juvenile attitudes. "I'm glad you think nothing is wrong with it. Surely I have explained to you many times over that the best thing a man can do is marry someone who is in accord with all of one's ideals."

"And you and Beatrice are in accord?" Kit queried idly.

"We've come to a good understanding," he

informed, thinking of her fearsome determination and her playful look during their boxing lesson. "And we actually do share many ideals."

"Such as?" Ben prompted, draping his arm against the bench back.

"The rights of humanity. The need to improve the lives of all those around us, to help people, to support them, to do good work for the country."

Ben groaned. "You two are going to be absolutely insufferable together. You will both be a walking cause."

He considered this. It wasn't accurate. He and Beatrice laughed a great deal together. He grinned triumphantly. "We both like the theater as well."

"Fair play," Kit said. "You won't always be insufferable, just most of the time, and when you aren't out at the theater."

William tossed back his gin, the suspicious East End liquor likely burning a hole in his esophagus as it traveled to his belly.

The truth was he was still a bit shocked about what had transpired the morning before. But his shock had not caused him to hesitate.

His lawyers had already made the contract with Beatrice's stipulations and ten thousand a year in funds allocated to a personal account for her. After signing it with a flourish, William had taken it over to her uncle's club.

He was not risking anything. Her uncle had wisely agreed to the marriage but had asked him to be discreet about the news of his ruination.

William had agreed because it wasn't his place to announce to the world a man's ruin.

But he did wonder if Margaret was going to be told before her wedding, because it was clear her father had no plans to inform her.

Beatrice was a courageous person; she might tell Margaret.

But it would take a great act of defiance to go against her uncle and share the information with her cousin.

If anyone was brave or defiant enough, it was his future wife. Who would no doubt see it as a sin to keep her cousin in the dark about such a thing.

And he admired her for it.

Secrets were often dangerous.

And when one tried to protect someone from such a serious thing, sometimes more damage was done. He wished that Margaret's father would confess it all.

He hated the idea of keeping it from Kit. But he wanted nothing to sully the marriage. Nothing would darken it for his brother. He'd be damned certain of that.

Everything would be a lot easier if Margaret's father told her, but people were very strange about this sort of thing.

Tragically, William had seen it over and over again—people so ashamed of how they felt over failure that they were unable to face their families.

Soon, all London would know what had happened. Perhaps he had a few weeks more, but probably not that much.

William was tempted to suggest to Kit that he procure a special license for himself and Margaret so that no one would say anything untoward to them on the marriage day.

But in the end, he wasn't entirely certain that was the best idea. Maggie and Kit had longed for such a large wedding, and pushing something up so quickly would mean that everyone would grow suspicious as to why. They would all be staring at Margaret for the next several months, waiting to see if a baby made its entrance into the world too soon.

It was possible that people might stare at him and Beatrice, too, wondering if Beatrice would suddenly begin to balloon with child and go into confinement in six months.

But of course that was not the case. He and Beatrice were not easily flummoxed by gossips.

Predictably, Kit said over his glass, "You swore that you would never marry before you were forty."

William rolled his eyes, draining his gin to the dregs. "Can a man not change his mind? Does his palate not alter as he ages? Must I be stagnant and intractable? I've never been so hardheaded that I could not alter my opinion on something. Indeed, it is a sign of intelligence to be able to grow and consider new paths," he said.

He nodded and smiled, pleased with his explanation.

"True," Ben said, "you have always been magnanimous and able to be persuaded to another side if given the right information." Ben looked to his own glass and frowned. "And Beatrice is a wonderful prize."

"She is not a prize," he countered, thinking that it was absurd to compare a woman to something one might win after a competition or game.

"I don't know. I think she's a bit of a prize," Kit declared, shoving his hand through his thick, dark hair.

"Whatever do you mean?"

Ben shrugged. "Shall we make a list? She's not intimidated by your position, she gives as good as she gets, is smarter than all of us, and she's a good sport. What more could you want? Also, she is capable of keeping us all in line—no easy task."

He glared at his younger brother, who had so astutely described Beatrice. Perhaps too well. "Ben, she is not your governess."

"I'm too old for a governess," he declared merrily. "And do not enjoy discipline as some fellows do, but there's something about her that's really quite wonderful, isn't there?"

"Yes," he agreed, "there is, and I'm glad you like her."

"She will be a brilliant addition to the family. I always wanted sisters." Ben swung his gaze to Kit. "And Margaret will be wonderful, yet I think that Beatrice will be just the ticket for us."

Will frowned before he lifted the gin bottle on the table and poured the last of it into his glass. "Do you indeed?"

Kit nodded. "Margaret will make us all feel loved and appreciated, but Beatrice? She'll run a tight ship and won't take any of our nonsense."

He thought about that as he took another swallow of gin.

It was probably true.

And he felt damned lucky.

It was well and good to have a lady flatter one

and make one feel special.

But to have one tell you the truth? There was nothing better.

Beatrice reminded him of a general who made sure her armies did not retreat or run wild on the field. She kept everyone charging forward, confident and passionate with a whistle here, a bark of a command there, and a rousing speech to lift everyone up.

And he liked that about her. A little bit of organization helped people do much better in this life. He rather hoped that she could help organize Ben, who was on the road to ruin if not absolute debauchery.

"I've procured a special license," he stated. "For Beatrice and myself."

Kit slammed his glass down. "I beg your pardon?"

Ben eyed the empty bottle, then lifted his hand and waved at the bar wench, who came by their table, swinging her tray high over her head. Her bosoms threatened to spill free, largely thanks to a tightly laced stay and gown meant to make male costumers leave her better custom.

She propped her hand on her hip and asked, "Wot do ye fancy, governors?"

Ben took her hand in his and gazed up into her eyes in that terrible Byronic fashion he had. "My brother is getting married in haste, and I need to get dead drunk."

"Absolutely." She winked at him, quite used to gentlemen. "Oi'll bring ye a bottle of the strongest, luv."

Ben winked and tossed her a guinea. She grabbed it in her hand, put it between her teeth, and bit down.

She winked back at Ben and sashayed off to the bar at a good clip, motivated by gold. She easily made her way through the crowded room without spilling a single drink on her tray. She was a wonder in balance and gravity.

"It's not that shocking," he protested at Ben's dramatic comments. "You needn't get three sheets to the wind on the acid they pass as gin here."

"Indeed I do," Ben intoned, narrowing his eyes. "Surely you're about to relay catastrophe. Something drastic must've happened if you're marrying her immediately."

Kit grimaced. "Did you ruin her?"

"You're not supposed to ask those kinds of questions," he snapped. "The very idea is an insult to Beatrice."

"Perhaps, but everyone will be whispering about it," Kit said. "Everyone's going to assume it's the reason for such a hasty marriage."

They wouldn't; not in three weeks' time, when the news of financial ruin broke. He needed to tell Kit the truth, damn it.

He adjusted his position on the bench and said firmly, "No, I have not ruined her." He shrugged. "I have simply decided it is time that I marry, and Beatrice is the perfect choice. As I said, we have aligned goals."

"Aligned goals," Kit mocked, "how terribly romantic."

He shuddered. "Romance is not to be a part of our marriage. Beatrice has promised me that she will never fall in love with me. And I shall never fall in love with her, so everything shall work out well."

Ben and Kit looked at him as if he was being irrational in the extreme.

"What?" he asked, swinging his gaze from youngest to middle brother and back again. Then he looked down to his burgundy waistcoat. "Do I have a stain on me?"

"What do you mean she promised she wouldn't fall in love with you or you with her?" gritted Ben, who looked as if William had kicked a puppy.

He cleared his throat, feeling surprisingly defensive. Still, he drew himself up and explained, "It is going to be the tenet of our marriage that we maintain we are just friends. There is absolutely no reason that we shall ever be in love."

Ben and Kit stared at him with pained but unsurprised expressions.

He grimaced, hating but accepting the look his brothers gave him. "Don't you see what happens to people when they fall in love?"

"Brother." Ben gave him an impatient shake of the head. "We know your opinions on this, but surely marriage to Beatrice will lead to love?"

"I don't think so," he said, palming his glass.

Once again, they both stared at him as if he was absurd.

"No, no," he insisted as the barmaid sashayed back and plunked a full bottle on the table.

Ben grabbed it and plugged out the clear liquid in his glass as if his life depended on it.

William rolled his eyes at his younger brother's dramatics. "Both of you can stop looking like codfish. I am a man of intelligence; I know myself, and I know Beatrice. Neither of us shall fall in love, and

we shall have a very good life, and we will never
have to be concerned about being foolish with each
other. We are committed to the improvement of all
society, and that is enough."

"Mm-hmm," Ben said, nodding as he drank his
gin in steady swallows.

"Oh yes," Kit said as he, too, took up the bottle
and poured a goodly measure. "I wholeheartedly
agree."

He scowled at both of them as he poured more
gin into his own glass and drank it apace. Clearly,
nothing was going to convince his brothers of the
sensible arrangement.

He waited until they were both drinking and
stated, "The wedding is tomorrow."

Ben sputtered on his gin, and droplets flew across
the table, landing on William's coat.

He wiped at it. "Bloody hell. Not my favorite
coat."

"Forgive me," Ben exclaimed, "but you've completely astonished me. Why tomorrow?"

"Why not?" he said with a shrug. "I didn't see any
reason to wait."

And the truth was he could not wait to get
Beatrice in his bed. A quick marriage was the only
answer. The fact that they would get to explore the
passion their kiss suggested was an added benefit.

He was slightly surprised that Beatrice had
agreed to it, but she did not seem to have any silly
notions about an elaborate wedding or a grand marriage.

No—quite wonderfully, she had suggested a
beautiful place near the city, in a small but stunning

Christopher Wren church. She'd also requested only his brothers, Margaret, and her uncle attend.

It would be intimate, simple, honest, earnest, *perfect*. And given the haste? It was bold.

Just like Beatrice.

CHAPTER SIXTEEN

"I swear, day is night and night is day, and the ocean has turned to dust." Margaret beamed, the morning light dancing over her shining face. As she arranged the flowers in the wedding bouquet, she exclaimed, "Beatrice, are you truly getting married? Today?!"

"Indeed I am," Beatrice replied, hardly believing it herself. "Life is full of surprises, is it not?"

Margaret's eyes widened, and she laughed her beautiful bell laugh. "Surprises? Miracles, more like; but when I saw you kissing him, I knew. I knew in my heart of hearts that he was the one for you."

Margaret crossed to her cousin and placed the bouquet on her dressing table so that she could arrange Beatrice's pelisse. "I cannot believe you are marrying before me, let alone at all. I keep thinking I will wake and find it all to be a strange dream."

"Are you angry with me?" Beatrice bit her lower lip, her insides tight. She cared about Margaret so much, and she knew the rush of her own wedding had come as quite a shock. "For superseding your day?"

"Don't be absurd!" Margaret exclaimed before blushing. "Well, there might have been a single moment in which I found myself wondering at it. But I am not angry. How could I be? If you're to be happy."

Beatrice let out a sigh of relief. "I would understand if you were put out. You've already planned so much of your wedding. Your name was on all of London's lips. Now…mine is."

Margaret gave her a kind smile. "I'm not marrying Kit to be noticed by the *ton*. Oh, I hope everyone is happy at my wedding breakfast. But the point of it is to celebrate our union. Just as you are about to do! Don't you wish you had a bit more time? You could have a grand wedding. He is a duke, after all."

She blanched. "I think if we had more time, we'd both find a reason not to."

Margaret's brow furrowed. "You cannot mean that. I've seen you two together."

"Neither of us wished to wed."

"Yet—"

Beatrice groaned, then laughed and adjusted her spectacles. "Never fear. We both have chosen this with clear sight."

Margaret's lips twitched. "Could you two do anything else?" As she smoothed the buttons, she said, "Truth be told, despite the surprise and rapidity of the date, I'm so glad that you have yielded to your love for him. And he you."

Beatrice all but yelped, "Oh! I don't love him. And he certainly doesn't love me." Her heart raced at the very idea. How absurd. Truly. She drew in a breath and said steadily, "This is simply a marriage of convenience."

Margaret pulled back and frowned. "What could possibly be convenient about it?"

Beatrice swallowed, uncertain how to answer. "Can I not alter my hopes and desires?"

Folding her arms over the golden belt just under her breasts that complemented her peach morning gown, Margaret pointed out with little of her usual sweetness, "Of course you may, but you have always been so adamant. You don't like the idea of marriage. It turns a woman into property and all that. You'll have no say over your children and those kinds of things. You're always telling me about it."

Beatrice let out a sigh and bit the inside of her cheek. She tried to pull at her gloves, a sheer sign of prevarication. But what was she to do? She was in the most terrible predicament with her cousin.

She'd never kept anything from Margaret before, and it felt wrong.

And she did not do things she felt wrong.

"None of that has changed," she said quickly. "I will be his property. My children will be his property. And you're right; technically, I shall have no say over anything, but William is not that sort of man."

She smiled at her cousin, wanting to reassure her and ease her mind. "And I insisted that the funds he allows me—which are considerable—and my ability to do what I like with said funds be put in our marriage contract. If he violates it, he shall not have a legal leg to stand on. Truly, I shall have a great deal of freedom in the end."

Margaret gaped at her. "I don't understand. You have a fortune yourself. That's very generous of the duke to wish to give you more money."

Beatrice's stomach sank.

How could she not tell her cousin?

Margaret looked at her with suspicion. She crossed to the bed and leaned against the tall, ivory-painted post. "What motivated you to marry him, Beatrice, if not love?"

"Passion," Beatrice insisted, but even though it was partly true, it felt like the worst lie in her mouth and tasted acrid.

She looked away. At last, she threw her hands up, crossed to her dressing table, and picked up the small paintings of her parents that were in connected, golden frames. She stared at their handsome faces. Faces she sometimes struggled to recall.

But in her heart, she knew they wouldn't wish her to be false to Margaret. No, they'd wish her to be true to herself.

And then she turned to her cousin and admitted, "Finances."

"Finances," Margaret echoed, shaking her head, which sent her perfectly coiled hair bouncing. "How is that possible, Beatrice? You have a larger fortune than I."

She ground her teeth, her own complicated feelings about the circumstances whirling around her middle.

She felt both relief that she had William and frustration that her life had gone in such a completely different direction than she had intended.

All because of the decisions of her guardian.

"I do not," she replied evenly, forcing herself to sound calm lest she overly distress her cousin. After all, she did not wish to arrive at the church with Margaret's eyes red as burned coals from crying.

Margaret grew still as she picked up the flowers that were meant to go into Beatrice's hair from the counterpane.

A single white rose dropped from her grasp. "I don't understand. You have money—"

"No, I don't," she cut in, not wishing to make either of them suffer any more than was necessary. She licked her lips, readying herself to break the news. Because she couldn't allow her cousin to live in a lie just because her uncle thought it best. Margaret was an adult, not a child. She deserved the truth.

"What?" she whispered, her voice barely audible. The color slipped from her already pale face, leaving her ashen.

"I'm not supposed to tell you this. Uncle told me only yesterday, and it is why I am getting married so quickly, without looking back." She swallowed, squaring her shoulders, determined to make the best of it and hoping Margaret would, too.

"You see, dearest cousin, I am charging into the future," declared Beatrice, trying not to shake as she shared the truth.

Though it was hard to force the unpleasant words out, she felt better for it. Men were always trying to protect ladies, but in the end it wasn't protection, was it? No, not at all. Women were not porcelain dolls one had to protect from cracking. No, they were living, breathing people with feelings, and they deserved to know their fate.

"Margaret, you have no money, either," she said honestly and as gently as she could.

Margaret scoffed, then laughed, though the sound was far too high for humor. "I have a very good dowry that will go to Kit. Although he's a second son, he doesn't have the kind of fortune his brother has. I shall be a help to him."

Beatrice closed her eyes, hating that Margaret

was about to have her feeling of assisting her beloved taken away.

She licked her lips and ventured, "Luckily, Kit has a good deal of money, thanks to his brother. You will be taken care of by the duke's fortune."

Margaret shook her head. "Impossible. Papa has a fortune."

"We are paupers, Margaret," she insisted patiently, recalling how out of sorts she'd felt when learning their circumstances.

"This is not a funny joke." Margaret flinched. "Stop it, Beatrice," she said, "this is not amusing. Your jokes are always clever, but this is just cruel."

"I'm not trying to be clever or cruel," Beatrice replied, wishing she could draw her cousin into her arms but seeing that Margaret did not wish it at present. "Uncle is in a great deal of trouble. He lost all of our money, yours and mine, and his. He thought he was going to increase our wealth with investments. He was wrong. It doesn't mean that he's a bad person."

"Of course he's not a bad person," Margaret burst out, even as her eyes shimmered. "He's my father, and he loves me. He loves you, too. He's always taken care of us—always assured that we were looked after."

Margaret was shaking her head, horrified.

"Margaret, Margaret," Beatrice cut in, crossing to her and taking hold of her hands. "Please, I understand it is tempting to become completely fraught, but you must not. You are going to be in very good hands. Kit will look after you now."

The words tasted like bitterness on her tongue.

The idea that Margaret should have to go from one man looking after her to another—it felt like bitterest gall.

Was a lady always to put her fate into a man's hands and hope he did not ruin her future?

What if Kit made some sort of error, as her uncle had done?

Beatrice was going to learn how to look after her own finances. She was going to demand that the duke teach her or have his advisors do so, because she was not going to have something like this happen to her again.

If she lost all her money, it would be her own bloody fault, not someone else's.

She hesitated and looked her cousin in the eye. "I did not know if I should tell you," Beatrice said, "but I did not feel I could keep the truth from you."

Margaret nodded, blinking. She sucked in a sharp breath, closed her eyes, then snapped them back open.

Surprisingly, there were no tears in her eyes, no hysterics.

Instead, shoulders back, head high, Margaret walked away from Beatrice and looked out the window. "Are we to lose this house?"

Beatrice was silent for a long moment, but then she ventured, "I don't know what will happen. But you and I will no longer be a financial strain upon him."

"A strain," Margaret repeated, lifting a hand to the glass pane.

And for the first time, Beatrice felt that room, the whole house was a pretty cage for herself and her cousin. They were trapped, with only the freedoms they could forge themselves.

"I never thought of myself as a strain before," Margaret said softly. "But I don't do anything for Papa, do I? I don't bring money in. I don't earn money. He simply must spend money on me to make me pretty for some man to purchase me like a bauble, I suppose."

"Kit doesn't think of you as a bauble," Beatrice protested.

"Doesn't he?" Margaret countered. "Just a bit. He thinks I'm terribly pretty, and he thinks I'm clever, it's true. But I'm an ornament for him. I'm not like you, Beatrice. I think that your husband will see you as a partner. I'm not sure Kit will see me thus."

"But he loves you," Beatrice urged, at a loss at her cousin's suddenly logical and blunt words. "Doesn't that matter to you? You've always said love matters."

"Of course he loves me, as best a man can love a girl like me," Margaret said firmly, but there was no softness to her tone. "And I do love him, but it's different for you, isn't it?"

Beatrice did not know what to say. "Oh, dear, I am sorry I've ruined your happiness."

"You cannot ruin my happiness, Beatrice." Margaret turned toward her, and it seemed that the happy young girl of but a few hours before was gone, replaced by a woman who understood her role in the world was a precarious one. "You don't have that power. I am the one in control of my happiness, and I shall decide now what I do with myself and my feelings."

Beatrice reached out to her. "Please, Margaret,

come here."

Margaret crossed the room, forcing a smile. "I shall not be in dark spirits for your wedding, dear cousin. I have longed for the day that you would find your match despite all your protestations of being a spinster for the whole of your days. Somebody who would be equal and worthy, and you have found him. And I know you say that you do not love him, but—"

"No, no," Beatrice rushed, lifting a hand to stop her. "Do not attempt to convince me I love him. I don't. And it's actually a condition of our arrangement that we stay out of love."

"*Out* of love? Why?" Margaret demanded.

Beatrice cleared her throat, feeling a strange touch of defensiveness. "It's very sensible, if you ask me. We shall be good friends, and that is all."

"Good friends," Margaret repeated. "You two?" Margaret began to laugh, a deep, amused sound. And she laughed so hard she wiped her eyes. "Oh Beatrice, that's ridiculous."

"It doesn't sound ridiculous at all. It's logical."

"You two are not a pair of Greek philosophers," Margaret pointed out with an arched brow. "And I can attest to that because I caught you in the most astounding of embraces. Goodness, I had no idea such passion existed."

Beatrice's cheeks flamed. "You have not kissed Kit?"

Margaret shook her head. "We've never had the opportunity. I'm never alone with him." She hesitated, nibbling her lower lip before she asked boldly, "Are you excited for the wedding night?"

Beatrice's insides fluttered. "Of course I am. Luckily I have read enough books to prepare, because I don't think Uncle's going to be giving me a lecture before my wedding to tell me what will happen."

Margaret let out a peal of laughter, which was a relief after her most serious expression but a few moments ago. She raised a hand to her cheek, mortified. "I cannot imagine it. Can you? Father coming in, sitting on your bed, patting it, and asking you to sit beside him so that he might initiate you into the mysteries of married life?"

"Oh God," groaned Beatrice. "The horror." She played her hand over her coiled hair, completely at ease with the subject. "I have read of animal husbandry, and I think that I shall do well tonight. After all, I understand the anatomy of it, and from books and plays, I believe it can be rather pleasurable."

Margaret's eyes widened with fascination. "Do you think he'll be a ravening beast? Many plays and books do suggest that men just turn into absolute wild animals at the event."

Beatrice laughed. It sounded a touch too loud to her own ears, but she smiled anyway. "He seems far too reasonable for that, but men are strange creatures, are they not?"

"They are," Margaret agreed. "But if anyone can tame a beast, it's you."

"Thank you for your vote of confidence."

Beatrice picked up her bouquet, for the hour was fast approaching.

She never thought she'd be a part of sexual passion, but here she was about to embark on that new adventure. She only hoped that it was as gratifying as some accounts suggested. That one kiss had been so wonderful, it would be quite disappointing if lovemaking would prove a letdown. She did understand that many ladies found it something to bear.

But many accounts from women suggested it would be a duty like cleaning the house, arranging for the sheets to be washed, or the curtains to be drawn. She prayed not.

"Come," Margaret said, picking up her gloves from the bed. "We cannot wait any longer. We must be off to the church." Beatrice nodded and scooped up her bonnet. She contemplated the bouquet of white roses and pink camellias. "Thank you, Margaret, for making this for me. I must admit— today, especially, I miss my mother."

"Of course you do," Margaret replied gently.

"I'm glad I have you," Beatrice said honestly, embracing her cousin.

She did not think of her mother as often as she used to, but on a day like this, she felt her loss. And though she was joyful and excited to unite with William and be able to do so many things, she felt a moment of melancholy.

She turned to the small portraits of her mother and father again on her dressing table.

Again, she picked it up, but this time, she pressed a light kiss to the glass. "I love you, Mama," she said. "And you too, Papa. I know you are with me today, even if it is only in spirit."

And with that, she turned to Margaret, drew herself up, and marched toward whatever future was to come.

CHAPTER SEVENTEEN

"Stop fidgeting, man."

Will tugged on his perfectly tailored black cuff again, then pulled at the linen shirt beneath, though it was already exquisitely arranged.

He could not stop himself.

Damnation, he could barely stand still.

"She's not going to come," he announced firmly, swinging his gaze up to the ornate ceiling.

"Why in God's name would she not come?" Ben demanded, leaning irreverently against a marble column. "You agreed to marry. You have a contract. You're essentially married already. Do you not wish her to appear? Is that it?"

Will swung his gaze to his devil-may-care youngest brother.

Bloody hell, Ben could be so aware it was sometimes harrowing.

Of course he wished her to appear, but a part of him was still deeply unsettled by the whole turn of events. He had not planned to marry so soon. So impulsively.

And that's what this was. An impulse.

He closed his hand into a fist, willing himself to calm. To reason. It had been the right thing to do. He needed to believe that.

"We won't be married until our signatures are in the registry, puppy," Will drawled.

He had gotten the special license easily; fifty

pounds had seen it done. And now he stood in the small Christopher Wren church of Beatrice's choosing, waiting for her to arrive.

Waiting was hard. If he slipped out the side door, he could be on the coast in a few hours' hard ride. He could flee this hasty marriage and the way his feelings did not seem to be obeying his mind's dictates.

Of course, he would never flee. He was not a coward, and he was a man of his word.

But neither he nor his bride were enthusiastic about this endeavor. That should have given him hope that this marriage was a good decision.

It did not. He prayed with more fervor than he had done since being a small boy willing his mother to return that this was not a mistake.

He drew in a long breath, forcing himself to patience, forcing himself to believe he would remain in control of his emotions as he always had done.

But if he was honest, standing at the front of the nave, waiting for Beatrice to arrive was testing his nerve.

Somehow, she seemed far more daunting than all of government or the king whose wits waxed and waned, leaving one wondering which George they were to meet with.

Now, that might sound ludicrous to some. Because obviously Beatrice did not have the power of kings, nor was she likely to skewer him with her hat pin upon joining him before the altar.

He should not have the unease that he did.

But this was probably now the most unexpected moment of his life, because he had not planned on wedding a woman as formidable as Beatrice.

Somehow, some part of him felt that there was absolutely no way it would come to pass.

She had agreed out of duress. He had proposed under duress.

The whole bloody thing had been under duress.

Kit eyed him like he was a stallion about to make for the stables.

He would not. He was made of stern stuff.

But perhaps in a fit of pique—not that Beatrice could suffer from such a thing—she might decide that the whole endeavor was a terrible idea and bolt to America.

He stopped his ever-escalating thoughts with a point of logic.

Women did not have rights in the newly founded republic, either. So, she might not leave and decide England, and himself, really was her best bet.

Still, it was all he could do to keep from shifting from one foot to the other like a schoolboy being forced to await an exam.

Kit slapped him on the back. "Now, now," he said, "I have never seen you lack confidence, brother. Square your chest, man. Take a deep breath."

Ben reached into his coat and produced a silver flask. "Would you like a nip of brandy?"

"I would not like a nip a brandy," he ground out, giving his brother a suitably chastising stare.

He did not wish to reek of alcohol when Beatrice arrived. He could only imagine the meal she would make of that. And he did not doubt that she would comment, for she was not easily daunted.

No.

Drunkenness was not the state he wished to be in when he said "yes" to Beatrice.

She was, unfortunately, intoxicating enough without the aid of alcohol.

Ben elbowed him. "You know, we could slip through the side door if you're deciding this is a terrible idea. Naples is always an option."

"Cease," he roared, and then he lifted a hand to adjust the enameled ruby pin in his cravat. "I am not running away from Beatrice. She needs me."

Kit frowned. "Whatever do you mean, she *needs* you?"

He said nothing.

"As in her loins burn for you?" Ben drawled melodramatically.

He gave Ben a hard stare. There were not enough stares to keep the puppy in complete check, though. Ben would be Ben. And truth be told, he was grateful for his lighthearted play with the world.

He needed a touch of it just now.

Honestly, he still had not told his brothers the facts of the case. He would, but it was not his secret to tell.

He would tell Kit before that marriage; it was wrong to let Kit marry without knowing it.

But today?

Today was not about that.

Today was about marrying Beatrice for herself, even if that was not the instigating motivator. He didn't want his brothers thinking that he'd been maneuvered into it. He hadn't. It had been a choice of his own, made freely. It had been his suggestion, in fact.

But it was a choice so precarious that they had decided not to wait. He wondered if it was because they both felt so off foot on this new and unfamiliar path.

Suddenly the organ let out its low hum as the organist pumped air into the ancient instrument. A surprisingly sprightly hymn struck up. One she had chosen.

He tensed but couldn't stop his smile. It seemed, with Beatrice, he was ever doing things he normally wouldn't. And it felt…unnerving. For he had controlled his fate so thoroughly for so long, ensuring his stoicism. But now, he felt as if he was heading down a path and he had no idea if there were curves or rocks ahead.

The music picked up, and a long chord resonated through the nave.

She was here.

Slowly, breath held, he turned.

There she stood at the back of the nave. Sunlight spilled behind her through the arched door, her golden dress illuminated by the equally golden rays.

He loved the way she looked with that glow caressing her, tracing fiery red strands through her hair and lighting up her spectacles perched high on her nose.

In that moment, she looked more like a goddess than she ever had before.

Bouquet of white roses and pink camellias held firmly in one hand, she did not look afraid at all. There was no trepidation to her, no nervousness, no lack of surety.

She looked as if she was more self-possessed than

any person in the entire world.

Her uncle looked significantly less so.

And as she took her uncle's arm and proceeded up the aisle, she met Will's eyes and smiled. It was the most mischievous smile he had seen in his entire life. Clearly, she had no intention of letting any of her present misfortunes get her down.

All of his concern lifted, and he felt lighter than he had for years.

Perhaps he truly had no reason to fear.

He and Beatrice would be the greatest allies England had ever known, far more fortuitous than any royal match ever could be. And likely they would actually be happy together.

Now that she was here, looking so bold, he waited easily. His brothers came to stand beside him, a veritable bastion of support, and he loved them for it.

He did not draw breath as she and her uncle moved steadily toward him. It was a moment out of time.

And when they arrived beside him, her uncle bowed to him. He clearly was far more nervous than she, as if he was afraid the whole thing might not come off.

As if all his duplicity, his hiding, would finally be exposed.

In the face of such worries, Will nodded to his future in-law, silently letting him know he understood the difficulties of life, hoping he would understand that he would support him even when things were hard.

Her uncle shakily passed Beatrice's hand over to

him. Beatrice flinched for a single moment, and he knew exactly why.

He leaned in as he took her hand. "I promise," he whispered, "you are not simply passing from one owner to the next. You are about to become the most powerful woman in England, aside from the queen."

"All because of you," she whispered back.

He was not certain that it was a compliment.

He definitely could not entirely argue that point. So, instead he countered softly, "But it's what you'll make use of what I can give you that is important. I believe in you, Beatrice."

She blinked rapidly, and for one moment, all her confidence vanished and she looked as doubtful as he had felt before she arrived.

Straightening her shoulders as one facing a firing squad with noblesse oblige, she turned to face the bishop.

The bishop looked at them both through glasses that were far less exciting than Beatrice's own golden spectacles.

Said spectacles had slipped down her nose, and, much to his delight, she pushed them back up, a clear sign she was about to do something with purpose.

It was the most endearing habit. And oddly, it set him at ease.

He loved it.

As the bishop began the familiar preamble, William's mind wandered. Wandered to Beatrice, wandered to the future, thinking what they might do with their days and their nights.

The very idea that he was going to get to spend the rest of his nights with Beatrice seemed almost impossible. And damned enticing.

He'd always known that in many ways he was fortunate, of course, because of all the things he'd been allowed and given in society. But the idea of endless nights with Beatrice? That was fortune indeed.

Some part of him had always been afraid that any joy he had would be ripped from him. After all, he'd known a great deal of tragedy. The idea that this could be taken away? He would not think on it.

No, he would not let himself linger in doubts. He'd think only of the possibilities ahead.

Beatrice and he would be triumphant when all had been tragedy in the past. They were choosing a different path, a different kind of marriage. And that...that would mean everything.

As the bishop finally asked him those fatal words, he said, without hesitation, "I do."

William allowed his thoughts to slip away, considering Beatrice, watching her. He loved her face, how animated it was as she listened. When the word "obey" was intoned, she cringed.

He'd wished that they could have omitted it from the ceremony. But the bishop had insisted such a thing was impossible; dogma stated that it must be said. And so he'd agreed, but as the word was said, he squeezed Beatrice's hand, an assurance that he would never expect her to obey him. How could you expect such a splendid creature to obey? That would be the height of insult to her, and any man who expected his wife to obey him was looking for a very boring life indeed.

No, it was the fact that Beatrice was so vital, so capable, so independent that made him want her so.

And finally, when it came time for her to say "I do," she said it so firmly and so fiercely, he knew that she was choosing to be as committed to this venture as he.

When he slipped the ring onto her finger, it did not feel like a moment of ownership. It felt like a moment in which they were both freeing themselves from all the expectations of society.

Will smiled down at her.

She met that smile with one of her own. A smile full of determination to succeed.

Yes, this was the beginning of something beautiful, and he would not let them fail.

CHAPTER EIGHTEEN

Beatrice wondered at the fact that the wedding had to take place in the morning.

It seemed terribly inconvenient and most stressful to the bride and groom to have to get married in the morning and wait for hours upon hours upon hours for the wedding night.

Really, it was a great deal of strain to put on a couple, especially since they were a couple that had enjoyed kissing so well.

She longed for night to come. After all, it was the one thing she truly had to look forward to with Will. Oh, she'd have all the trappings of a duchess, but that wasn't truly him. That was his position. No, she wanted to feel his arms about her again.

The breakfast, thank goodness, sped by quickly, for they had not bothered to invite a hoard of guests. Why should they? They did not need to proclaim their marriage to the world.

The gossips would do that for them.

Eventually everyone would know that she was the new Duchess of Blackheath, and she was not worried about it in the slightest.

She did not need the approval of others to do a suitable job. All she needed was her own approval and the support of her husband.

Her husband.

What a shocking word; one she'd never imagined to think, let alone say with regards to a man like him.

But here she was, thinking the word.

Husband, husband, husband.

Goodness, it was true.

William was her husband, and she was his wife.

Ben and Kit had already departed to their shared bachelor lodging.

And after she bid her uncle and her cousin good-bye and they'd departed in their coach, Beatrice turned to William in her new foyer and asked, quite mystified, "What do we do now?"

"What, indeed?" he asked, sliding his hand to her waist. They were in his house, now, where the wedding breakfast had taken place.

It was all a bit of a puzzle being a wife, and she had no particular line of study to which to turn. Especially a marriage, which specified accord but not love.

There was no book written out for the actions that a young lady should take the moment that she and her husband were alone together. And if there had been a book written, it would no doubt say that she should wait for him to lead the way.

But Beatrice was not particularly good at waiting for others to lead the way. And so she asked, savoring the feel of his palm just above her hip, "Has the wedding night already begun?"

His sensual lips parted. "Not quite."

"Do you think that we could commence with it?"

He choked on a laugh but then sobered, his eyes darkening with that look of hunger she had seen before.

"Of course," he said. "May I show you to your chamber?"

"That sounds like a marvelous idea," she replied even as her insides fluttered.

While she was capable in many things, it was always nerve-racking to be new at something. And she was most definitely new at this.

"Will, can you explain—"

But as she was speaking, he swept her up off her feet and cradled her against his hard chest. A chest she admired greatly.

"Whatever are you doing?" she asked, her voice far breathier than usual.

"We're not crossing a threshold. So, I must carry you to my bed."

"Aren't I too heavy?"

He quirked a brow. "No."

And as if to prove his point, he easily took the stairs. He climbed to the landing with no effort, then strode smoothly toward the west wing.

They passed endless pictures of military exploits and ancient Greek vases placed precariously on Grecian columns.

The house was magnificent. Elegant. And yet she only had eyes for him. She loved the feel of her arms about his neck, his body so comfortably carrying hers.

Will paused before an elaborately engraved door. "Would you be of assistance, Beatrice?"

She blinked, still in a reverie at being so carried, then looked at the door handle. "Oh! Of course."

"My hands are quite full," he teased gently.

"So they are," she hastily agreed. Quickly, she turned the golden handle, and the door swung open on well-oiled hinges.

He took her through and kicked the door shut behind him.

It was a surprising and rather exciting gesture.

She bit her lower lip. She'd never thought she would get this chance. Yet here she was, about to experience carnal delights.

It was both thrilling and a touch daunting.

Moonlight spilled in through the many windows at the end of the long chamber, blue rays bathing them in a summer silver light.

Slowly, he slipped her down so that her body pressed to his as her slippered toes touched the elaborately woven rug.

The sensation of her sliding down his front sent a shiver of anticipation racing through her. "Should I…? Are you going to…?"

He cocked his head to the side, contemplating her. "Are you nervous, Beatrice?"

"No." She grimaced. "Yes. I confess I am. I have no idea how this goes. No one has explained it."

His brows drew together. "No one?"

She swallowed, determined not to be embarrassed. "Just books…"

He smiled at her encouragingly. "I dearly love that you love to read."

"Thank you, but they're not very instructive in what I should do or say."

He lifted his hand and gently stroked a lock of hair back from her face. "There is no script, Beatrice. Nothing is prescribed. We can do what we wish. What do *you* wish to do?"

She gazed up at him, amazed by the offer. She had been rather led to believe that husbands controlled these things. But he was offering her a choice. Her heart swelled with appreciation and relief. "I want to know what it's all about."

He shook his head. "All about?"

"Why people are so excited about it," she explained quickly. "Why there's so much gossip."

He nodded, understanding dawning on his features. But then his breathing changed. It grew heavier as if he had been walking for a long time. "I think I shall have to show you."

She swallowed. "Will…"

"Yes?" he queried, though he seemed distracted by whatever he intended to *show* her.

"I have a request," she whispered.

His brows rose ever so slightly. "I'm glad. A lady should always make requests of a gentleman when they are together intimately."

"Truly?" she asked, surprised again.

"Indeed." He stroked his thumb along her lower lip. "It is the only way I can truly learn what pleases you. Of course, I can observe you, but requests are most welcome."

She kissed his thumb instinctively, and his eyes grew hooded as if it had been the right thing to do.

How strange.

"Will, may I see you without your clothes?" she blurted before she could stop herself.

But from his pleased look, she was quite glad she had not.

He blinked but then smiled. Oh so slowly. "It would give me a great deal of pleasure. Let us start there."

He took a step back, then began removing layers.

First his dark coat. Then he unbuttoned his waist-coat, which he allowed to join his coat.

He tugged at his cravat and unwound it.

She bit the inside of her cheek, having absolutely no idea what to do with herself or her hands as she watched.

With each layer that he removed, she grew warmer and warmer…and her skin positively tingled.

She was alone with a man who was growing ever closer to being naked.

"Come," he said softly, holding his hand to her.

"What?" Surely he was not about to cease?

"Will you help me with my shirt?" he asked.

"You don't need help," she scoffed.

He laughed. "No. But you might enjoy it."

"Oh." She blushed. "I see."

This was so odd. Usually she felt so in control. So capable. Not now. This was unknown territory.

Tentatively, she reached out and took his linen shirt in her hands.

She pulled gently. It did not budge. She smiled at him, then tugged, and the hem flew out of his breeches.

He pulled her to him, stealing her lips in a hot kiss.

She melted to him, savoring the feel of his mouth on hers as his hands roved down her back.

His embrace was voracious, and she was shocked at how much she loved the feel of his hand cupping her bottom, cradling her hips up toward his. Amazed, she felt the hardness of his sex through his breeches.

Before she could think twice, she lowered her hand and gently caressed that hard length.

He groaned.

Her mind went blank, but instinctively she worked his shirt upward until at last, due to his significant height, he assisted her with pulling his shirt over his head.

It spilled from her fingertips to the floor.

His mouth still on hers, she traced her hands over the hard planes of his body. They were both discovering each other, using their hands as their guides.

The wildness of it charged her with a need. Oh how she loved the feel of velvet skin against her palms. She wanted to feel him skin to skin.

"Your turn," he whispered against her mouth as if sensing her desire.

He reached for the pins at the front of her gown and made easy work of them.

She decided not to think overly long on how he had acquired such skills.

For he had her gown removed in a trice, and she stood in nothing but her chemise and stockings within moments.

His gaze trailed over her as he guided the thin garment up and over her head until she stood in nothing but her stockings and shoes.

The cool air of the room touched her hot skin, and her nipples hardened.

His gaze drew to them, and he let out a moan of anticipation before he dipped his head and took one into his mouth. She arched against him, shocked by the pleasure of such a thing.

He swept her up again and walked to his great

bed. Then he pulled back the counterpane and set her down on the cool silk. She gazed up at him, vulnerable, feeling more alive than she could remember ever feeling.

It was difficult not to try to cover herself. She'd not been fully naked in front of anyone in years. Not since she was a girl, really.

Beatrice pressed her hands into the mattress as he trailed his gaze over her breasts, then looked lower and lower.

That look was as powerful as any touch.

She felt sensations in places she had not known she could feel excitement.

Wordlessly, he lowered himself beside her. Gently, he traced his fingertips along her stockinged calf, traveling upward past her knee, then her thigh.

He skimmed the thin skin of her hip and slid upward over her belly to cup her breasts.

She gasped, astonished by the power of it and the strange need growing between her legs.

"Do you like that?" he asked.

She nodded, unable to express herself for the first time she could recall. But it was all so much.

"I want to touch you," she finally murmured.

William's eyes widened, but he nodded and climbed onto the bed.

He slipped off his boots and breeches and pulled her against him.

She gasped at the feel of his long, hard body. In all her life, she'd felt nothing like it…or his sex.

She hadn't been able to imagine it. The feel of it pressed against her was nothing like she imagined the sketches or statues might be like when aroused.

It was hot, hard, and big. Far bigger than she'd anticipated.

She felt a hint of trepidation. But she trusted William, and she wasn't about to act the silly miss.

He kissed her again, only this time, his tongue teased the line of her lips and she opened her mouth to him. And as he slipped his tongue into her mouth, his fingers slipped between her thighs.

She tensed, but as he kissed her and he slid his fingers along her slick folds, she felt herself trusting him more and more.

For it felt…

There were no words as he circled his fingers.

She tossed toward something. Something wild and indescribable. Something that was beyond control and rules. His fingers, confident yet gentle, traced over her delicate folds until they found a spot that caused her to gasp with a wave of such pure pleasure she was stunned.

At her gasp against his mouth, he continued to circle and stroke that suddenly aching spot, urging her body to some unknown yet seemingly impossible destination.

Just as she was certain her body was about to come apart, he pressed ever so slightly against her. She cried out at that sure stroke. Wave after wave of bliss rippled from her core.

She could not think—a very strange state of affairs for her. But she savored it. In this moment, there was only their bodies, so close together, and the fact that she had just found a new place on her own horizons, heretofore undiscovered.

He gazed down at her face, full of triumph.

She clung to him as she shuddered with the ongoing ripples of pleasure.

How was such a thing possible?

She smiled up at him, full of wonder at her discovery and his participation in it. "This is what it's about?"

"Partly. Are you ready for the rest?"

"More?" she gasped, but she supposed of course there was more, for their bodies had not been united at the hips as books claimed they should.

She nodded. "I'm ready."

"This will hurt. Or so some say."

"I will manage," she replied, determined not to be afraid.

• • •

Will struggled to maintain control.

He'd always been a master of pleasure. Pleasure was important.

But with Beatrice? He wanted to be wild. Something inside him was driving him to let go. To make love to her without thinking and to let instinct take over. But it was imperative he was gentle, as he understood a woman's first time could be most difficult.

He'd never made love to a virgin before, and he was taking no chances.

He eased himself between her thighs, sliding the head of his cock against her slick heat.

He bit back a moan of sheer bliss. She felt like perfection.

He spent time at the seat of her pleasure until

she began arching her back and moving toward him, a sign she was ready.

Carefully, he rocked against her opening. She slid her hands up his back, pressing him forward.

Bloody hell, this was too good.

He longed to be inside her.

And so, as gently as he could, he thrust forward.

Tight. She was so very tight, and he tensed. Willing himself not to hurt her.

She tensed beneath him as well. Frowned. And wiggled.

The wiggling nearly undid him.

"Why have you stopped?"

"Does it not hurt?"

"It could be far worse," she replied. "Will it get worse?"

"I don't think so," he said.

"Then do not hold back," she urged.

Do not hold back. It seemed her lifelong maxim.

And so he followed her words and thrust deeper into her body.

The perfection of her was too much. He'd never expected to feel...so *much.* So alive. So like he was going to rattle apart in her arms.

She embraced him, and he continued to thrust against her, building a rhythm, arching his hips to caress her most sensitive spot, and she cried out with pleasure.

Her face was a mask of bliss.

God, how he loved her face and seeing pleasure upon it.

He rocked his body against hers, building her need again.

He did not know if he could hold, for his own body was tightening.

And just as he was certain he could not wait, she tightened around him. And the way her muscles embraced him, he could not hold back.

As pleasure crashed down upon him, he called out her name.

Again and again that pleasure crashed upon him.

Until finally, Will collapsed against her, careful not to crush her. Breath ragged, he tucked her beside him.

He stared up at the ceiling and flung his arm above his head.

What had just happened to him?

She placed her hand over his heart, then pressed a soft kiss to his skin. "That is what it is all about."

"Yes," he replied. But he knew that until this moment, until the power of the pleasure he had felt with Beatrice, that he hadn't truly understood what it was all about until just now.

And that was alarming indeed.

CHAPTER NINETEEN

Dawn light spilled over the enormous, ancient bed, and Beatrice stretched, feeling positively delightful.

She felt languid, pliant as she smiled to herself.

The night had been delicious, full of shocking wonders. It had proved far better than she ever could have imagined. In fact, she did not think she could have imagined at all what had occurred between herself and her husband.

Husband.

Although she would not use the word as most ladies did, for she understood that their relationship was not typical. It was still quite a realization that her status in the world was very different in the light of this day than the previous one.

Beatrice let her hand slide over the cool linen, searching for his hard body.

Quickly, she realized that she was alone in bed.

She blinked in surprise and stretched again, allowing herself to take in the canopied bed. Its green silk hanging shone verdant in the morning light.

Biting her lower lip, she felt a wave of excitement crashing over her.

A duchess.

With ten thousand a year to do whatever she pleased. And a duke to lend his power to whatever cause she chose. How many could say such a thing? Few.

Birdsong greeted her as she pushed herself up

onto one hand and contemplated the vast, empty chamber.

It didn't feel lonely.

Quite the contrary. Everything about the chamber reminded her of his presence.

No doubt he had gone about his business.

She loved the fact that he bounded out of bed and met the world to fulfill his duty. It had been kind of him to let her sleep, and she vaguely recalled a soft kiss and murmured adieu.

Beatrice lifted her fingers to her lips.

Delicious scents wafted toward her, and she perked toward them.

She pushed herself up and clasped the linen sheet to herself. She looked about his large chamber and beamed, despite the nerves that would not quite dissipate at their union.

It was such a beautiful room, so very masculine with its mahogany wood, green leather chairs, and desks and tables strewn with books stacked carefully.

She laughed at that.

Her books were never stacked so carefully.

They were always a shambles with whatever she had looked at the last moment on top, but his were meticulously organized.

In fact, they were squared from largest to smallest in towers.

She would have to remember and leave everything intact as she found it, or perhaps she could bedevil him and put everything out of order. No, she would never be so cruel as to do something like that.

Then she spotted it.

The tray that was emanating such compelling

aromas. Suddenly she was ravenous. Her stomach growled loudly, and she bounded up from the bed, linen sheet wrapped about her body, and crossed to it.

The scent of strong coffee drifted up from the ornately engraved silver coffeepot. Several flaky rolls with butter and jam awaited her on a blue-painted porcelain dish, and fat purple grapes tempted her, waiting to be popped into her mouth.

There was also a note on thick ivory paper. She snapped it up quickly and peered at it, scanning the bold handwriting quickly, and she quirked a brow.

My dear Beatrice, I have gone to the House of Lords. Several important bills are being read today, and it is important to give my presence. If you would like to come and visit me, you are certainly welcome to come to the Stranger's Gallery and watch the debates. Or, which might be more suited toward you, you can organize your bedchamber. The duchess's room has been made ready at your disposal, and you may do whatever you like with it.
Yours, William.

She stared at that note and frowned. Quietly, she put the note back and paused.

So, they would have separate rooms.

It was quite common for married couples, and given the fact that they weren't meant to be swooning over each other and claiming inseparability, she was not surprised.

Still, it was a bit interesting. He was getting rid of her already.

Not getting rid of, she amended, but perhaps setting his boundaries. She was to have her space, and he his. She couldn't complain, though. It had been a wonderful night, and he was inviting her to come watch him debate.

But that was rather odd, too.

The idea that she would be a spectator to his life rather than a participant. Of course, wasn't that the way of it? Men were the active, and ladies were the passive.

She swiped up a roll, tore it open, and spread thick marmalade along the fluffy white inside.

William was going to get quite a surprise if he thought she'd spend the day ordering curtains or being his audience.

She already had several engagements for the day that had been arranged before their marriage. She had not bothered telling him because she didn't think he would be particularly interested.

As he had made plain in the note, they would have separate lives in this marriage.

She poured out a cup of coffee and drank the heady dark liquid with a sigh of happiness. It was so delicious she almost swooned.

The bread, too, was so light and perfect that she nearly groaned with joy as she ate it with the hunger of one who'd spent a great deal of energy.

Yes, she would surprise the duke with her resiliency and independence. She would do very well on her own. She would not lean on him. He already had given her far too much support as it was.

She would not be some silly fool, enamored with her husband just because they'd spent a splendid night in bed.

Even if she found herself wishing that perhaps, for once, she could indulge in just a bit of romantic silliness.

She shook her head. Permitting such thoughts would only lead to dissatisfaction.

Beatrice wiped her hands on the accompanying damask napkin, then ran for the bell pull. It was time to have a bath.

She had been quite active the night before, and she would need her ablutions before she met with the Ladies' League of Rights outside of Parliament.

Today, she was going to look her very best.

It was her first day as the Duchess of Blackheath, and she planned to make an impression.

• • •

William strode out onto the wide steps of Parliament with Viscount North beside him, debating the last points of the bill on the corn laws.

It was a shambles, of course.

The price of bread was going to be astronomical this year. No doubt there would be revolts all over England. They were going to have to do their very best to ensure that people did not go hungry.

And he was concerned. The price of bread had been a leading factor in the French Revolution.

When mothers could not get bread for their children, leaders such as himself and North needed to act.

They came out to dull, overcast skies and the shouts of ladies.

As usual, there was a thick crowd on the street that lined Parliament. But today there seemed to be a particular crush and rush of movement. He let his gaze wander to the people petitioning outside the halls.

Viscount North stood beside him, cocked his head to the side, and said, "I say, is that not Lady Beatrice?" North cleared his throat. "I beg your pardon—the Duchess of Blackheath."

He shook his head, tucking his hand behind his back. "It can't possibly be. She's engaged today in the organization of the house."

But then his gaze snapped to the woman to whom North was pointing.

Dear God.

It *was* Beatrice.

She stood in the center of a vast crowd, handing out pamphlets. Her brown hair was curled in a most sensible fashion on top of her head with a simple straw bonnet with burgundy ribbons.

A single coil of dark hair laced with fiery red bounced over her Burgundy Spencer. And her glasses, as always, glinted in the sunlight.

She beamed at the crowd as she happily thrust flyers into hands, even at people who walked by her with no interest.

She and several of her friends shouted, "Ladies' rights! Support ladies' rights! Petition Parliament!"

And he stared agog.

In that moment, he realized he'd never seen her in action.

What the devil was she doing?

This was how she was spending the day after

their wedding?

As that rather absurd thought shot through his brain, he recalled he was also doing work the day after their wedding.

He was not a bloody hypocrite.

Truly.

Still, this was not exactly how he imagined she would spend her time as a duchess. Accosting people on the street.

He strode toward her, determined to make a point that ladies did not petition person-to-person with leaflets.

And then he stopped himself.

What the blazes was he about to do?

Metaphorically hang himself, that's what.

This was Beatrice.

She was an independent woman, and if he attempted to lecture her, she might murder him in front of everyone. And it'd be the greatest dishonor to her, for he had assured her he did not want some other lady who would bend to his will and act as society dictated.

No, he had liked her for her independent spirit, and here he was, the first day of their marriage, preparing to castigate her for it.

Men really were the devil, but he was determined to turn a new leaf.

He had to. He was the one who had blurted out a proposal. It did not matter that it all felt so…strange. As if he were standing on sand, waiting for it to slip out from under his feet.

So instead of marching up to her, a lecture on his lips about duchesses and suitability, he paused, drew his shoulders back, and pulled in a breath.

What bothered him about all this?

Was it because she was doing something that was slightly different than what he saw as correct?

Ladies did engage in such endeavors in crowds.

Several aristocratic women had campaigned for Charles Fox and other politicians over the years. They'd gone door to door, for goodness' sake.

Some even gave out kisses.

How was this different?

Actually, this was quite tame.

This was not undignified or below a duchess. This was her actively trying to make change.

And so he swallowed his silly prudishness, bid North adieu, and strode into the crowd, which, spotting him, immediately parted like a veritable Red Sea.

His wife continued to shout "Ladies' rights! Ladies' rights!" until at last she swung and thrust a pamphlet in his direction.

He took it in his hands. "Hello, Your Grace," he said to her.

She hesitated for a single moment as if she was certain that he was going to say something unkind, and he was abruptly very glad that he had checked himself.

When he did not, she smiled up at him, her eyes dancing with delight. "Hello to you, too, Your Grace."

That delight alone had been worth his self-assessment.

"May I be of assistance?" he inquired.

"Please do," she said with enthusiasm so great

that her cheeks flushed with joy. "We always need more hands."

He felt a wave of such satisfaction at her look he was convinced he could pass out pamphlets for the rest of the day and not complain.

What the blazes was happening to him?

Beatrice grabbed a stack of pamphlets from one of her friends, a dark-haired girl with a red hat, and put them into his hands.

"You are not above such a thing?" she queried.

He paused, then said earnestly, "I am never above working with you, Beatrice. And I think we should do more. I think we must unite and create an organization that strengthens the Ladies' League of Rights."

"What an excellent reply," she marveled.

"Thank you," he said with a wink. "It was impulsive."

"I'm glad to know that you did not have to practice it," she teased.

Bloody hell, how he wished he could kiss her right there and right then.

Seeing her out and about, doing what she loved was positively invigorating.

Inspiring, even.

His work took place largely in back rooms with taciturn old men determined to keep gold and power in their gnarled grasp.

He wondered that he had never done such outside work before. Why hadn't he gone out amongst Londoners?

He did want to begin something new with her. Something they could strive for together.

"What did you have in mind?" she asked, holding those beloved pamphlets.

"No," he said firmly. "What do *you* have in mind? You lead on this."

Her eyes widened with astonishment, and she swallowed. "Let us work side by side, then. As one. Surely we can organize and begin a speaking tour. We can set up stages and bring the voices of those who do not have rights as of yet to all."

He nodded, feeling waves of excitement. "To all of London. To Manchester, York, Bristol, Glasgow, Edinburgh, Dublin," he enthused. "We can organize it and bring speakers to areas that might never hear of the injustices being done daily at home and abroad."

She beamed at him. "Together?" she whispered. "How can we lose?"

With a squeeze of his hand, Beatrice then turned back to the crowds passing her and continued her work.

As he looked about, he realized that it would be better if Beatrice had more opportunity to speak to people, for she was making claims right, left, and center without quaking.

And many were listening to her and taking the pamphlets.

"Support ladies and their seeking rights and independence," she called, brandishing her literature.

"Support women and their right to keep their children," she added at the top of her lungs.

His throat tightened, and his eyes burned. And he thought of his mother. The pain of it sped through his body like poison, and he fought a gasp.

If only his mother had been given the rights Beatrice now fought for. If only someone had championed his mother...she might not have had to abandon him.

He might not have had to be alone.

He forced himself to draw in breath after breath, digging his nails into his palms before the agony at what could have been overwhelmed him.

"Support women and their right to be protected from violence within the home!" she called, turning to another group.

"Hear, hear!" he roared, driving back the darkness threatening to steal over him again, and he began passing out pamphlets to the onlookers, who were positively stunned at his presence.

He focused on those shocked faces.

The truth was, a duke was a veritable god amongst the people, and they were all staring, surprised that he had come down amongst them.

Usually, he did go directly from Parliament to his coach, because sometimes he could be mobbed if he was not careful, but here, standing with Beatrice, he felt *right*.

And so, embracing the change, he passed out more and more pamphlets. He even took up a few of her slogans, using his loudest House of Lords voice.

Eager hands took them and immediately began to read the words, gossiping and chatting with one another.

He found himself chanting, "Rights for ladies! Support rights for ladies!"

Beatrice beamed at him, and that was all the reward he needed.

If ladies were able to attain their rights because of his support, he of course would be thrilled, and he was going to have to do a great deal more than pass out pamphlets to help Beatrice make that happen.

Men were going to stand against him. That note dimmed his pleasure. But he did like seeing the joy upon her face.

That? That was a great thing indeed.

He paused for a moment and looked about. She needed more resources and opportunities to reach more people. Will leaned over to her and said above the bustle and noise, "Perhaps next time you can tell me when you're going to do this. I can build a stage for you, and you can make speeches."

She laughed. "That sounds a bit grand."

"No, it doesn't," he said honestly. "You would be perfectly capable. I think you would make a tremendous orator."

"Why thank you, Your Grace," she said. "I take that as the highest compliment."

"You had best not start calling me Your Grace now that we are more intimate than ever," he whispered against her ear.

She flushed red, but then she lifted her chin. "All right, William."

He burned at the sight of her flushed cheeks. Marriage still felt like a minefield. A negotiation he wasn't entirely certain of. But this didn't feel like defeat. This felt like victory.

Clapping his hands together, he declared, "Now, where the devil are more of those pamphlets?"

CHAPTER TWENTY

If it had not been for the fall of night, Beatrice might never have known that she was married.

William was so busy that she scarce saw him from sunup to sundown.

And she, too, was so consumed by all her new tasks and opportunities to further her present causes that he scarce saw her.

She marveled at the fact that they both had such full schedules.

As the Duchess of Blackheath now, she found there was no moment to spare. There was so much to run, and she relished it. She'd bought several large ledgers and had them placed in her office. And in that office were quills, and ink, and more books than she had ever hoped to acquire. She'd spent several hundred pounds on books ranging from poetry, statistics of London populations, philosophy, science, politics, to, of course, Shakespeare.

Yes, her own office.

It was absolutely magnificent.

At her uncle's house, she'd had a shared library that she'd done most of her work from. But here in William's expansive townhouse, she had her own suite of rooms, and it was sheer perfection. Here she could scatter pages out and work with them all about her, picking up what she needed and then putting it down in a system that made sense to her and few others.

And there was no one to make comments about her unique methods.

Her own library had cheerful azure silk walls meant to lift her spirits. The furnishings were functional and beautiful. She had selected her favorites from the hundreds of paintings in the house and hung several Turners.

All of them were stunning ocean pictures with great ships, making her think of voyages to far off lands, something she had never been able to do. And she had so much to do that she probably never would.

During the day, she went to her usual meetings, whether it be to her foundations in the East End or meeting with friends to discuss what next move they could take with the Ladies' League of Rights.

In the last several days since becoming the Duchess of Blackheath, she had also spent time learning about the various necessities of a duchess, with which her butler, Forbes, and the housekeeper, Mrs. Marshall, were assisting her.

They were patient and a veritable font of information.

Mrs. Marshall was a wonder, for she did seem to know everything about the duke and every previous generation.

The housekeeper had taken her through the house on a grand tour, filled with pride, as if every family member on the wall was connected to her personally.

They'd paused before portrait after portrait, battle scene after battle scene. Mrs. Marshall had regaled her with tales of war-minded dukes who

toppled rebellions and duchesses who had lent their
support to political upheavals, artists, and a surprising number of young scholars.

Many of whom had gone on to various academies
and then proceeded to shake up the world order.

Perhaps she was joining a tradition rather than
starting a revolution.

When they came to a portrait of an absolutely
striking woman dressed in the highest fashion of the
previous century hanging in a place of pride in the
grand ballroom, she gasped aloud.

Mrs. Marshall had hesitated, then smiled sadly.
"She is lovely, is she not?"

Lovely? Yes. But there was an intensity and intelligence to the lady that shook Beatrice to her core.
The eyes were so intensely dark, she felt as if the
portrait might suddenly come to life and the lady
would join them in conversation.

The woman looked so much like William it was
almost frightening.

"Who's this?" she asked Mrs. Marshall, though
she had an idea.

Mrs. Marshall folded her elegant hands before
her black bombazine gown. "That is the duke's
mother, Your Grace."

"His mother?" she breathed, comprehending.
The resemblance, intensity, and intelligence now
made perfect sense.

"Yes, Your Grace. That's correct." Mrs. Marshall's
eyes widened slightly as if she was gauging
Beatrice's reaction. "I'm sure you've heard of her."

And she had.

Everyone had.

There was no one in all of England who had not heard of The Bolter.

Though she would never use such an appellation herself.

Beatrice let her gaze linger on the picture of Sylvia, Duchess of Blackheath, and wondered what had made her choose a life abroad away from her children.

Love.

Or at least that's what she'd been told.

Legend had it that she'd had a torrid affair with an officer.

Duchess Sylvia had not been able to bear separating from her lover, and she had run away with him. Away from her sons, never to see them again.

She wondered at the power of such passion that could make anyone do such a thing.

Had her husband's father been so unpleasant and impossible, keeping his boys from her? Or had the power of love truly been so strong that she'd been willing to abandon everything, including her sons?

The law of the land made children the property of the husband. And she hated that her husband's father had not allowed his mother to come back into his life. But such was the way of things in England.

A husband punished a wife who left him by ensuring that she never saw her offspring again. And for a duchess to run?

It was a dire thing indeed.

From what she understood, Sylvia had never returned to England and had died abroad.

It was terribly sad—the saddest thing that she knew about her husband. Her heart ached for him, standing before his mother. She noted that the portrait was not hidden but put on full display. Almost defiantly.

When she considered her own life, she had never known any scandals or gossip.

It was true that her parents had died when she was quite young, and that had been very hard, but at least she'd had the love of her uncle and her cousin. And she had the memory of how perfectly her parents had treasured and supported each other. A beacon for her own standards in this life. She'd never achieve that. It caused her heart to ache desperately. Knowing that her parents' sort of love would prove ever elusive.

But she was fortunate compared to most. She had to remember that. Even when life seemed to refuse to take the path she had so carefully desired.

Poor William had lost his mother in such a painful way and his father so very young.

He spoke so little of his parents.

It was no wonder that he and Ben and Kit were so close. They'd needed each other over the years. Frankly, she was astonished that they were not all bitter and angry.

They were remarkably amiable young men.

And after the tour of the house, Mrs. Marshall had presented Beatrice with stack upon stack of notations and information about the various estates the duke owned.

Like the few other truly powerful men of England, he moved from house to house throughout the year, and she would have to make certain those transitions occurred smoothly. And it wasn't just a moving of houses. It was a dance with tenants, farmers, staff, villagers... So many depended on the duke in each area of his lands.

Come fall, they would go to the North of England. In the winter, they would go to Cornwall. And in the spring, they would come to Sussex and then London.

It was quite a lot to take in.

She'd never lack for funds, but this was wealth and power that she'd only ever been adjacent to, not directly a part of.

It was tempting to wish to do away with it. To break it all up and give it away as had been done in France, but it was all entailed to the duke's title, and it was her job along with her husband's to make certain that it was run efficiently, safely, and kindly for all in their care.

How they ran the vast thousands upon thousands of acres that encompassed the estates determined the lives of those who lived upon his land.

And she was determined to make certain that everyone lived well.

When not engaged in her usual activities? She read, and read, and read, taking in as much information as possible about each estate. How many people lived on it? How many houses were on it? What was the way that people made their livings, and how many schools?

She noticed that there were several boys' schools, which she thought was quite a good thing. But most of all, she was amazed to find that there were several schools for girls as well on her husband's holdings.

She had not expected that, and suddenly she was

rather annoyed at herself for having been so difficult about William in the beginning of their relationship. He had not been lying.

He truly did support the rights of ladies.

Only he had not wished to be in league with a lady to do it. Now it seemed he was changing, just as she had hoped. Now, instead of charging forward, his own voice the loudest, he was taking advice from one of the people he was helping.

And she loved the fact that he'd been able to listen to her and to others.

So many men could not; so many women, too.

But she wasn't certain she would ever truly know William. He was ever just beyond her grasp. His true self momentarily revealed, then drawn back and hidden behind the highest of barricades... His kisses, his kind smiles, and his unwavering assistance.

But not once had she seen him suffer or struggle or reveal weakness to her. Not in truth.

He was a rock, but she wondered, if he never allowed himself to be free in his emotions, would he not crack underneath the inevitable strain?

"Hello, dearest Beatrice. How goes the war?" he asked with that rich rumble of a voice as he leaned against the wide, polished-wood doorframe. "Do you mind if I bother you?"

"No, not at all," she said, looking up from her ledger. She adjusted her spectacles and stretched her shoulders. "The war is ever taxing, sir, and you are often on the side of the enemy. But I shall finish up, and you and I can gather under the flag of marital truce. I was about to have a glass of wine. Would you like to join me in a libation?"

She loved that he had waited to be invited in.

So many husbands would have just barged in, seeing the house as theirs—their presence in any room as a right.

"I shall take whatever terms you dictate," he declared, crossing into the room. "Would you listen to one of my speeches and give me your opinion on it?" He winked, giving her an exaggeratedly suspicious look. "Or should I not trust you even under the white flag?"

"I should like nothing better," she said, laughing as she pushed her chair back. She'd been sitting far too long. "I'm amazed you would trust the opinion of a mere woman."

"Ha!" he exclaimed. "I shall not fall for that trap. There is nothing mere about a woman. Remember you are to tell me what is wrong before my true enemies can."

She arched her brow and gave him a playful look of warning. "It will be my pleasure, and I shall hold nothing back."

And it was, and she wouldn't.

In his presence, she felt heard in a way she never had before.

Beatrice stood and went to the decanter of wine that Forbes had brought up when the hour had tolled five. She poured out two glasses of ruby-red wine into Italian crystal goblets and passed one to him.

Their fingers brushed. His gaze warmed at that barest caress.

He took the wine, held her gaze, and took a long drink.

Heavens, how she loved the way the muscles of his throat worked and the way the ruby wine stained his lower lip.

It was…tempting. Tempting to push him back upon her settee and demand a kiss.

Soon…

She lifted her glass in salute to him. "And were you triumphant in your endeavors?" she asked before she took her own sip of the heady wine.

"It's more of a draw at present, but I shall prevail." He sighed. "Lord Buxton will keep insisting that working-class people are owed no protections. Children should have to work down the mines and be thrust up our chimneys to keep them clean. I don't know how to explain to him that children — and women and men, for that matter — should be able to work in conditions that are humane. He has no sympathy. I wonder if we were to open his chest if we would find a heart at all."

She groaned, empathizing with her husband. "Unfortunately, there are a vast many aristocrats like that. They have no value for human life except their own."

"Do you think it would be a great difficulty if I took him out to Cornwall and thrust him down a mine? Do you think anyone would notice?"

She laughed. "Perhaps no one would care. Should we try it? I'll fetch some rope from the stable. We could go over to his house this very evening."

He stared at her for a long moment, then let out a booming laugh to match her own. "It is tempting. But I think that even I might get in trouble for something like that."

"Murdering a peer is even too far for a duke?" she teased.

"Perhaps if I lived in Henry VII's time," he mused, "I might be able to get away with it. But the War of the Roses is long since gone, and the Glorious Revolution has made it clear that Parliament is important. Not just the Lords. The House matters as well."

She nodded her approval. "Hear, hear. Power to the peasants."

He closed his eyes, then drank deeply before he groaned dramatically. "Do not say such things, Beatrice; I am a duke. My family hasn't espoused revolution since the seventeenth century."

"Oh, I know, my dear. I know," she assured. "But one of us must call for more drastic reform. I'm not even a person to most of your sex and won't be for the foreseeable future. And you must admit there were certainly good things about that revolution."

A pained look crossed his face. "Revolutions can lead to bloodbaths."

"I refuse to give up or give in," she stated firmly.

"I'm not entirely sure how we'll sort it out," he ventured before stating with surprising passion, "but I have faith that good will prevail."

"I'm glad you have faith," she said, trying to join him in that sentiment. "But our actions will dictate the future."

He studied her. "I'm damned glad you'll never let me grow complacent," he said. "Do you have the list of speakers you think best? I have arranged engagements in the city center of Bristol and York and Manchester for two months hence. And I've arranged protection, in case there is an unsavory element that doesn't like the idea of change."

She drew in a long breath. "I am almost finished with it. Do you think they shall throw more than tomatoes?"

He stared for a long moment. "If I personally attend? No."

"Will you?" She gasped.

He nodded. "You pick the speakers, and I shall stand behind them. No one shall dare throw stones at me."

No, she did not think they would. Not at her indefatigable husband. Surely he could wither a naysayer with a mere glance.

"And you will be beside me," he stated. "As the main voice in our organization?"

To her shock, tears stung her eyes. It was all so much more than she had dared hope for, months ago, when she had begun writing him letters. "I will. I will be proud to do so."

And in that moment, she became overwhelmed by her feelings for him.

He sat, still determined, still hopeful, even if he had faced a tide of resistance his whole life. She could see how his constant striving left him exhausted. A lifetime of attempting to change those who had no desire to change? It was no easy thing.

William hesitated, turning his drink, catching the spark of the glass in the light. "Have you heard from Margaret?"

She frowned. "I have not. She's been so consumed with wedding preparations."

He gave a tight nod. "Bridal nerves, no doubt.

That's what I said to Kit. But he did seem concerned."

"I'm sure all shall be well. After all, she insisted on marrying your brother" — she winked — "even when I begged her not to."

"You did what?" he asked, astonished.

"The very idea of having to see you at every family function was simply too much to bear."

He laughed. "How life turns. Now you see me every day."

Barely, she almost said. But she swallowed it back. She refused to slide into the recriminations, slights, and sarcasm that were the entryway to every miserable *ton* marriage. If she could not have love, she would not have bickering.

But as she studied him and wondered about Kit's concern, she felt her own wave of fear. Was this enough? Could she bear being on the outskirts of a man's existence? Even if she was a duchess?

Oblivious to the trepidations rattling through her brain, he said, "I have been looking forward to this all day."

"What?"

He winked. "Being your three-leg stool."

A shocked note escaped her lips as he referenced *The Taming of the Shrew*.

"Shall I sit on you, then?" she teased, her cheeks burning as desire lit with in her.

He sprawled on the settee before the empty fire, for the weather was fine.

With a surprisingly boyish gesture, he pulled at his cravat and cursed, "Damned strangling thing."

She enjoyed watching him achieve a state of deshabille as she strode over to him.

Meeting her gaze slowly, he took her glass of wine from her fingers, placed it on the table, and put his own wine beside it. He reached forward then, his gaze hungry for something very different than wine, and grabbed her waist.

In one steady move, he pulled her onto his lap so that she could indeed sit upon him. "Before this speech, I find that I should like to have a moment with you."

She blinked oh so innocently, even as Shakespeare's text began to reveal just how naughty it was. Now that she was perched on her husband's lap, she felt the hardening evidence of his need for her. "We are together. How is that not a moment?"

He cupped her cheek. "Let me show you."

And he took her mouth in a fiery kiss.

She was desperately glad that he wished to kiss her so.

She loved the feel of his mouth upon hers. She would have kissed him every hour upon the hour if such a thing were possible. Nothing was better. Not even the Ladies' League of Rights, which seemed like a terribly treasonous thing to say.

But in his arms, the whole world slipped away and there was not a single bit of trouble to think on. There was only pleasure.

Only him.

Will slid his hands to her skirts and lightly took the silk in his hand. He guided the hem upward, exposing her stockinged calf.

"Here?" she asked, stunned.

"Here," he replied. "I want to have you in every

room, Beatrice."

Her cheeks burned at that idea whilst it thrilled her to her very toes.

Did he want her so much?

Did he think of her throughout his long work hours, as she did him?

He trailed his hand up her thigh, under her chemise, then slid to the softness at the crest of her legs.

She bit her lower lip, holding back a moan.

He stroked her for a moment, but it did not seem to be enough to him.

And then he was sliding down to the floor, bracing his knees on the dark blue rug.

"What ever are you about?" she demanded, rather disappointed.

"Do you wish me to stop?"

"I don't know," she countered. "Will I like it?"

Desire darkened his eyes. "I believe so."

"Then no," she breathed, "do not stop."

"Good," he said as he placed his hands on her thighs and pulled her toward him.

A cry of surprise escaped her throat.

He tugged her into the position he wished before he tucked the cushions about her so she was comfortable.

"Now I want you to think only of me," he demanded.

How could she think of anything else?

She was most curious. He was acting so mysteriously. And she felt quite odd, her thighs nudged apart, laying back.

And then William kissed the inside of her thigh.

She jumped.

"Does it tickle?" he asked.

"Not exactly," she breathed.

"Mmmm." He began to trail kisses upward. Sliding his lips along her skin until—

A cry of astonishment tore past her lips as he kissed her most intimate spot.

Surely he was not supposed to do such a thing!

But he was…and it felt marvelous.

His tongue teased and circled her, the pressure more delightful, more intense than his fingers had been.

She began to toss her head back and forth, and she grabbed hold of the cushions, need building inside her.

"William," she gasped, stunned at how it made her feel.

But he did not stop. Quite the contrary—he increased his efforts. Not through vigor but through delicate caressing of the perfect spot.

And just when she thought she could take no more, he pressed his tongue to the most sensitive spot, and her world exploded into stars. The exquisite bliss of it took her in ebbs and flows until she could think of nothing but the ecstasy ruling her body.

She held on to him.

And as soon as her bliss eased, he climbed up, sat beside her, and pulled her onto his lap.

"What about you?" she asked, barely able to draw breath.

"What about me?" he asked. "I wanted to give you pleasure, Beatrice. And that is enough."

She shook her head, her fingertips taking his cravat.

"But I wish to give you pleasure, too."

"Do you?" he asked, his voice rough.

"Oh yes."

And without waiting, she trailed her hand down to his breeches, unbuttoning them one by one.

An idea occurred to her.

When she'd undone the last button, she reached into the placard and freed him.

His sex looked incredibly excited to see her.

His head arched back at her touch.

"How fascinating," she said.

He groaned.

And then she dared herself to ask, "Will, do I always need to be beneath you?"

His eyes snapped open, passion burning in them. "No, Beatrice. You don't."

"Then I should like…"

She straddled his thighs, experimenting. It was a trifle awkward, but then she found the way to guide him to her entrance.

He gazed up at her, allowing her to take the lead.

And then she slid down his hard shaft and, given the exquisite release she'd just received, the sensation was delicious.

He grabbed her hips and bucked. Gently, he guided her hips with his hands. She braced her feet onto the floor, then found a rhythm of her own.

She placed her hands on his shoulders and studied his face carefully as she rocked against him.

The pleasure on his face mounted, and she loved every moment of it. The feeling it gave her, giving him that.

And just when she was certain she was about to

feel her release again, his hips jerked against her, and she cried out.

They held on to each other for dear life as they both tumbled into bliss together.

Beatrice collapsed against his linen-clad chest, amazed. Amazed at how he trusted her and gave her power.

He wasn't just her friend.

Will was so much more. Her world had grown by leaps and bounds in but a few days, and here in her office, the remarkable moment still pulsing between them, she could only imagine what new horizons awaited them.

CHAPTER TWENTY-ONE

Beatrice put the final pin through her hat decorated with a single jaunty peacock feather, just as they were about to go to the Ladies' League of Rights meeting.

She was thrilled that William wanted to attend with her, and he seemed positively intent on going to several meetings, to observe, take note, and listen as to how he might best assist.

She kept her composure. But only just. She was thrilled by his enthusiasm.

And she knew her friends were looking forward to seeing him again after he had stepped in so gamely, passing out pamphlets. His suggestion of a stage had been admired by the members. All the better to holler at passing parliamentarians.

At first, many of her associates had voiced concern that he would take her away from them and make a dutiful wife out of her. Instead, they had seen that instead of losing her, he was joining them.

Much rejoicing had occurred. None of them were foolish enough to turn their noses up at a duke who could further their endeavors exponentially.

But just as William raced down the wide stairs to meet her in the foyer, there was a loud pounding on the front door.

She turned to her beautifully dressed husband.

The pounding was not subtle.

He looked as astounded as she.

Forbes, almost ghostlike, swept in and swung the door open.

Margaret stood on the threshold, looking quite distressed. Her dark brown hair, usually perfectly curled, was wild about her face, and her cloak, too, was askew.

She stormed in without waiting for Forbes's admittance and stumbled into Beatrice's arms.

"Whatever is it, dearest?" Beatrice asked, alarmed, as she held up her cousin, who seemed on the verge of collapse.

"I cannot marry him," Margaret declared, her voice strong for one so upset.

Beatrice and William exchanged a horrified glance. "Whatever do you mean, Maggie?"

"Please," Maggie pulled back, her gaze urgent. "I need to speak to you. I'm so sorry, Blackheath. I admire you greatly, but I need to speak to Beatrice alone."

William raised his hands, making no protest. "I completely understand. Everyone needs to have a confidante, Margaret, and I wouldn't wish to invade upon your privacy. So please go with Beatrice, and I shall go to the Ladies' League of Rights meeting on my own."

Margaret let out a cry of dismay as she blinked. "I am so sorry. I did not mean to interrupt anything important."

"No, no," Beatrice said firmly. "You are important. This was just to be a regular meeting. You will be fine on your own, Will?"

He nodded. "I think that I shall be able to hold myself together."

The members of the league could be formidable, but if anyone could negotiate their numbers, it was him.

And with that, he gave her a bow and a worried look, then headed to the door. He paused. "Send word to me if you need assistance."

She nodded, and she knew he would return immediately if she called. It was one of the reasons she adored him.

And then he was gone. Full of purpose, as ever.

She took Margaret by the hand and led her into the morning salon. Forbes, who was trailing behind like a worried mother cat, hesitated at the door.

"Please send tea at once," she instructed. Relieved to be given a task in the face of female distress, he headed off.

Beatrice clasped Margaret's hand in hers, guided her to a settee, and eased her onto it.

But immediately, Margaret popped up and began striding about.

Alarm rattled through her.

Margaret did not stride. She usually glided with feminine elegance.

"I have been thinking about this since the day of your wedding," Margaret began. "I can't stop thinking about it. And...I cannot marry."

Margaret kept saying this, and each time, she seemed to grow more resolved. Still, Beatrice would not leap to conclusions. She would stay calm. She had to. Otherwise, disaster could ensue.

"Your marriage is in but two days' time," she reminded gently.

"No, it is not," Margaret declared firmly, stopping,

swinging a gaze so hard Beatrice nearly gasped at her. "I will not marry Kit," she announced, her delicate hands balling into fists.

It was all she seemed to be able to say. Repeating the same firm maxim again and again but not explaining why.

Beatrice stopped her cousin's striding by gently but firmly touching her arm. "I understand you will not marry him. But...why?"

Margaret's face twisted with anger and pain. "I have tricked him into marrying me. It is false."

"No, it is not," Beatrice protested. "Kit loves you."

"He loves some image of me that is not true," she rushed. "I am not the heiress he believed, Beatrice. He has no idea what I truly am."

Her heart began to beat wildly in her chest. She didn't know what to say to Margaret's claim.

She'd never thought that Margaret would feel so strongly. After all, Kit had declared his love for her, and Margaret for him, even before her father had lost all their money.

This was an astonishing happenstance, and she began to feel the ground slipping out from under her feet like sand at the seashore.

"Margaret, perhaps you are being rash in this," she urged. "You do not wish to reject Kit, do you?"

"Indeed I do," she said, her voice breaking. "It is a mistake. Marrying him is a terrible, terrible mistake. When he asked me, he thought I was an entirely different person."

"You haven't changed at all, Maggie," Beatrice insisted. "You're just..."

"Financially ruined?" Margaret ground out fiercely.

She did not cry.

There were no tears in Margaret's eyes; there was only outrage.

"And Father kept this from me," she stated. "And William, even though he knows, would keep it from me. Only you, Beatrice, are honest, and that's because you're a woman." Margaret's face transformed into a veritable firebrand. "I have no wish to marry into the world of men, where men betray ladies daily."

Beatrice did not know what to say, because she wasn't entirely certain she could argue with her cousin.

The terrible, unrelenting truth was, most men did deceive women. In little ways.

Keeping secrets from them, doing things behind their back, lying to them, pretending that they knew what was best for them.

But many men just simply believed they knew what was best for a woman, without bothering to ask them what they thought or taking their own wishes into account.

Her husband, she knew all too well, was unique.

Will was completely singular.

It was why she had married him with haste without fear.

She didn't know if Kit would prove as wonderful as William. Kit was several years younger and not as experienced or as staid.

And Maggie... Until this moment, she had not shown the audacity that Beatrice had had in her interactions with the male sex.

"Margaret," she said softly, unwilling to let her cousin throw everything away on a whim. Though Margaret did not appear to be acting on impulse. "Don't do something that you'll regret. You love him."

Maggie grew very still. She did not look away or flinch. Something deep had shifted within her.

She drew in a long, shuddering breath. "I do love him. But my entire world has changed. I have changed. Beatrice, I cannot ignore the way my life could change on a whim of a man. What if Kit does something like Father did? Am I a buoy in a man's sea, floating wherever he takes me?"

"It is the risk all ladies take when they marry," Beatrice said gently.

"Then I shan't marry," Maggie gritted. "I must find my own way for now. I must find who I am without a man. As you did all your life until the duke."

Beatrice let out a sigh, wishing she could rail at fate. Wishing she could tell Maggie she was entirely wrong, but who was she to contradict her? Beatrice had spent her whole life seeking independence.

Yes, she'd had a guardian who'd had ultimate control of her funds, but she had never allowed her uncle to act as her father.

She had to try hard facts. Reality to persuade her cousin and not philosophy. "If you don't marry and your father is ruined, you are ruined. It is why I married…"

"William?" Margaret put in. "You married him because you feared being poor?"

"If you do not fear being poor," Beatrice said firmly, "you know nothing of what poverty is like.

You and I have led privileged, lucky lives, Margaret. You do not wish to be impoverished."

"Perhaps I do," Margaret bluffed, though fear shone in her eyes. "Perhaps I wish to see."

"No," she countered, unyielding. "You don't. And if you wish to see, I will take you to the East of London right now, where you could see how ladies live. You will not like it."

Margaret flinched.

"Women do not have many resources," Beatrice continued, determined to make Margaret understand the potential dangers of her choice. "Margaret, you can read. You can sing. You can play the pianoforte. You can embroider, and you have very good conversation. Unfortunately, that only secures you for two roles: that of mistress and that of wife. Perhaps you could become a lady's maid or a tutor, if you wished."

Margaret let out a bitter sound. "How could I be so foolish not to see as you have seen? Ladies have almost no choices."

Beatrice's heart ached for her cousin. How was this right or fair?

It was not. And she could not stand by and watch Maggie be tossed by fate. She reached a hand out to her. "Of course *you* have choices, my dear. I will take care of you. William has made certain that I have a great deal of money, and I won't make you marry Kit to secure your own future. You will not have to make that choice."

"Can William forgive you, though, if I break Kit's heart?" she asked, her voice so low it was barely audible.

That sentence struck her like a blow.

Would Will forgive her?

It seemed like a terrible cruelty to use his funds to break Kit's heart. And yet, how could she force Maggie to choose as she'd had to? Though she would not regret marrying Will for the world.

"I don't know," she replied honestly. "I chose to marry William because it was the right thing for me to do. If I did not, everything that I had worked for would be over; it would be done. But that is not your life, Margaret, and I can offer you help. If you wish that help and you need it, of course I shall give it to you."

"Then I will write Kit, and I will tell him that I cannot marry him at present," Margaret rushed, determined in her decision. "Until I know myself better. Because, Beatrice...I no longer do."

They stunned Beatrice, those words.

She knew that it could happen—that women could suddenly realize the situation that they were in, and it would change them irrevocably.

Much like Hero in *Much Ado About Nothing*.

Hero had realized the circumstance she was in, and it had been a bit of a shock to realize that the world could treat her so foully, even though she had done nothing wrong.

Margaret had done nothing wrong, but she had woken up one day to find out that the world was not at all what she'd thought it was.

That it was dangerous, that it was difficult, and that her value was based entirely upon what a man thought of her.

And apparently, that was no longer enough.

CHAPTER TWENTY-TWO

The meeting with the Ladies' League of Rights had gone exceptionally well. Support for Beatrice's vision with his organization of a countrywide speaking tour was now truly in development. He had organized lodging, music, pamphlets, and continued lectures in various schools with content to be developed and approved of by the league.

Everyone had been particularly welcoming to him, which had been a surprise. Will wasn't entirely certain how well he would be welcomed, but the ladies had encouraged him to join their discussion and had been far more inviting than he thought most men might be in a similarly reversed setting.

As a matter of fact, he knew that gentlemen would not be welcoming at all.

Case in point, he entered his club—a club for men that did not allow ladies, even as guests. But it was a place that was traditional and a place that he had been going to all of his adult life. Perhaps he'd put in a letter suggesting that a ladies' room be opened so that women might be admitted to the club.

He had a strong feeling it would not be passed, but one could always try.

And keep trying.

He climbed the stairs, eager for a brandy and hoping all was going well with Beatrice and Margaret. He did not wish to intrude on their meeting, and so an hour at his club would be just the thing.

Besides, it was imperative he keep a certain distance from his wife. He liked her. He liked her very well, and that was how it had to remain.

No, he couldn't allow the way it felt to have her body next to his in the night to lead him down a path that couldn't be reversed. He couldn't allow himself to give in to the temptation.

Steady friendship was the key.

He turned past the tall ionic columns and headed down a long hall. Just as he was about to enter the smoking room, he met one of the porters, whose face look positively white.

"I say, Geoffrey," he observed. "You look as if you've seen a ghost."

Geoffrey, usually implacable, let out a pained sound. "Your brother is here, Your Grace."

"Is he?" he asked, pleased. It would be nice to share a drink. "Which one?"

"Lord Christopher, Your Grace."

"Oh, where is he?"

Geoffrey swung a slightly strained expression to his left. "He is in the green room, Your Grace. On the floor."

Will shook his head, certain he'd misheard. "I beg your pardon?"

"On the floor, Your Grace," Geoffrey reiterated. "We're not entirely sure what to do with him. We have ushered everyone out of that particular part of the club."

"Bloody hell," he replied, stunned. Kit did get drunk on occasion. What young buck did not? But two days before his wedding? Dread pooled in his belly.

"I wonder what the devil that's about."

Geoffrey sniffed. "A lady, Your Grace, as best we can tell. We have continued to supply him with brandy. After all, it seems his heart has been broken."

"His heart has been broken?" William echoed, his throat strangling the words.

"Yes, Your Grace. He's quite undone about it. Would you like me to take you to him?"

But then Will heard a long, loud bellow of a sonnet.

He closed his eyes. This was going to be hell. "No, Geoffrey, I do not think you need to take me to him. I think I can follow the sound."

Geoffrey bowed and left him to it.

And Will did indeed follow the sound.

He turned in the direction of the rather loud and poorly recited sonnet.

It did not take him long to march down the hall, turn, and then come to an open door. His brother was sprawled on the burgundy-and-gold Aubusson rug, propped on one linen-clad elbow, a brandy bottle in his hand.

His coat, cravat, and waistcoat were in a pile on the chair beside him.

Kit spotted William and proclaimed with a dramatic opening of his arms, "Come in, brother, come in. I am so glad it is you." He scowled. "I'm drinking alone, which is never a good thing. Come, come share a cup with me."

William groaned inwardly.

It was going to be a long evening. And he felt a deep wave of concern.

What the bloody hell was happening?

He strode in, lowered himself down beside his brother, as one can only do with a man in his cups, and took the offered brandy bottle...which was nearly empty.

Kit angled himself to his brother and grabbed his arm abruptly. His face folded into deep lines of distress. "Will, love is terrible."

"I know," Will replied honestly. "I've always said so."

Kit scowled. "You needn't be so awful in my moment of woe with sentiments of I told you so," he said.

"Yes, you're right," he agreed. "I'm a bloody tosser. Do tell me how this rotten coil has come about."

"Margaret," Kit intoned.

Will swallowed, thinking of Margaret bursting into his house today. "What about Margaret?"

"Cruel woman, bloody...cruel," he drawled before reclaiming the bottle and taking a swig of brandy. Kit leaned back and cried to the stucco ceiling, "She has ripped out my heart and crushed it to pulp."

He cleared his throat. "That's very vivid, but I don't follow. How has she done this?"

Kit snorted. "She won't marry me."

"I beg your pardon?"

"She sent me a note this afternoon. She said she refuses to wed."

Will grabbed the brandy bottle and took a drink.

Surely this was all a mistake. "But you're getting married in two days' time."

"No, we're not," Kit said as he swiped the brandy bottle and drank again. He let out a dry laugh. Then he stared at the bottle. "I thought whoever laughs last, wins. But that doesn't seem to be my case. I'm laughing now. And I have lost."

William shook his head. "Why in God's name would she break it off?"

Kit wiped a hand over his face, then searched his pockets. He pulled out a crumpled note and handed it over. "Something about tricking me—something about her father. Something about the truth."

"Oh God," William groaned, realization hitting him like a hard blow. "That's what this is about?"

Will drove a hand through his hair.

"What do you know?" Kit demanded.

He blew out a breath. "Her father is in a financial situation."

Why the devil hadn't he told Kit right away? Out of honor? Out of some sort of noblesse oblige about protecting a man on the verge of a scandal?

"Her father has lost everything," he said flatly, his insides quaking as the ramifications of all this began to fall on him. "She must feel terrible about trapping you into marriage with no money."

"No," Kit protested. "Well, yes. She said that, too, but read it. She said… She said that she could not marry me because she no longer knew who she truly was. And that she couldn't trust her fate into the hands of men."

"Oh God," William bit out, "that sounds like Beatrice." Could Beatrice have instructed Margaret in the writing of the letter?

No, his wife was too sensible for that.

She had tried to persuade Margaret not to marry Kit before, but things were different now. She wouldn't go against his family and, by extension, him.

This all sounded very strange. And he suddenly felt...off foot. It made him slightly ill, and he was forced to draw in a slow, deep breath to keep his nerve.

What the bloody hell was going on?

And then, much to his horror, Kit allowed a tear to slip down his cheek.

"Are you crying, Kit?" he asked softly, his own damned heart twisting.

Kit dashed his hand across his cheek. "No," he protested. And then Will wrapped his arm around his brother, as he had done when they were small and alone. "All of this will be sorted; I promise. You love her. And she loves you. And that's all there is to it."

"But you said love is the devil," Kit lamented. "And I heartily agree in this moment. If she loves me so much, why would she write me a letter like that? She's the devil herself. I'll never take her back. Breaking my heart like that two days before the wedding. I should find another wife immediately."

William pulled him closer and sat beside him. "You're not going anywhere. Not at the moment. I don't even know if you could stand."

"Do not disparage my honor. I can hold my drink," Kit declared, and then he tried to shove himself to his feet. He paused, tumbled down, and groaned. "Why is the world spinning? Who's letting the world spin? William, you're a duke. Tell the world to stop spinning."

Will grabbed hold of him and kept him down. He clapped him on the shoulder but did not let go. He would keep care of his brother. As he always had done. As he always would.

"If you stay down, it will stop spinning," Will said firmly.

"Fine. I shall remain." And Kit slumped. He threw his forearm over his eyes. "I didn't know it could hurt so much."

"What?" William asked.

"Love," Kit said.

Will was silent for a long moment, then replied, "Love always hurts. It's the cruelest thing of all."

Kit nodded. "I should have listened to you."

"I'm sorry," William replied gently, squeezing Kit's shoulder. "I truly am. I never wished any of it."

"Of course you didn't, William," Kit declared passionately. "You're a good brother." He groaned. "Love. Never again," Kit vowed before he reached for the next bottle of brandy and thrust it at Will. "Come, you have some catching up to do."

William took the bottle, tilted it back, and took a drink. He hated being right about something like this. He was correct so often, but he would have truly preferred to have been mistaken.

He hated that his brother was learning that love was a mess.

But surely it was a vast misunderstanding? It had to be. But whatever the case, he would protect Kit. As he had done when he was a boy and their mother had left. He'd never blamed her. He'd blamed society. He'd blamed the foolish notions of love that caused people to abandon what mattered, what was important.

Pain laced through him as echoes of the past washed over him. As the brandy slid down his throat, a wave of the fear and loneliness that had been his constant companions after his mother left crashed over him.

Love caused agony. He had loved his mother. But it had not been enough. And she had run away for love.

He knew those were a child's simple views of what happened. But he'd seen it again and again. People throwing their lives and duties and happiness away for a moment of love.

It was why he had chosen action, dedication, stoicism. Why he would always choose a steady life over a passionate one.

He studied his brother, his own heart lacerated with his inability to stop Kit's suffering. He'd failed him.

Now, he had to right things. He would always protect Kit. It was his lifelong role. And he wasn't going to allow him to be abandoned, not for anything and not for anyone.

CHAPTER TWENTY-THREE

The loud singing would have woken up people as far away as China.

Beatrice was convinced of it.

She rushed down the stairs, her sapphire silk dressing gown wrapped about her. A single candelabra filled the foyer with a golden glow, awaiting the duke's return.

And return he had, for she could not mistake that rich baritone.

Forbes stumbled to the door, ready to open it.

"You should go to bed now, Forbes," she said. "I shall take care of everything."

"But, madam, what if they need..." As the door opened, her husband and Kit stumbled through, barely able to stand.

They were singing at their loudest.

She couldn't identify the individual words, but she was fairly certain that the song had to do with the horrific nature of the betrayal of women.

It sounded like an Irish shanty. She'd heard it before on one of her visits to the East End. Something about pistols being misloaded and his handsome Jenny turning him over to the British army.

It struck her as odd that her husband should know an Irish shanty, but he was a man of many parts.

Forbes lingered by the door, clearly certain he would need to serve.

He was likely right. Forbes was probably almost always right.

There was no better butler, except perhaps Heaton.

"There's my wife," William declared, grinning at her, confident. "She will assure us that all will be well."

Oh, how she wished she could.

From their state, she felt certain that Kit had told Will some part of what had occurred today.

"Kit knows the truth about your uncle," Will proclaimed magnanimously as he took a surprisingly strong step toward Beatrice. "And that this is all a vast misunderstanding. And now, of course, Margaret will marry him."

Any reply she had died on her lips.

She said nothing, because she couldn't tell him what he wished to hear. He was not nearly as far gone as Kit in the sea of drink, but likely he had flung himself three sheets to the wind, too.

And poor Kit looked like a drowned rat. Sunken in sorrows.

Men really were baffling. If he was so bloody upset, it might have been better for him to come and talk to Maggie.

But no one seemed to be using their reason.

"We shall sort it all out in the morning," she assured, because she wasn't about to start a long discourse with two brandy-soaked brothers. "Come now, let us get you settled and into beds. Forbes, will you assist me?"

Forbes all but hopped forward. "Oh yes, yes, Your Grace."

She nodded her thanks to him. "You take Kit to his room, and I shall pour this one into bed."

"Yes, Your Grace," the butler said with a great deal of relief, obviously concerned he wouldn't be able to handle two brothers himself.

Though it was likely he had seen and dealt with this kind of thing before.

Brothers did have a tendency to go on the town together, or at least so she understood.

She braced her arm around her husband. "Will, do you think you can manage the stairs, or should we put you both on couches?"

"I am still completely dignified," William drawled as he leaned against her.

"Bed, then," she stated. "Off we go."

And with that, she began leading him.

But as soon as they reached the first step, she realized it was a terrible decision.

Her husband, whose physique she admired so much, was positively massive, and his earlier steadiness now seemed deceptive.

If he fell on her, she'd be crushed like a bug.

"Never mind, Forbes," she declared before they could head once more into the breach, only to discover retreat impossible. "Let us tuck them up in the green salon."

Forbes nodded, his eyes bulging as he guided Kit along. "Thank you, Your Grace. That seems like a very wise decision."

They staggered into the long salon, Kit and Will occasionally reuniting in song.

Beatrice sat Will down on one of the settees, and Forbes tried to put Kit onto one as well, but Kit groaned and rolled onto the floor.

"Water, I think," she said, propping her hands on her hips, eyeing the two sorry fellows without a great deal of sympathy. "And perhaps some charcoal to soak up the nastiness in their stomachs."

"Yes, Your Grace. Whatever you say, Your Grace," Forbes agreed, clearly glad of her assistance in this endeavor. How he might have managed alone, she had no idea. Perhaps a host of footmen usually stormed to his aid.

She nibbled her lower lip, then added, "And a few blankets. I think we must wrap them up. And I will sit by the fire just in case one of them decides to wander off. As I understand, drunkards can be very troublesome."

Forbes gave her a surprising smile. "Indeed they can, Your Grace, indeed they can. Your sensibility is most admirable."

"Thank you, Forbes," she said, pleased at her own good sense. She plunked herself down on the couch and grabbed the complete works of Shakespeare from her husband's side table. Apparently, he'd been reading it and had marked in the pages. She flipped it open, drawing in a long breath.

Tomorrow was going to be the very devil.

CHAPTER TWENTY-FOUR

"My darling? My darling, wake up."

William stirred in his bed, flinging a single arm above his down cover.

He blinked against the heavy weight of sleep. He was so warm and comfortable in his bed, and it did not feel right to wake up. He blinked again, trying to make sense of why he was drifting upward toward that voice and away from dreams.

It was still dark in the room, save for the golden glow of a candle.

"My darling, wake up," she urged again, gently but with a hint of urgency.

"Mama?" he asked, wiping his hand over his tired eyes.

He knew that voice, that deep, lovely, beautiful voice, which had soothed a thousand hurts and sung him to sleep hundreds of times.

William opened his eyes and met the face that had lingered over his bed night after night, kissing his forehead before he fell into sleep. Her dark hair was curled and floated around her pale face like a cloud. Her bright blue eyes shone like stones in the candle-light. They reminded him of the river stones he and his brothers skipped and played with. Usually, they danced. But now? They glimmered with emotion.

"Mama?" he queried again at her silence.

She sat on the edge of the bed, her dark green travel skirts sweeping over his blankets. He reached out, and she took his hands in her gloved fingers.

"Yes, my love, it is Mama." She paused, her lips tightening, but then she smiled at him. "I have come to bid you goodnight."

"But, Mama, I'm already asleep," he pointed out.

She nodded, and her face changed slightly. There was something different about it tonight. Her dark curls bounced against her shoulder as she bowed her head slightly. "Yes, my sweetheart. I know. I'm sorry for waking you, but I wanted to come and say goodbye. I'm going away."

"Going away?" he echoed, confused. He did not feel alarmed, for his mama was often away for the weekend or sometimes for several days. She attended many house parties. It was the role of a duchess, he knew. He'd been told all his life about the duties that she fulfilled and how she was doing good things for the family and the country.

But she'd never woken him in the middle of the night before.

She squeezed his hand.

"Yes, my pet," she affirmed softly. "I could not bear to go without coming to kiss you. And hold you. One last time." She swallowed and said, her voice strained now, "I shall miss you so much."

"I shall miss you, too, Mama, but I shall see you again soon," he assured, hating to see her sad. He would be strong for her now as she had been strong for him so many times tears had flowed from him. He would hold her hand and make sure she knew all would be well in but a short time.

William reached up and placed his hand on her cheek. Her eyes shone with tears, and a single one slipped down her face. Gasping, for he had never seen her cry, he brushed it away. "Do not cry, Mama."

"Oh, my sweetheart," she said through her tears. "I love you so." She licked her lips and drew in a shaking breath as she smiled, assuring him now. She took him into her arms, holding him to her chest, wrapping him in the arms he knew and loved so well. "Now, you must take care of Ben and Kit whilst I'm away."

"I will, Mama." He felt odd. Unsure. But he needed to show her how big he was. How capable. He pressed his face into her neck and whispered, "We have been promised to go for a swim in the lake tomorrow. It shall be wonderful."

"Of course it will, my dear," she said firmly, squeezing him. "Promise me you shall have adventures, and love your brothers, and be as good as you possibly can. Be happy, my darling. Promise me."

"Of course, Mama." He tried to pull back, but she held him fast to her, and he felt a hot tear splash onto his shoulder. "Will you bring me back a treat when you come?"

"I love you, darling," she replied, and then she eased him back onto his bed. Quickly, she dashed her gloved hand over her cheeks. She bent and kissed his forehead. "Goodbye, my sweetheart."

"Goodbye, Mama," he said, even as he knew in his heart something was wrong. Something was very wrong. But he always trusted everything would work out. His mama had always promised it would. So he smiled up at her. "I shall see you again soon."

Again, she said nothing but pressed a kiss to the top of his head. She stroked his cheek, then slipped off the bed. As the rustle of her skirts filled the room, he tried to go back to sleep in the darkness.

But he felt alone... So very, very alone.

William jolted awake.

Sweat poured down his back, and his heart slammed so hard in his ribs he was certain it was going to spasm.

That dream had sent ice spilling down his spine. Will sucked in air.

God's teeth. He had spent years trying to forget that memory, the night his mother had woken him in the middle of the dark and bid him adieu.

After staring into the shadows, he had finally drifted back to sleep with the safe assurance of a child who knew he would see his mother again.

He never had.

And he would never forget the softness of her cheek against his hand or the way her tear had felt as he'd wiped it away. He would never forget the scent of lavender and vanilla that had wrapped him up in safety. Or the feel of her lips against his forehead.

He would never forget the way she had looked as she said goodbye.

He had not understood it then, but she'd not been saying goodbye for a few days. She'd been saying goodbye forever, because she had fallen in love with someone—someone besides his father.

It had been years before he'd realized his father had sent her away. And she'd run with her lover because she had so few choices as a lady.

The pain of it washed over him as he sat up and cradled his head in his hands.

His head pounded. He blew out a long breath, feeling as if he had run to Cornwall and back. Lifting his gaze, he surveyed the room.

His heart beat anew.

Beatrice sat before the empty fireplace. Sleeping. Keeping vigil.

He didn't deserve her. No man could ask for a better friend. Or so he prayed, as he swung his gaze to Kit.

His brother was curled up on the floor under a blanket. He recalled Beatrice maneuvering them into this room, tucking them in, and making sure no one wobbled or broke their neck.

He felt a wave of appreciation for her, but also a crash of doubt as he remembered that everything had gone terribly wrong the day before.

What role had Beatrice played in that? He couldn't think on it. Not yet. He needed cold water—and fast.

Quietly, Will stood, took his blanket, and oh so carefully tucked it around Beatrice. Her spectacles drooped on the edge of her nose. She was so damned perfect.

And yet…

No, he did not know what happened with Margaret. He wouldn't judge.

She must've been exhausted, poor thing, putting up with him and his brother in the middle of the night. Drunken fools, the both of them.

Will headed down to the kitchen.

Dawn's first gray light barely touched the windows. It was not yet six a.m. Mrs. Riley, the cook, was still abed, and the tweeny had not lit the fires.

He was glad that he was alone in the vast, perfectly clean kitchens.

Soon the rooms would be a riot of action. Trays readied, bread baking. There'd be no peace then.

He found a jug of cold water, poured it out into a simple clay bowl, and splashed his face and hands. A cold bath would arrive in his room by six. But he needed this now. Anything to shake his dream away and the feelings it had brought.

God, he had not seen his mother's face so vividly in his mind for twenty years.

It was almost as if he had touched her…

He closed his eyes at the bitter sweetness of feeling her embrace again, even if in a dream.

He'd spent most of his life trying to forget that memory, to forget the pain, to forget the realization that love was the very devil.

That it stole people away and broke them.

Margaret had abandoned Kit.

Why was love so cruel? Surely, it shouldn't make people abandon…

He swallowed, crushing that thought.

Love should have made it impossible for Margaret to hurt Kit. Instead, it was that love which was causing Kit insufferable pain now.

What the devil did that mean?

Poets were all bastards. There was nothing sweet about love or the pain it brought.

In one day, love could bring devastation. Yesterday morning, Kit was a happy man, excited to wed his bride. By nightfall? Heartbroken.

Love could destroy quickly.

He, too, recalled how quickly he had transformed the morning he'd discovered his mother had abandoned them.

Gone was the carefree boy of that time, replaced by a young man who knew he had to look after his younger brothers. He'd quickly understood that the world was unsure, unsafe, and dangerous. That one could have safety one moment and complete lack of security the next.

He'd failed Kit.

He supposed he could not blame Margaret.

No, *he* was to blame. For not hardening Kit's heart to love.

Now? Now he had to find a way to make it right for his brother. To protect him as he'd promised his mother he would.

What did Margaret need to make her feel she could trust Kit or the male sex in general?

He did not know, but he had to find it, because he had to find a way to make Kit safe again.

He sighed. It was such a coil. But a few days ago, he never would have expected that they would all be hurtling toward disaster. Yet, he should have. He had the experience to predict it.

And he did not even know what to think of Beatrice.

For that letter…the words in it…

Had she been an instrument in Kit's misery? He couldn't bear the possibility.

He placed his hands against the long wood table in the kitchen. He only thanked God he had not made the mistake of falling in love with his own wife, or letting her fall in love with him.

No, thank God. They had not done that. Such toils and troubles would never face him and Beatrice. It was a relief beyond measure.

As he shoved himself away from the table and turned back toward the door, he winced.

Winced at how brutally cruel emotion could be.

At how it could destroy lives on a whim, because that was what had happened.

Margaret's unreliable emotions had destroyed it all.

In one decision, she had chosen not to marry his brother, and now his brother was a broken young man.

No, he could not stand by and do nothing—he had to fix it.

Somehow, he would. After all, he was a duke, wasn't he? Dukes could fix anything.

CHAPTER TWENTY-FIVE

Beatrice blinked awake, startled.

Something was different.

No, not different. Something was amiss. And not just two-foxed-fellows-asleep-in-the-salon amiss.

She stretched, her neck positively throbbing, and noticed the dark green blanket draped carefully over her. Trepidation raced through her as she looked to where the two men were sleeping.

Will was gone.

Kit still slept on the Aubusson rug, snoring loudly, sprawled out without apology. Standing, she let out a groan as her muscles protested the long night in the chair.

Beatrice crossed over to him and checked on her brother-in-law. He seemed to be in a deep sleep, but otherwise he was not unwell. No doubt, he would wake feeling positively dreadful, and she would ensure that beef tea was awaiting him.

Yes, a good, strong bowl of that would see him right.

She hurried out of the room, wondering where the blazes William could have gotten to. She rushed up the stairs to her own chambers, wishing to get dressed and face the day quickly.

It was going to be a difficult one.

As she crossed into her chamber and shed her dressing gown, she heard William's boot steps coming down the hall from his own chamber.

She dashed to her door and flung it open.

Was he trying to make an escape?

She stood in the empty doorframe in her night rail and met his gaze.

William looked fresh, clearly having bathed himself. His hair was wet, and he wore new clothes.

But his gaze? It was guarded, not at all as it had been for the last several weeks.

He looked at her as if he was uncertain if she were friend or foe.

"Good morning," he ventured, but it was not his usual welcome tone. There was something wary about him.

She pressed her fingers into the doorframe, willing herself to stay calm. "Is it? You are acting oddly."

"Am I?" he queried, standing still, neither giving or taking.

"You are," she affirmed quietly.

"Well, I am not certain if it is indeed a good morning," he replied, a muscle tightening in his jaw as he eyed her with an assessing quality she had not felt since the first night of their acquaintance. Yet, somehow this was *different*.

He'd withdrawn somehow.

"Likely not," she replied honestly. "At least not for Kit."

Will cocked his head to the side. "Then it is not good for me, either. He is my brother." His mouth pressed into a hard line, and then he asked, "Will Margaret marry him?"

Her heart began to slam against her ribs—a painful sensation, for this time it was out of alarm and not desire. "She says not."

Will gazed at her with a sort of forlorn hope mixed with hard resignation. He took one step toward her, as if she might be able to still solve this conundrum. As if she had the key to it.

And perhaps, to him, she did. She was Maggie's cousin and dearest friend, after all.

"Can such a thing be of any good sense, Beatrice?" he asked, his voice brittle. "To throw her entire safety and life away simply because of a"—his lip curled ever so slightly—"*feeling.*"

"A feeling?" she echoed, stunned. In fact, it so stunned her she could make no further reply at present. The comment was so…dismissive of Margaret, so appallingly male as to suggest Margaret was a typical purveyor of hysterics. A creature of emotion not to be trusted.

Which was the usual line of the male sex and why women were denied power—because their brains were always overcome by emotion.

Her mouth soured.

This was a new tack from William.

He had always proved so practical in response to her. This did not seem to be a rational response. He seemed as if he was humming with something she could not quite put her finger on. But it was bitter and cold.

"Yes," he said firmly, warming to the argument. "Margaret is throwing away her own happiness, as well as Kit's, because of a feeling—a feeling of inadequacy. And, frankly, a whim." He gave a terse nod as if this explained everything. "She's not inadequate. She is still exactly who she was. She's still worthy of him."

Her jaw nearly dropped. It was terribly cliché, but the words coming out of his mouth? Was it even William?

"*Worthy of him?*" Beatrice challenged.

His eyes hardened with resolve as if he'd found the key to bringing Margaret and Kit together. "Whether she has money or not does not qualify her as worthy or not for my brother. She shall be a good wife to him. She shouldn't throw that away. She'll regret running away for the rest of her life."

"She's not running away—she's finally understanding her true position." Beatrice blinked. "Can you hear yourself?"

"Yes, I hear myself very well," he countered, tugging on his clothes, dismissive.

A look of frustration furrowed his brow as if Margaret's actions were so disappointing he could hardly stomach speaking to her. And, in his eyes, it seemed the whole thing could be righted in a morning. "I am discussing the fact that Margaret is still perfectly acceptable to be a member of my family, and I do not even know why she would consider *abandoning* it."

There was such rancor in his tone she nearly stepped back.

"I do not follow," she said.

Dropping her hand from the doorframe, she took a step forward, not caring she was in naught but her night rail. "There was never a question of Margaret's worthiness," she ground out. "I have no idea why you mention it. She is the dearest person. She is the one who has been treated poorly by those around her."

"Not Kit?" he mocked coolly. "His feelings and pain matter not?"

She winced. What was this? It certainly was not her reasonable, collected duke. He was raw with anger and emotion. "She does not wish to marry him when she is no longer the silly, innocent, trusting girl that she was. She can no longer simply put herself into a man's hands and assume that all will be well. She has seen what can happen now. And that takes some adjusting to."

"Does it?" he barked. "Has she truly seen what can happen when a young lady goes from her family into some fantasy? She is abandoning my brother for what? A dream of equality that has never been and may never be? Does she know the actual ending to that story? My own m—"

He broke off, his gaze flashing with pain, and he turned away swiftly.

She gaped at him; then it dawned on her, and she closed her eyes, trying to steel herself for the agony she was witnessing. "This is not about Margaret, William. This is about something else."

He looked back over his squared shoulder, his jaw tightened.

"Tell me," she said. "I am your friend. Who else should you tell but me? What is this about?"

William did not reply, and as she stared at him, she understood too well the word that he had used: *abandoned*. "This is about your mother," she stated, even as her stomach tightened.

There was something wild about him. He thought he was acting logically, above emotion, but he was far more in it than she or Margaret.

William jerked back. "Don't be a fool."

"I am not a fool," she countered, shocked he would say such a thing. Her voice grew lower, firmer in the face of his own lack of reason. "I can see right now that you are tremendously upset by Margaret's choice. It, I think, affects you as much as Kit. Why?" she asked, fearing she already knew the answer.

"Why?" he growled, his shoulders tensing as he whipped back toward her. "Why do you think? She has broken my brother's heart. It has been broken once before, and I cannot allow it again."

"This is not about you," she pointed out, locking gazes with him. "This is not something you can allow or not allow. You cannot make Margaret choose him. And you cannot make Margaret stay in love with him. Nor can you control if Kit will behave like an adult or a wounded Romeo. This is beyond your control." She lifted her chin. "Even if you are a duke."

"Nothing is beyond a duke," he said harshly. "And this debacle is why love should never be trusted."

"What?" She gasped, stunned by his passion and his completely ludicrous claim.

He shook his head, his anger and pain humming through him and filling the air around them. "This is why I insisted that when you and I married, love would never be a factor, and I am grateful that I do not love you and that you do not love me."

She stared at him, aghast. Her own heart ached. It ached so intensely she could scarce believe the power of it. "I beg your pardon."

He squared his jaw. "I am grateful that we are not

so weak. If Margaret was not so colored by emotion, she would see that Kit was the best decision for her. I wish she was as ruled by logic as you."

"Colored by emotion," she repeated quietly, trying to grasp the way her life was unraveling so quickly.

"Your Grace," she began. "Right now? You are naught but emotion. You are the one who is living in the past, living in the pain of when your mother left you. And by God, I am truly sorry for what happened. It must've been terrible to lose your mother that way, to have her run away from you, to take a chance on love so great that your father refused to let her see you."

"Love," he scoffed, his voice a growl. "That could not have been love. And if it was love, it ruined everything. She left us. She abandoned—"

"No," Beatrice cut in. "Your father did that."

He sucked in a sharp breath.

"My darling friend," she said, refusing to back away from his pain. "You strive to be perfect and untouched by emotion, but you are the one who fools yourself. No one can hold so tightly to perfection and not break, Will. It doesn't exist. And because you so desperately wish to be seen as above feeling, you are trying to push me away. You have forged a shield with your pain, but it does not protect you. It is creating the very agony you fear."

She balled her hands into fists, feeling her own sorrow and desperation building to a pitch within her. "Your mother did bolt, but it was your father who kept you from her. It was your father that owned you. Do you not see?" she demanded, wishing she could be softer, kinder, but there was too much at stake. "She had no rights to you at all. It was *his* decision. And I'm terribly sorry for it. I fight for women like your mother every day, and I will not hear you speak the lies society has taught you."

Tears filled her eyes as she watched his shoulders sink.

"She did not have to go," he gritted. And in that moment, the duke was gone. William, a boy lost and confused and suffering, remained.

"No, she did not," she agreed, her own eyes stinging. "Perhaps she hoped your father would allow her to visit. It is impossible to know. But I cannot make Margaret marry your brother to assuage the wounds of the past—to assuage *your* wounds."

He gazed at her, and yet he seemed empty, his eyes hollow. "You're going to support her, aren't you?"

"Of course I'm going to support her," she said. "Margaret is my cousin, and I believe in her. And I believe in her right to make the choice to marry Kit or not."

She waited for him to make some comment about the money. To throw that in her face.

Instead, William nodded. "I see. So, two young people shall be brokenhearted, and you and I are in discord." His face twisted. "That is what comes of love."

"I suppose it is," she said, "because the truth is…"

It hurt so much, what she was about to say, she couldn't believe that she was going to say it, but she couldn't leave it unsaid. She couldn't ignore it any longer. He needed to know. He needed to understand how his plans had gone thoroughly awry and that the world was not his to control, even though he was a duke.

"Will," she began, her own voice far shakier than she would have liked. "You insist that I do not love you. You've said it more than once. And you insist that you do not love me."

She swallowed the pain tightening her throat. "And that is fine. I never expected you to fall in love with me. But you cannot control other people's feelings and emotions. You cannot dictate them as if they were pawns on a chess board, pieces of logic in an argument, or figures in a ledger."

Her shoulders tensed as her throat tightened. She struggled for breath to speak.

Dear God, she was going to cry. Now that she had grown accustomed to the idea of being his duchess, of working with him, of sharing so much, she couldn't imagine losing that…

It hit her then. And she couldn't stop herself.

Beatrice sucked in air, and her whole blasted body trembled, devil take it. "Because the truth is…I love you, Will. I have loved you now for days; for weeks, even. I knew the moment that you began to pass out pamphlets with me before Parliament that I loved you."

He blanched, and his whole body winced as if she had struck him.

She flinched.

It was the most horrifying response, and yet she was not surprised; he was so averse to love. "I cannot take it back, and I know that you hate it. But there it is. You are the love that I never thought I'd find. We respect each other. Believe in each other. Support each other. And I love you."

He shook his head, unrelenting. "No. It's not possible. I planned… We agreed… Beatrice. I am not going to fall in love with you. And I do not want you to love me. And I do not see how you could, if you will help Maggie abandon Kit."

The words cut down to her bones.

But she couldn't ignore his resolve to cling to his pain in spite of what could be theirs. Though her heart was breaking, she drew herself up. "I love Maggie and will support her," she said, "just as you are protecting Kit."

"If all this is love?" He shook his head. "No wonder I do not want it."

She gasped, the words like icy water to her face. His pain—his old, dark grief—coated him, directing him to this cruelty. But she couldn't excuse it. "I think that we should spend some time apart until all of this is sorted. Our separation should not bother you too greatly. Since, as you insist, you do not love me."

He blinked, uncomprehending. "That is not necessary."

"It is." She rolled her hands into fists, longing for the accord they had felt that day of her boxing lesson. Or in her office. Or even yesterday morning when they'd prepared to go to the Ladies' League of Rights.

It seemed a lifetime away now. "Until you understand that we cannot bring Kit and Margaret back together by decrying either of their needs or feelings, until you can see that it is not bad that I love you…I cannot bear to be near you."

She threw her gaze to the ceiling as if some answer might lie there. "Can you not see, Will? No one is listening to Margaret. And that is why she feels as she does—because everyone has acted for her and not allowed her to act for herself. She did not understand what was happening behind her back, and now she does. So, she wishes to make a decision based upon what she now understands to be the truth."

She let out a frustrated growl. "And you don't wish that for her because of feelings." She began to shake. Shake with the power of her own feelings as she raised her gaze to meet his, which was dark with memory.

Beatrice refused to look away. "Love is not awful, Will. Love is not the source of pain. Love is a source of great joy. You make me happy, but right now it is fear that is making us miserable. Margaret's fear, your fear. And I will not be a party to it."

And with that, she took a step back and slammed the door.

As the panel trembled on its hinges, she pressed herself against it and slowly sank to the floor, holding back sobs.

She wouldn't cry.

She would not be the roiling pot of emotion he thought all women were.

For he was just as wild with emotion as she. And his fierce denial had brought them both into hell.

Her body shook.

She could not believe the things that he had said. That she had said.

She could not believe how cruel he had been.

Not love her? Determined not to love her?

It hurt. Dear God, it hurt. And she was a fool, just as he'd said, for thinking that she could have a marriage with mere logic.

Because the more she considered it, the more she thought it possible that she had loved him from the moment she had strode across the ballroom to speak to him and he had turned and asked her to dance...

It was a disaster. All of it.

And she could not stay.

CHAPTER TWENTY-SIX

Will could not tear his gaze from her door, all his control slipping away from him. That shield she had asserted that he possessed? It shattered within him, and the pieces were piercing his heart.

That complete lack of decision jarred him. His insides coiled with...panic. She had shut him out. Everything he had fought against and promised himself wouldn't happen was happening. Bloody hell, how could he have done this?

He'd failed everyone. He hadn't protected or kept anyone safe. The hell of it coursed through him, and he wanted to collapse with it.

Half of him insisted that he storm forward and pound on the door and gain admittance. *Mine*, his heart growled.

After all, she was his. She belonged to him. By every law of England, he owned her and he could force her to stay with him. He could rope her to him, and somehow he could make that horrified look on her face vanish. He could find a way to make his laughing Beatrice come back.

Surely he could make her understand. If he but said the right thing. If he could but make her feel as he had felt trying to hold his brothers together all those years ago, she'd see. She'd see and let him back in.

But he couldn't.

The way she'd looked at him, with pity as if he

was some broken thing that could never be mended. And who could ever want a broken thing?

He pressed his eyes shut and turned. What a sodding fool he was.

Who the hell had he been trying to convince that they could be friends?

He snapped his gaze open and caught a flicker of his reflection in a gilded mirror glowing with dawn light.

But he couldn't make himself lift his gaze and meet his own eyes.

He couldn't bear to see what she had seen. All these years... All these damned years, he'd kept the dam in place and the emotions firmly pooled behind.

With one look and a few words, she had cracked that wall, and he could feel the force barreling down on him.

Her words had ripped him apart.

She *loved* him?

And then she'd slammed the door?

He could not make sense of the world. It had turned upside down.

He staggered down the hall. He couldn't stay in the house. In this hell. In this hurricane of memory.

She was not supposed to love him. It was against all his plans. All their agreements.

Will picked up his pace, pumping his legs as if they could carry him away from the cut she had opened in his heart. He stormed through it, then down his sprawling stairs.

The wildness of his thoughts and feelings made him feel as if he was rattling apart.

He got to the foyer, ready to rush out, only to

crash into Ben.

His brother staggered back. "I have heard rumors of great drama afoot, but I had to see for myself." And then Ben stopped and looked at Will. "Oh God," he said. "Who murdered your dog?"

"I don't own a dog," Will ground out, needing to get away from Ben. He flexed his hands.

He'd never noticed it before. How had he not noticed? But Ben was the perfect image of their mother. With his curling dark hair. His playful eyes and his teasing.

Ben had barely known her, but he saw the world with her humor and light.

Will's throat closed. He missed her. God, how he missed her. And that missing had finally come to complete catastrophe this morning.

"It's a figure of speech, old man," Ben said softly.

Will shot him a fierce glare. "Margaret is not going to marry Kit, and apparently my wife loves me."

Ben's brows rose. "Felicitations." He folded his arms across his chest and gave a carefree shrug. "I knew it all along, of course. It's a wonderful and happy event that Beatrice has finally told you. And now you can get over your foolishness and tell her that you love her, too."

He recoiled, appalled Ben would say such a thing. "She's asked me to leave."

Ben gaped at him, his dark hair wild as he shook his head. "What the devil are you talking about?"

"I do not love her," he bit out, furious that people kept bandying the word *love* about. It was like salt in his wounds. "I can't."

Ben rolled his eyes. "Will, that is the greatest lie

I've ever heard."

A muscle clenched in his jaw, and anger burned inside him. It did not matter that he admired Beatrice more than anyone in the world or that he longed for her presence like the night longs for the dawn.

"It is not," he stated. Could no one see but him? Was he alone in his determination to keep them all from pain? "I have been very careful to keep my feelings—"

"What?" Ben cut in. "Dry, boring, unimportant."

He was a complete disgrace, and the weight of it crushed him. Because everyone was in pain.

He'd failed at the only thing that had ever mattered to him.

"I've been patient with you, but there is a limit for even this absurdity," Ben challenged, throwing his hands up. "*Everything* that you have done is a shining example of the way that you *love* Beatrice. For God's sake, man, the way you look at her every moment of every bloody day is evidence that you *love* her."

"Cease, Ben," Will snapped, refusing to believe the rising tension in him was panic. "You are being ridiculous. I admire her. I respect her. I think she's marvelous. But love?" He scoffed. "I would never lose myself in that emotion."

"Bloody hell," Ben exclaimed. "You actually believe what you say."

He glared at his brother, unable to respond. He didn't love Beatrice. But God, he wanted her right now. He wanted her to wrap her arms around him and tell him it would all be well.

But perhaps there was a poison in his line. Perhaps all he could do, like his mother, was hurt people.

"Where the devil is Kit?" Ben demanded. "I heard—"

"Do not ask me about Kit, since you are such a fan of love," he bit out, knowing he was being a total arse but apparently unable to stop himself. "Ask Beatrice," he added, so full of emotions now he thought he might explode with them. "She seems to have all the answers."

With that, he turned away from his brother and strode out into the street.

He could not stay in the house.

Not that house.

The house that had been his mother's jewel for years.

A house that had been full of parties and fun and love.

Memories crashed back in on him as luxurious coaches raced passed on the road: memories of his mother's departure, of his father's misery, of looking for letters that never came.

Apparently, he was not going to be able to out-run that any longer.

Pain had been such a significant part of his life.

The loss of love.

He knew it so very well, he couldn't do it again.

Beatrice loved him? Surely she could not. And worse, if she did, such a thing would just be a precursor to a greater disaster. He could not risk that sort of pain again. He could not risk the erosion that it could cause in his life.

In *their* lives.

Look what was happening to poor Kit, who was asleep on the floor right now, blessedly unaware of the drama unfolding.

No, surely Beatrice did not mean it. Soon, she would come to her senses. Yes, she would make Margaret come to her senses, and they could all go back to the way things were. Staid. Careful.

He stopped himself and let out a curse.

Careful.

When had he chosen such a word by which to rule his life?

He'd always been so certain that he was bold, making decisions and living life to his fullest.

Being happy, as his mother had made him promise to be.

Bloody hell, he wasn't happy. Not at all.

He was living in fear, as she said, but fear had protected him.

Fear had protected Kit and Ben.

Fear kept them safe.

And by God, he was not about to throw his entire future away on the whims of a woman in love. He would not do that. His mother had died abroad; he had never seen her again.

The cruelty of that was beyond anything. And truly, only a fool would choose to risk their whole life on something so transitory as love.

Will walked, and walked, and walked.

He walked until his legs nearly gave out from under him and he was far out into the countryside beyond the new buildings that lined the West of London.

Soon, all of this would be city, he knew, but not yet.

Now, it was still wild.

The fields were full of rich, verdant grasses, the trees towered into the sky, and today it was blue.

The sun was setting slowly, its yellow hues turning to purple and gold.

Stars were coming out to dot the night sky.

He felt cold and alone and broken and more like a little boy than he had in his entire life.

It was hell.

He had faced brutal men and courts that happily would have crushed half of humanity, but Beatrice telling him that she loved him had been the worst of all.

For some men, no doubt, a declaration of love from such a woman would have been the greatest moment in their life.

Not for him. For him, it had woken the feeling of his entire life being yanked out from under him.

What was he going to do?

He wanted Beatrice.

He'd come to need her. Like air in his lungs. How would he breathe without her?

He wanted her so much he did not have words for it.

She brought a peace and a purpose to his life that he'd never felt, a joy and amusement and a feeling of accomplishment. She saw him in a way that no one else did. But love?

What would happen in a few years' time when that love caused them to act like fools, to do and say things, to have arguments that could not be bound or fixed or made better?

Was he attempting to live his mother's past?

Legs worn, he dropped down onto the cool, long grass of a field aside the deeply grooved, empty road out of London.

Night fell, and the stars glimmered overhead. He caught sight of a bright star.

It did not flicker; it shone steadily.

He stared at it and stared until he was not certain how much time had passed, but the night breeze blew through his hair, and for a second, he felt as if all the pain and all the fear had been blown away from him, because that star reminded him of something.

It reminded him of Beatrice—steady, strong, fierce, unwavering in her fire.

He doubted Beatrice, because he had known pain and loss, but she was not the past. She was not that pain or that loss. She was a star, blazing bright in the sky, casting light all the way down from the heavens to earth, touching him, teasing him, correcting him, daring him to do better.

He drew in a shuddering breath.

Did he love Beatrice? Had he been pretending all this time that he did not, when he did?

He tried to imagine his life without her now, letting her go, and all he could see was a black void without starlight.

It was a life he did not want to live, for it would be empty and cold and without reason.

She made him stronger, and she had cast a light on the fear that he had been living his life by. All this time, he had been so certain that he was the strong one, the one who was guiding everyone else, when in fact it had been his fear of letting go that had been ruling everything.

His fear of losing control and the safety that he had created.

All his cold swims and long walks and bold declarations in Parliament couldn't change one thing.

He was terrified that if he gave his love away, he would lose it. Once again, he would be abandoned and alone.

But there was one true thing: for the first time in his entire life, he'd felt safe, truly safe, with Beatrice, and he had thrown it away with a few words.

• • •

Beatrice forced herself to dress as she did every morning. She went through her rituals of bathing her face in cold water, of dressing her hair, of putting on a simple gown, of writing in her diary.

The words she wrote in it did not please her.

I dared to hope and told Will I loved him. I have never tasted the ash of such defeat. I cannot express how it feels. Perhaps, it would have been better, as he said, to have never fallen in love at all. But I cannot believe it to be true. I cannot feel as Will does. He claims it is nothing. But I know he lies. His heart is dark with mourning and has never shed its black weeds. He feels, oh, he feels so very much. If he would but let himself love, I know he could step into the light again.

Those words had been incredibly painful to scratch out in jetty ink.

In fact, her entire heart and soul felt as if it had been cut open, left to twist in pain with no recourse. In this moment, she almost wished a heart could break, for then she might not have to feel this deep dread that her life was going to be unbearably hollow now.

Much Ado About Nothing and all its joys seemed long gone. *Hamlet* came to mind instead. For she was no longer in a comedy. Tragedy had seized her up. There would be no happy endings, no merry weddings.

Only bitterness and grief.

How was it that but weeks ago she had been as content as one could be? But now? Having love and lost it was so full of discontent that she could scarce tolerate her own shadow.

Man delights not me, she thought to herself. She understood the doomed prince in a way she never had before. There was nothing to delight in man.

Everything they worked for... What would become of it? Oh, she did not doubt he would keep his promises, but the joy of doing it together? Of building something with him? That was gone now. And the grief of it tore through her with merciless force.

Still, she would not give way. That was not the kind of person that she was. There was still much to be done. People to help. And wrongs to be righted.

In fact, she realized as she drifted down the hall, attempting to walk with purpose but feeling leaden, those pursuits were all she had left. Luckily, they were valuable.

But her heart... Her dratted heart.

Beatrice swallowed, unable to think on it another moment lest she turn and go back to bed.

She headed down the stairs and into the foyer, wondering if Kit had woken yet.

When she came into the green salon, her brother-in-law pushed himself up onto two hands and stared blankly.

He swung his gaze to Beatrice, confused. "What the blazes happened?"

Beatrice folded her arms under her bosom. "The entire world has erupted in catastrophe."

"Has it, by God? My head certainly feels as if it has." And then his face crumpled. "Margaret..."

"Yes," Beatrice said, her heart sinking for him. Everyone was unhappy. She couldn't think of a single joyful soul at present. "Margaret."

"Whatever will I do?" he lamented.

"I do not know," she replied honestly, hating to see him like this but wishing he had chosen actions over such grand melancholy. Perhaps if he had, she and Will would—

No. This was not Kit's fault.

She gave him a sympathetic look, even as she felt her own sadness lacing its tight bands around her. "I do hope you're not going to sit here and wail away the rest of the day. Such a thing will not aid you."

She drew in slow breaths. Her own hopes for a great love were over now, but Kit's didn't have to be. After all, he was pining for it.

And Margaret did love him; she knew it. But her cousin needed to understand her new position before she could give herself to anyone again.

Kit eyed her warily. "I thought you might be a touch sympathetic. I always liked you, you know?"

"Yes," she returned, trying to be kind. "I do know. And the reason why you like me is because I am not silly and I will treat you as an equal and tell you the truth. Even if you don't like it."

He flinched. "Don't hold back."

"I shan't," she said, crossing to him and crouching down. "You have drunk yourself into a stupor, feeling sorry for yourself, because you do not understand Margaret's decision."

"She's here, isn't she?" He gazed upward, his voice thick. "I can sense it. She's upstairs."

Beatrice rolled her eyes. "Focus, Kit. Focus. Do you actually love her?"

He snapped his dark gaze back to her, his russet hair flopping over his forehead. "I love her greater than the sun, greater than the moon." And then he said, "Doubt thou the stars are fire? Doubt that—"

"No, no, Kit," she cut in, not having the patience. "Do not launch yourself into Shakespeare. Whilst I love the Bard, this is not the moment to use his words. Use your own."

"I love Margaret more than I can possibly say," he said honestly. "I felt so alone until I met her. Her smile, her eyes—"

She groaned and grabbed his hand, willing him to finally understand her point. She clasped his big, warm palm and gazed into his eyes, which resembled a poet's at present. She sighed, resigned she was going to have to get past his romantic notions to the core of his love. "No, no, Kit. Not her smile, not her eyes, not her beauty. Those are not things that will indicate that you love Margaret. Those are all physical; those will fade. What do you love about her?"

He gaped for a moment, apparently astonished by this idea.

Blowing out a breath, he easily began, "I love the way that she always sees people in their best light, how she always trusts that the darkest situation shall see the rise of the sun, how she always feels that things will turn out well, how she lifts people's spirits whenever she walks into a room, how she adores the written word, how she adores dancing…"

"Then you must tell her," Beatrice rushed, squeezing his hand, feeling hope for the first time that it might not end in total tragedy. Indeed, she felt far more hope for him than she could for herself. "You must tell her how much you love her and why, for right now she does not know if she is loved for herself or if she as loved as an ornament. And it is a very confusing thing for a young lady, for we are taught to be nothing more than our smiles. You must love her for more than her smile, Kit."

"I do," he swore. "So much."

"Then do something about it," Beatrice said tightly. Wishing the man she loved had not so easily run away. But he had, because, just as he had insisted, he did not love her.

He never would.

"Goodness," Kit said. "You really are fierce about this, aren't you?"

"It is your life," she pointed out, a bittersweet smile tilting her lips. "Would you wish me to be less?"

"No," he confessed. "Now. Would you be so kind

as to get me—"

"No, Kit," she said quickly, patting his hand. "I will not sort this out for you. You must do it yourself. But I have ordered you beef tea, which will at least get you started. You shall take care of yourself."

She looked away, her own sorrow heavy again now that Kit seemed to be on his way. "If only Will were sorted out so easily."

Ben strolled in behind them. "Yes, Will is in quite a state."

"I'm glad you agree," she said, standing. "I've never seen him like that. In fact, I had no idea he could be like that."

"Nor I," Ben agreed, worrying his lower lip.

"Do you think it's because he's finally been defied as a duke?" Kit asked.

"No. It is far worse," she whispered.

Ben nodded, his face creased with worry. "I do not think he's felt so much since he was a boy. Before Mama left us. It's an age-old wound. He's been covering it for years, and finally it's coming to the surface. I hope to God he doesn't really destroy everything because of it."

Beatrice dropped her gaze, wondering if her own future was slipping away with Will's wounds. "I hope so, too. I don't know if I can bear it."

Ben crossed to her, and, much to her amazement, he folded his arms about her. "I hope you don't mind me giving you a hug."

"Not at all," she said, her voice straining suddenly. "I could actually use one."

"Beatrice, we all love you," Ben said, holding tightly to her. "We all adore you, and he loves you, too, if he can but admit it."

"No," she lamented. "I don't think he does." A bitter laugh rolled over her lips. "Everyone loves me but the man I love. The irony is terrible. But I will not be so foolish as to not value my friends."

Ben did not argue or try to convince her that Will would come to his senses. A sob tore from her throat, and much to her horror, she buried her face against Ben's chest. "F-Forgive me."

Kit jumped to his feet and joined her and Ben in an embrace. "We shall always be here for you, dear sister. Even if our brother insists on his path."

"He's so bloody determined that none of us should ever be hurt again." Ben winced. "But damnation. The destruction of his determination is quite a thing to behold."

Those words silenced her. She contemplated how alone Will must have been for so many years to act so. "I do not think he will change. And I cannot blame him. He warned me before we wed. And like the fool I am, I wed him anyway."

"Oh, Beatrice." Ben shook his head. "He's damned stubborn, our elder."

Tears slipped down her cheeks, and she dashed them away. "What a coil. I'm a water pot."

Ben whipped out his handkerchief and dabbed at her face. "A marvelous water pot that we love."

She nodded, but she could not ignore the unsaid words: *even if Will cannot.*

CHAPTER TWENTY-SEVEN

"What the bloody hell are you two doing?" Ben demanded.

Kit and Will circled each other in the boxing arena.

They were looking for ins. Both ready for a damned good fight.

Will kept his guard up, as did Kit. They both eyed each other, hoping to find a moment, an opening in which they could swing at the other.

"We are taking out our feelings in the only way that men know how," Will replied drolly.

Ben rolled his eyes. "That is not true. The vast amounts of verse in the history of the canon of poetry suggest that men are absolutely capable of using words to describe their feelings."

Kit scowled, then jabbed forward.

The punch struck Will's jaw, and his head jerked back.

He laughed. It felt so damn good. Since his long walk and night with the stars, he'd been thinking. But now? Now, he needed to work it out with his fists.

"Perhaps," Kit said. "But I do not have adequate words right now to describe my distress at the fact that Margaret is traipsing about town, following Beatrice to every political event and charitable meeting that Beatrice has on her list."

"You should be damn glad that's what she

actually likes," Ben retorted. "And let's be correct. She's attending those *and* every art gallery in London."

Kit scowled again and pulled his guard up, but this time, Will swung in, spun round, and jabbed his fist into Kit's back. Kit winced, nearly went down to the floor, but bounced up fast and circled around the ring.

It was impossible now not to think of boxing and Beatrice in the same sentence. How he longed for the accord that he'd felt with her that day.

But they could never go back.

No, there was only forward. He had no idea what that would be yet, but he would not hold himself back any longer. Of that he was certain.

And he hoped the same for Kit.

Will had made a complete muck of things with Beatrice.

He cringed at the things he'd said. It had struck him that the best thing he could do was give her and Margaret time. To realize that he was not going to sweep in and attempt to control their every action.

He was a duke. It was difficult not to storm in and make everything right. Or at least the way he thought it should be.

But there was one true thing in all of this. Every damn day without Beatrice was hell; there was no questioning it.

He *needed* her by his side. In one short month, that had become utterly clear to him. But he had no idea if he could win her back.

He couldn't go on merely existing. And that's all he would have without her.

Right now, he was putting on a show for his brothers. He didn't wish them to worry. But every damn moment was agony, a battle not to choose a gin bottle or a dark room that matched his soul.

He'd been capable before, and he would continue to be capable, but without her by his side, it was so meaningless and brutal.

He hadn't known joy until Beatrice. And now, joy was gone. Hell, he didn't even have mere contentment. Every breath was riddled with pain.

Yes, Beatrice was his air. Without her, he was in a suffocating wasteland.

Like an arrogant duke, he'd not realized how she'd made herself absolutely integral to his life. He loved hearing her thoughts on his speeches and positions at the end of every day. No one critiqued him like she did. No one skewered his mistakes with such wit. And she prepared him the best for debates because she had a better mind than most of the men around him.

He missed the way the light played on her skin, as if it adored her as much as he did. He missed the caress of her long hair across his chest as they slept. He missed the feel of her body next to his, taking up most of the great bed.

Consumed with Beatrice, he didn't see the blow coming.

Kit drove his fist into his belly, and he realized he was doing the exact thing he had told Beatrice not to do. He was standing still.

Standing still in life, too.

What a bloody disappointment he was.

He maneuvered around the boxing ring, light on

the balls of his feet. People were gathering, watching, wondering, because gossip had broken, of course, that Kit's marriage had not taken place.

So other club members were now taking bets on which brother would win, because rumors, too, had made the rounds that Beatrice and he were not on speaking terms.

Rumors were the bloody devil.

Ben leaned against the ropes. "I never knew that I had such unintelligent brothers. I always looked up to you, my elder brothers, my wonderful brothers, capable brothers with awe and respect. I always thought, yes, those are the men I should aspire to be. Now I think, good God, please save me from your fate. Can you not pull yourselves together? Can you not deduce what it is that you are meant to do?"

Kit and Will swung him hard glares.

"You've never been in love," Kit growled. "You have not set yourself into the arena of it. You have nothing to say."

Ben scowled. "That is not true. I think I understand ladies far better than the two of you. I have a great deal to say. And I say, there's only one thing to do."

"What?" Kit demanded, turning toward him.

Ben gave them a look that suggested they were completely without wits. "Listen to them, listen to what they want, and then give it to them." He folded his arms across his linen-clad chest and concluded, "It is the best way forward."

Will marched over to the ropes, grabbed Ben by the collar, and hauled him over. "Kit, you take a break. This one needs a go around."

Ben laughed. "Whatever you command, old man."

He rolled up his sleeves, brought up his guard, circled round with Will, and launched a punch so hard into Will's cheek that Will staggered back.

"I'm going to give you matching sets of bruises," Ben said. "You're in need of them."

Will leveled his youngest brother with a startled look, shaken. He'd always protected Ben. He could still remember when he'd toddled to him as a baby, wishing no one else to pick him up when lost after their mother's departure. It seemed Ben had abandoned sentiment in favor of hard blows. "What have you been holding back all these years, puppy?"

"My disdain for you," he bit out. "I've always held you in respect, elder, always kept myself in check because I did not want to bring you low. But now? I'm not sure. How can you keep Beatrice waiting?"

Each word cut. Did Ben think so little of him? Of course he did. And he was right to. He'd failed everyone. And he did not know how to lift himself out of shadow. "Puppy, I had no idea that you were so capable."

"I know," Ben said tightly, bouncing. "You do not think that I'm capable. You did not think Kit was capable. Or at least not capable of taking care of ourselves without you to pick us up. You're always protecting us, Will. And I have loved you for it," he said loudly.

Will winced. "You needn't use that word."

"Why not?" Ben countered. "It's true. I *love* you, brother."

Each use of the word "love" was like a dagger driving into his heart. Or…was it something else? Was the pain purging a poison that had festered far too long?

For how else could he describe his feelings for his brothers, if not love?

But surely that was different?

The crowd gathering around was milling and making quite a lot of noise, for men did not usually use this word.

But they'd all known so much gossip as of late that they no longer seemed to care what people thought.

It was damned refreshing.

He stared at his brother, who seemed to be standing on a precipice, waiting.

And in that moment, Will realized he'd never told Ben.

"I love you, too," Will admitted at last, his jaw nearly sticking. But it felt damned good to say it. For he did. He had carried his baby brother. He had picked him up when he'd fallen, sobbing as only small children could. He had soothed his hurts and held his hand in the dark whilst they laid alone, all motherly love gone.

"Glad to hear it," Ben drawled. The admission was not enough, it seemed. "Glad you even know how to use the word aloud."

Ben leveled him with a hard stare. "You should try using it with someone else."

Will dropped his guard and pulled Ben over to Kit. His gut twisted as he tried to admit his feeling, his fear. The words died in his throat. He couldn't say it. He just couldn't. And so, he said, "I had a come-to-reckoning moment in a field with a star."

Ben coughed. "I beg your pardon? I did not see you at the gin, but—"

"Beatrice is my lodestar," Will cut in. "Truly. There is no way around that, but the problem is I have made her furious, and rightly so. I have no idea how to allow myself back into her good graces. She may never allow me to, because I have made the worst of all possible errors."

Will could not stand still. He had too much energy. Too much emotion trapped within.

So, Ben nodded for them to begin again.

Again, they circled, eyeing each other.

But this time, his true feelings beginning to break to the surface, Will spun in and drove his fist into Ben's kidney.

Ben let out a yelp.

"I'm not defeated yet, puppy," Will said as emotion of a different kind began to take hold of him.

"Never thought you were, brother; otherwise, I wouldn't be here," Ben wheezed. "I have not yet given up hope. Hope springs eternal, after all. What have you done, then, that is so heinous?"

Ben and Will put down their fists, and the crowd let up a groan of disapproval, no doubt hoping for a clear win.

He and Ben ignored them.

From outside the ring, Kit threw him a linen towel. "What did you do that was so unforgivable?"

"I blamed Margaret's emotions for the whole situation."

Kit cringed. "She is not to blame, Will. She's a

victim in this."

Will hung his head. "You've better sense than I, but I saw your suffering—"

"You can't protect me from being hurt, Will. It's life, for God's sake." Kit threw him his shirt.

He stared at his brother, trying to make sense of Kit's simple acceptance of his wounds. How was it that both of his younger brothers seemed to understand the world so much better than he?

And how had he made such vast mistakes? Mistakes from which he might never recover.

Ben reached forward and grabbed his shoulder. "Mama left us all, but she made a bold choice. It didn't end well, it's true, but you don't have to have the same fate that she did. You don't have to be unhappy. And you don't have to be alone."

Will sucked in a long breath; his lungs tightened, and his chest began to shudder. Ben grabbed him and pulled him close. At first, he thought he was about to wrestle him, but then he realized that Ben was embracing him.

He sucked in another deep breath at his youngest brother's kindness.

"It's all right, you know," Ben said softly. "If you want to cry, you can. You've been strong long enough. We don't have to be so very English all the time."

Will held on to Ben tight. "I know I can, scamp. I know I can with you if I want. I'm sorry for everything. You're the best of brothers, Ben." And he turned to Kit. "As are you."

Kit yanked on his shirt, then joined the embrace.

And the three of them stood there, hugging each

other, while people stared as if they'd lost all sense of propriety.

Will didn't give a bloody damn. He didn't care what other people thought anymore. He only cared about his brothers and Beatrice and Margaret, because the truth was, that's all that was worth caring about. He did not have to suffer the same fate as his mother.

He did not have to be afraid, and he could take a chance, and perhaps he would be happy.

Just as his mother had made him promise to be.

It was certainly worth the risk, because he wasn't going to spend the rest of his life living like this.

But was it too late? He'd already shoved Beatrice out of his life. The things he said. She might never let him back in.

He grabbed Ben by the shoulders, looked him in the eyes, and said, "Thank you. Thank you for telling me exactly what I needed to hear."

Ben's eyes lit with hope. "I'll do it every day for the rest of your life if you like. I don't mind."

"You'd better, brother," he said, pulling him back into a hard hug. "I'll need constant reminding. It's too easy to slip into one's old ways."

"Now?" Ben asked. "Now that we've eschewed all that stoic nonsense, what the devil are you going to do? She's heartbroken, Will."

And she might never forgive him. Perhaps she shouldn't.

Will bit down on the inside of his cheek, hating himself for hurting her. It was the one thing for which he could never forgive himself. But he had to try to make it right. It was time to make peace with his past.

• • •

Will stared at Sylvia.

The portrait of his mother hung in such pride of place. He'd put her there after his father had taken her down and put her in a back room with her face to the wall. He supposed it was because the old man had not been able to bear looking at her, a painful reminder of his failures.

But it also meant that Will and his brothers had not been able to look upon the glorious portrait by Gainsborough, either. And he'd felt the loss for years, until finally he'd become the next Duke of Blackheath.

After his father had sighed out his last breath, Will had brought the portrait back, and he had hung it up so that everyone could look upon it and know that he was not ashamed of her.

He'd never understood why she'd left, but something had happened to him in the last few days. He'd torn through the chests and boxes in the attics. He'd gone through every last box and every last desk drawer.

Driven.

Driven to find answers.

And he'd found them.

He'd found letters.

Stacks and stacks of letters bound with red ribbon.

The missives were between his father and mother. He had no idea how they'd all been brought together. Perhaps his father's letters had been sent back on his wife's death and his father had put them together.

Will had not been able to read them without breaking down. And it had felt like a great tide had picked him up and swept him out to sea. A sea of so much regret, but finally…understanding.

Over the years she'd been abroad, she'd sent countless letters, begging to see her children.

His father had refused.

Beatrice was right.

And the law had been on his father's side. His mother had had no rights whatsoever to see her children again.

Will had thought of all the nights he and Ben and Kit had cried themselves to sleep, pretending they weren't letting tears fall. Hiding under the blankets, holding on to one another.

And in that moment, he wished he could throttle his father.

His father and his pain had caused so much more suffering.

And those letters — the words on them had burned into Will's soul forever.

With those pleas from his mother and denials from his father, he had come to a single understanding in almost an instant of transformation. It echoed Beatrice's claim.

His mother had not abandoned them.

She had been *kept* from them.

And if he could find a way to choose love and gain Beatrice's forgiveness, perhaps he would be choosing happiness for his mother.

If he chose to take a chance, he would be honoring her.

He would be bringing a better end to the

suffering she had engaged in and make her loss have some meaning.

He had also noticed in the letters that she was not entirely unhappy, that she had indeed found love with this man abroad, but it had never been quite able to fill the vacancy of being forced from her children.

Time and time again, she'd asked to see them, and time and time again, she'd been denied.

Because of the law. Because of power. Because of his father's pride and arrogance.

Tears stole down his cheeks, and he wrapped his arms around himself, thinking of her longing for her children so many miles away.

He held a different stack of letters in his hand as he gazed up at his mother. Letters written by Beatrice. Those letters had stolen his heart long before he had even met her in person. And he had clung to lies and the expectations of his father when he had denied himself her love.

He had denied so much.

But Beatrice was right. Perfection was not possible—and he no longer wanted it. There was only one thing he wanted now, but he feared he had thrown it away. He tightened his grip on the letters, as if he could somehow bring her back, holding them as if he'd never let them go.

But he had let *her* go.

She'd tried to make him see, but he had clung to familiar lies. Lies about his mother. Lies he had told himself about who he had to be...

At long last, he let the suffering out. In shuddering waves, he knew there was nothing to forgive his mother for. She was the one who needed amends.

And there was only one way to give it.

He would not be the taciturn man that his father was. Oh, no. He was going to be greater. He was going to be more.

He had to be. No matter if she could forgive him, he could never let Beatrice down the way his mother had been let down.

CHAPTER TWENTY-EIGHT

Every day was brutally hard—far harder than Beatrice had expected.

She grimaced as she strode toward Parliament along Pall Mall. Spotting the Palace of Westminster and the cathedral usually invigorated her. A sense of purpose and determination typically flooded her as she made ready to do battle against those determined to keep her in her place.

Not today.

Today, each step felt as if she were slogging through mud. But a short time ago, she was content, independent, and pursuing her cause.

Now? There was a hole in her heart where William should have been but chose not to be.

How the devil was she going to survive this? She would, though. She knew one couldn't die from a broken heart, but oh, how she felt but a shadow of herself.

It seemed terribly cruel to have discovered a partner with whom to face the world, only to have that partner abandon her.

Margaret was but a step behind her, talking with one of her friends, veritably skipping along in her sense of purpose.

If she could be happy at all, it was for Margaret, who had seemed to discover herself. It was truly a wonderful sight to behold, seeing Margaret realize she was more than just a beautiful young lady destined to wed.

There was an air of melancholy about her cousin, though. As if the cost of her newfound knowledge had been high indeed.

The box of pamphlets weighed Beatrice's arms heavily today. This outing did not seem to be as helpful as she hoped it might be.

But she could not stay in William's great town-house alone and stare out the window, wishing that he'd come to his senses.

Though her heart ached, she wouldn't allow her-self to succumb to misery. Even if she felt miserable.

It was interminable, her present state. Not that her worth was based on a man's love, but that she had lost her dearest friend.

And for what?

She winced.

She wouldn't allow herself to think on it.

No, she'd allow the day's work to carry her through. It was the only thing that did. Besides, she absolutely loved making trouble for the stodgy old men who would pass her by.

Or at least she had.

None of it filled her with the cheer it had once done.

It wasn't fair, the way things had gone, but it had also been unfair of her to expect him to behave dif-ferently than he'd promised.

He was a duke, after all, and dukes did have a tendency to be distant, arrogant, and emotionally cold. He'd warned her.

And yet, hope had sparked in her heart. It had been a ridiculous thing to hope. She had no one to blame but herself.

Yes, Will had made it very clear what he wanted and did not want.

And he didn't want to love her.

It was she who had not been able to abide by the rules. In all events, she was glad she had stood by Maggie, because Maggie was blossoming every day.

Their poor uncle was in his house, awaiting financial disaster, which had not yet seemed to come. He sent them missives often, asking if they were well. And of course, every time he saw his daughter, he hoped that she had reconsidered and would marry Kit.

She understood why. Of course he wished to see Maggie safe and secure.

He loved his daughter.

But such petitions would not maneuver Maggie. She'd learned she had her own will, and she'd also learned that knowing herself would allow her to know if she *truly* loved Kit.

Perhaps one day soon, perhaps love could blossom again…if Kit could wait and still loved Maggie's adventurous new self.

Beatrice, too, was discovering she was stronger than she had ever known, but she didn't always enjoy it.

Sometimes strength was painful.

Sometimes she wished she could just run back to Will and tell him that yes, of course she would do whatever he wished. Love was indeed a preposterous thing, and it was ludicrous that she'd even consider it.

But she knew she couldn't do that. It would be a

lie and disservice to all of them.

She trudged on as they neared the towering facade of the cathedral and sprawling old palace. Her
feelings continued to match the gloom of the gray
clouds.

A vast crowd milled before the palace, and she
hesitated.

There was something different transpiring this
day.

Usually there were vast amounts of people making their way along the bank, but today there were
hundreds, and they all seemed gathered, waiting for
someone to speak.

They were gathered around a temporarily erect-
ed stage, the type usually used by parliamentarians
when speaking to their voters. The smell of fresh-cut
wood played in the air—a much nicer aroma than
London's usual scent of so many living cheek by
jowl.

She blinked as her booted feet slowed on the
cobbles.

Atop the stage stood a rather imposing figure in
a long black coat and top hat. Fawn breeches clung
to hard legs, and a sapphire pin winked in his black
cravat. The jewel matched his brocade waistcoat.

And today, it matched his eyes, too, for they
shone with determination…and an emotion she
couldn't quite identify. He did not seem like his
confident self. Oh, he was strong, and his presence
dominated the gathering, but there was something
else.

She gasped, her heart leaping into her throat.

Will.

He stood, shoulders back, coat swinging about his long limbs as he called out to the crowd that had clearly gathered to watch the famous Duke of Blackheath.

Those raucous Londoners from every walk of life, united in their desire to listen to the duke, might have come to see him, but Beatrice knew that stage was a promise he had made to *her*.

The pace of her heart increased, and she couldn't draw breath. Did she dare hope? Or did that make her a greater fool?

He'd been so emphatic in his denial of love. Did he think he could win her back with mollification? She could not endure empty gestures.

In fact, dread began to pool in her stomach. For surely a man as powerful as William was certain she would give in and yield to a marriage of convenience in which he could deny vulnerability and love.

As she listened, she caught snippets of the importance of supporting the Ladies' League of Rights. His deep voice boomed in the air, and people applauded.

It was refreshing to hear a duke defend the cause of women, and it filled her with a melancholy so deep, tears stung her eyes.

He was a wonder. She only wished that he was *her* wonder.

The duke caught sight of her, and he stilled. For several seconds, he held her gaze across the crowd. For a moment, the cacophony of the rowdy audience dimmed, and there was no one and nothing but the two of them before the old palace on the bank of the mighty Thames. Tears stung her eyes, but she refused to shed them. Oh, how she had missed him. But she couldn't have him. Not like this. For she felt deep in her heart, after all he had said, that this would be naught more than a grand gesture to appease her.

Grand gestures meant nothing without love. Such a thing would prove as rotten as the decaying palace that held Parliament.

"I have an announcement," he declared in a voice that soared easily through the din. "So, if everyone could please listen."

One man piped loudly, "Oh, governor, we'll listen to you all day. You talk good things, you do."

Will grinned at that. "Thank you, sir. Thank you. I shall count on your vote in the next election when my man stands for a seat."

"And you shall have it," another voice cried from the crowds.

"And the ladies will vote, too, when we have a chance," a lady shouted, her bonnet bobbing.

Will bowed to her. "I shall fight to make that happen," he announced.

And there was a great cheer and round of applause.

He held out his hands to silence them. "But this is a different announcement. If you will all make way for the Duchess of Blackheath."

The crowd turned in waves and spotted her.

Just as the duke commanded—something he was entirely used to, no doubt—they parted to allow her to walk easily to the stage.

"Beatrice," he called, holding out his black gloved hand to her. "Duchess, will you join me?"

Under the watchful eye of so many, for a

moment, she couldn't move. How she longed to go to him. To take his outstretched hand and feel his arms about her again.

But she couldn't betray herself. And so, she took a step back into the thick crowd and then another.

If he couldn't love her, she would have to love herself, and she wouldn't be made a fool of simply so that he could have his duchess returned to him.

She was more than that. She desired more than that. Even if it hurt more than she could ever say.

CHAPTER TWENTY-NINE

The plan was failing before his very eyes.

William stood atop the platform, his brain stuttering as Beatrice stepped in the wrong direction. Away from him.

Failure loomed, and the darkest part of him whispered that he should simply accept it. Beatrice had made her decision.

But he couldn't. He couldn't let her go without giving it every last bit he had.

He dropped to his knee before the vast crowd, stretched out his gloved hand, and called, "My dear Lady Disdain, do not give up just yet. I beg of you to stay and listen to my case. Join me."

She stilled, her shoulders tense beneath her green spencer, as if she feared the worst from him. "I don't have a speech prepared, Your Grace."

"You don't need one," he said honestly, keeping his hand aloft, willing her to take it. Willing her to give him one last chance. For how would he be able to do anything but merely survive without his Beatrice? "I'm the one giving a speech today."

The world seemed to pause on its axis as he waited to see if she would take up his hand and at least listen.

She did not let her gaze swing from his, and though there were shadows of pain in her eyes, she boldly crossed through the parted crowd and climbed the roughly hewn wooden stairs to stand before him.

He lowered his hand and cleared his throat, desperate to begin. "Will you put the box of pamphlets down?"

"Oh!" She looked down, clearly having forgotten she was carrying the box of her precious papers. He loved that she had not ceased in her endeavors these weeks. Nothing would daunt her. Not even a damned disappointing duke.

She nodded, then placed the box carefully on the stage. "I will be passing them out later," she informed him.

Gently, he took the box, and their gloved fingertips brushed for a single instant—and in that instant, he could not speak as a flash of longing went through him. Carefully, he placed her box down and slipped his own paper from his pocket.

Beatrice folded her hands before her. She shifted on her boots, and he realized that, for the first time ever in the time he had known her, she appeared nervous.

"I would expect nothing less," he replied, full of admiration for her. Full of hope and fear at once. "Now, if you will but listen?"

"As you wish," she whispered, her voice barely audible above the gathered people.

There was something about that voice of hers that did the most powerful things to his soul, and he knew he couldn't lose it. For if he did, it would be no one's fault but his own.

The crowd went oddly silent as he took a step forward.

Even the bustling carriages and coaches on the

road by them did not seem to penetrate the reverie
that took them all up.

Will drew in a long breath, trying to shake the
apprehension in his body that she would not be won
by his words. He unfolded the thick paper, scanned
his scrawled hand, and then he folded it again and
held it to his heart.

He closed his eyes, willing himself to have the
strength he needed to be honest.

"Ladies and gentlemen," he began, his voice
rougher than usual, for he understood what was to
be lost and won. "I am a difficult man; I know this to
be true. I like things the way I like them, as dukes
often do. When I met the Duchess of Blackheath, I
was prepared to loathe her."

He caught sight of her standing but a few feet
away.

She flinched. And his chest tightened. He
couldn't make a muck of this. He couldn't, but it appeared as if she was ready to flee.

He refused to back down. For such a woman as
Beatrice? He had to be willing to risk it all.

She stayed standing as still as a column, her face
a mask.

At that look, he forced himself to continue, "I
hated the way she castigated me. I hated the way
that she corrected me. I hated the way that she made
me feel as if I was not doing enough. I hated the way
that she made me feel as if I was not listening to her.
And I hated the way that when I danced with her on
that first encounter…"

He hesitated and met her gaze again, trying to
infuse his deep love for her into that look. Would

she see it? Would she understand?

"I tripped on the floor because she distracted me so. I hated the way she made me wish to throw all the things that I had promised myself away. I hated how she showed me my fears."

His voice grew rough, and he drew in a steadying breath. "I hated that when I was with her, I could think of nothing but making her smile and pleasing her. I hated the way I could not shake her from my thoughts, no matter what I did. And I hated the fact that I could *not* allow myself to fall in love with her."

Her breath caught in her throat, and she covered her mouth with her hands to stifle a gasp, but not before he heard it. Suddenly, his heart soared with hope. Perhaps it was not all in vain.

Emotion flooded through him as he finally gave his heart its freedom.

Tears filled her eyes, and her hands seemed to clasp even tighter as she waited. Waited for him to dare.

Every instinct told Will to swallow back his emotion. To remain stoic. But he was done with that. So instead, he quieted and listened to the whispers of his heart.

His passion shook him and poured out on a tide with his voice reverberating for all to hear. "You see, I had promised myself I never would love, and I had never meant to break a promise to myself."

Unable to bear the distance any longer, Will crossed to her and took her hand, lifting it reverently. He turned from the crowd and spoke to the woman he loved. The woman who had changed his life and woken him up from a never-ending nightmare of loneliness and sorrow.

"But the truth is, I love the way you make me feel not alone in this world. I love the way you correct me and make me better. I love the way you help me build a better world, and I love you, my darling Beatrice. All of you. From your passion to your pamphlets to your perfect person. This is for you," he said gently, handing her the pamphlet he had written that cited everything he had spoken of just now.

His words trailed off as he looked down on his wife. The silence echoed in his ears, and he felt as a man waiting to hear if he was to dance at Tyburn.

She took the creamy paper in her hands and was silent as she took in his words written in black ink. Her gaze seemed to linger on the top line, *Why I love Beatrice*, printed in bold letters.

Her eyes shone with emotion as she shook her head in disbelief.

"You love me," she whispered.

He took a step forward, his boot caressing the hem of her skirt. He cocked his head to the side, taking in his magnificent wife, and nodded.

She stared up at him, lips slightly parted, as if she could not quite reply.

For one brief moment he feared she would tell him it was not enough.

But then she seized the lapels of his wool coat and hauled him downward. She popped up onto her booted toes and took his mouth in a wild, wonderful kiss.

As their mouths met, the tension and fear left his body, and he knew with all his being that the world was well and all would be right.

Joy coursed through his veins, and he wrapped his arms about her, sweeping her up into a deeper kiss, not caring two whits who was watching. He wanted the world to know that he had finally admitted his love. He was the luckiest man upon the globe, after all.

The crowd erupted in cheers and applause so loud he could barely countenance it.

With a sigh of relief and contentment, she pulled back and held her hands behind his neck.

"Do you like the stage?" he asked, his eyes alight at last, as if all the love he had been hiding was now on full view. "Shall we take it around the country?"

"Oh yes," she breathed. She beamed at him, still stunned. "Am I dreaming?"

"If you are," he said over the crowd, "let us never wake. You are my lodestar, my shining light, my partner, Beatrice." He brought her hand to his chest, his eyes searching her face. "And I hope and pray that it is not too late and that I have not lost you. Will you stay by my side?"

A tear slipped down her cheek, and she bit her lower lip before her mouth curved into an irrepressible smile. A cry of happiness burst past her lips. "Yes."

"Can you love me, too, then?" he breathed, finally feeling as if the weight of all his sorrows was lifting.

"Oh, Will." She laughed as she wiped a tear away. "Need you ask? I love you with my every breath, and I always will."

And with that reply, his life changed forever. Gone was the fear, the distance, the control.

All of it replaced by his love.

CHAPTER THIRTY

"Right, Queensbury rules. Nothing below the belt! Keep it clean," Ben called from the center of the empty ballroom, which they had made up as a makeshift boxing ring.

Ben strode around, his boots thudding on the waxed wood floor, waving a white handkerchief as if to imply someone was going to have to surrender in a war.

If there was going to be a war, it would be a merry one. And if someone was going to have to admit defeat, it certainly wasn't going to be Beatrice—of that she was certain.

Today, she felt undefeatable. And why shouldn't she in her new set of clothes? She absolutely loved the feel of her fawn breeches and linen shirt. They easily hugged her frame, skimming her body like a caress, and she felt so free she wanted to skip and dance.

Who wanted to dance a waltz or a quadrille in a skirt? Not she! Goodness, she would be able to take the ballroom floor like a bounding mountain goat in this outfit. No wonder gentlemen led in dances; they had such freedom of movement. She could not wait to try boxing in it.

The Hessians? They were trickier. New, she hadn't been able to get them on herself. Will had helped pull them on, which had resulted in fits of laughter and an embrace or two that had nearly made them late for their boxing appointment.

Will gazed at her with that look he had, one that ignited her blood and filled her with so much love she did not know how she could contain it all. It was tender, but it also…smoldered, sending a heat through her that tempted her to grab his hand and drag him back to the bed chamber.

Ben cleared his throat. "Now, now," he said. "I don't want to have to vacate the premises already. I have come here to see a match."

The three of them had been spending a vast deal of time together since that day at Parliament. She adored Ben. He was such a good brother to her. She'd had so little family for so long, having only her cousin and uncle to keep her company, and now she had found a veritable army of brothers to make her feel at home.

It was wonderful. And Ben was always teasing her, which was the very best. She gave her brother-in-law a bow. "And we should hate to disappoint you."

"Hear, hear," declared Ben. "Well said."

"I know it is novel, but I wish to spend time with my wife, and we were quite occupied—"

"Yes, thank you," cut in Ben. "I'm delighted for your connubial bliss and all that, but I have an appointment in an hour at… Never mind where."

"You're going to get sent down from Oxford again, aren't you?" Will groaned.

Ben grinned cheekily. "One can only hope."

"Then we best get on with it," Beatrice announced, knowing how Ben loved to tease his brother. "Are you ready to face me, husband?"

Will gave her a grin. "I'm quaking in my boots."

"That doesn't sound like you," she pointed out, rolling up her cuffs to bare her forearms.

"I have turned a new leaf," he replied, mirroring her, revealing those muscled arms she loved so well.

They had been boxing with each other now every day for several weeks, and she adored it. She loved the feel of his body against hers when they would collide, and he was such an excellent instructor that she felt quite capable.

If anyone ever accosted her in an alley, she was ready to pop the blighter right on the nose. Not that she was planning to go down any alleys anytime soon, but it was quite nice to feel accomplished and self-possessed in more than ways of just political bent.

And she'd never have to worry about drunken lords letting their hands wander during a dance ever again. She was considering the benefits of having Will instruct the ladies of the league in the art of boxing.

She knew he'd say yes. He'd come to realize just how impossible gentlemen could be when a lady attempted to declare herself equal to a man.

Beatrice walked across the line that framed the temporary boxing ring. Her husband came in, too. They touched knuckles and took their stances.

"All right, Beatrice," Ben hollered from the sideline. "Shuffle! Shuffle to the left."

She did as her brother-in-law instructed, for he was an equally good coach as her husband, and she had a strong feeling he had a vested interest in her besting his brother. If only for the amusement of it.

Though she did not think she ever truly could. Will was such an excellent boxer, but one never knew; with enough practice, anything was possible.

Will circled the other way.

Both of them eyed each other, looking for an in.

She did not try to get close to him. No, she had to be patient and clever.

She did as he had taught her so many weeks ago. She began dancing right, then to the left, whirling about him, making him maneuver and go about the ring, chasing her.

Her cheeks flushed, and his eyes sparked at the game.

Will did his best to stay at the center, but if he wished to land a blow he would have to come after her, and so she kept him on his toes.

She grinned at him. "Tiring out, are you?"

"He's an old man, after all," Ben drawled. "If you work him hard enough, he'll collapse like an ox."

She laughed.

The very idea was absurd, of course. Will had the stamina of…well, an ox. It was one of the things that she absolutely adored about their married life. Nothing slowed him. Certainly not their merrymaking.

As they went about the ring, Will kept his guard up. For though he would never hurt her, he would also not humor her. It was something else she admired about him. He did not treat her like a doll, even if he was careful.

And then she spotted an in.

Beatrice darted forward and aimed a jab. Will blocked her blow with his sculpted forearm, and she winced at the strength of his body, which was akin to a brick wall. But she reveled in the fact that she was so strong.

He'd shown her strength of body. And it was a delicious thing.

Will gave her a quick nod. "Well done, Beatrice."

"Come on now, Beatrice," Ben called from the side. "I've got money on you—a whole bag of gold. I don't want to lose it to my elder."

She smiled at his encouragement but did not look at Ben, because if she did, of course, she could end up flat on the floor. Will had a deft way of being able to get her down on the ground without harming her. Then usually he would kiss her, which led to other forms of exercise—something that he would not do with Ben present, thank goodness.

She quickly darted back, and as they circled again and again, both of them began to breathe heavily. The exertion was quite something to behold. She found that boxing was far more taxing than a good long walk or a ride upon a horse or even a dance. She loved the feel of her body in her clothes, stretching, working, testing its limits as she'd never been allowed to do before.

She felt so liberated, so exhilarated with Will as her ally.

Will moved to the right a little too fast, and she spotted another chance. She wove nimbly in, and this time she jabbed right into Will's lower back.

He let out a grunt, then whirled around and grabbed her in his arms.

"I've got you now," he said as he headed for the edge of the ring.

And just as he gave her a satisfied smile, she delivered an uppercut, and his chin went back.

She beamed up at him, and he gave her a wolfish look of pleasure at her success. Pride shone in his eyes.

At that look, she felt overcome with feelings for him.

Will smiled down at her as he adjusted his jaw. "You're learning so fast," he marveled.

"Well, I have a wonderful teacher," she said, her guard still up, and yet she couldn't deny the fact that she longed to be in Will's arms rather than circling him.

Will's gaze warmed as he recognized her feelings, and his fists lowered ever so slightly.

Ben cleared his throat. "And me," he pointed out. "You've got me, too, but suddenly I am feeling rather malaprop. I think I should make my departure, for the two of you are exchanging glances that are completely inappropriate for boxing partners. The scandal."

She laughed, her heart so full of happiness. "Ben, you are the wisest of men and know exactly when one should retreat."

He waved his white handkerchief. "Indeed, sister mine. I know the moment when a man is no longer wanted, even if he is loved."

With that, Ben gave a bow and quickly departed through the ballroom door.

She gazed up at her husband. "I loved your gift," she said, stroking her hand along her linen shirt, which was now damp with perspiration.

"I would shower you with as many gifts as I

possibly could," he said softly.

"A lady doesn't need to be showered with gifts," she replied. "She just needs the right ones."

"And you find the breeches and the shirt to be the right ones?" he asked, crossing to her with that languid, self-possessed walk she loved so well.

She nibbled her lower lip. "I appreciate that you listened to me that night at the theater and that you recalled how much I longed to try these."

"I remember," he said, stroking a lock of her hair back from her face. He tucked it tenderly behind her ear. "And I valued then what you explained to me: the importance of a lady's ability to feel free. Beatrice, I would make it possible for you to climb any mountain that you chose."

She tilted her head back and felt her whole body fill with wonder. "I have the best gift of all, Will, without a mountain. I have you."

His eyes flared, and he pulled her into his arms.

"I'm so bloody lucky, Beatrice," he began. "So lucky you wrote me so many letters. So lucky you infuriated me. So lucky you did not give up on me."

"I?" she countered with faux shock. "Give up? Never say such a thing. I am not capable of it."

He cupped her cheek with his palm as love softened his hard visage. "Forgive me," he said. "I never should have disparaged you so."

"No," she agreed. "But I can see how a gentleman like you might wear others down. And it is I who am lucky."

"Oh?" he queried. "How so?"

"Because I found my equal," she confessed. "You are my partner, my friend, and my love."

"And you are mine," he replied as he trailed his thumb along her lower lip.

"Now, as much as I adore the cut of your clothes on your fine form...I think I should like to see you out of them."

"My sentiments exactly, my love," he replied. "Shall I help you with your boots?"

Beatrice tilted her face into his palm. "Absolutely, my love," she replied, happier than she'd ever been, ready to be in his arms. Now, forever, always.

EPILOGUE

A rumor was circulating London that Lord Christopher—Kit, to all who knew him—had, in a fit of romance, played the highwayman, kidnapped Lady Margaret out of her coach by the light of the moon, and stolen her away.

Of course, this was completely false.

Kit had approached Margaret right beside the stage that Will had set up by Parliament.

It was a day for proclamations and invitations.

And Kit, being a man determined to help his lady love achieve her desires, had suggested that they travel abroad and discover each other and the world.

Chaperoned. Because he had the good sense not to ask her to marry him that day.

Margaret had found the idea most appealing.

And of course, Beatrice was happy to fund Margaret's exploration of the world.

If she hadn't been so consumed in the running of so much of England, going abroad would have seemed an excellent plan for her, too.

Enraptured letters arrived almost daily, having been sent from coaching inns from Plymouth to Rome.

There was also rumor circulating the *ton* that they had been married in Naples.

This was blatantly true.

Ben had been in attendance.

He had written several long letters about the

getting of licenses and the creative negotiations at which he had excelled in that far-off land. His letter had also suggested that Kit and Margaret had discovered a shared passion for outdoor pursuits.

They were forever running off together into the forest, Ben complained. Though he seemed highly amused.

They brought her daily joy, those letters that proved that Margaret had come into her own. Apparently, she quite enjoyed the fall of evening.

Just as Beatrice did. Though Will did not limit himself to moonlight. Something Beatrice was quite grateful for.

She put her quill down and stretched, happily thinking about this morning, being awoken in their bed chamber by Will's exceptionally skilled mouth upon her—

There was a knock on her office door, and she stood. She knew that knock. Self-possessed and determined, could it belong to anyone but her husband?

Most definitely not.

"Come in," she called, and Will entered, a stack of pamphlets in his hand. He clutched them, full of eager enthusiasm as he strode across the room.

She laughed.

It reminded her dramatically of the night they had met, when she was so determined to make him see her point of view.

"Oh, dear," she said, "are you about to try to convince me of something?"

He arched a brow. "I am not about to convince you of anything," he said, "but I wish you to come and see something. Will you come?" he asked, brandishing the pamphlets.

She gazed at him suspiciously. "I suppose I shall. You're covered in ink, Will."

"Am I?" he asked. He stared down at himself, then laughed. He indeed was covered in black smudges.

"Damnation," he replied, his brows crooking with dismay. "I think I might be giving away what I'm about to show you."

"It has not," she assured, crossing around her desk. "I cannot guess."

He took her hand in his, winding their fingers together, his pamphlets still cradled in his arm, the fresh ink wreaking havoc on his linen shirt.

"Trust me," he said. And he guided her out of the room, through the hall, down the sprawling stairs, and into one of the studies on the first floor.

"What the devil are you doing?" she asked, completely flummoxed.

He positively beamed at her, so pleased it was like Christmas morning.

"I have something for you," he announced. He stood before her, leaned in, and whispered, "Close your eyes."

A laugh slipped past her lips at his infectious mood. "Will, we aren't children!"

"Beatrice, I thought you were made of bold stuff," he said with his eyes melodramatically wide with innocence.

She could not hide her grin, but she did as instructed. She was happy to humor him; he seemed so happy. It was a joy indeed to be with Will now, since he had eschewed the walls and glowering arrogance so inherent to dukes.

Will opened the door, and she stepped over the threshold with his guiding hand.

The decided scent of ink assaulted her senses.

"Open them," he instructed softly, his lips brushing her ear ever so slightly.

She did—and then she gasped with joy.

A great metal monstrosity met her view. "A printing press," she cried out.

"It is the best, the most up-to-date, and the finest," he declared, studying her, waiting for approval. "It will print more pamphlets for you faster than before, and you can do the typeset over here," he said, leading her to a beautiful set of block letters.

She leaned over, ready to examine them. But when she did, her throat tightened with emotion.

Will had already arranged the block letters, which could be rearranged in any order for the printing press. The letters formed a simple but profound quote.

I love you with so much of my heart none is left to protest.

Overcome, she reached out and stroked the words. "*Much Ado About Nothing*," she breathed.

Slowly, he reached out and lightly touched her hand. "Do you remember? When you set your hand on mine at the theater?"

She nodded, unable to reply.

"From that moment, I was yours, Beatrice. Always and forever."

She took his hand in hers and placed her other atop his. "Always and forever," she replied, her heart so full, she had no room for anything but their love.

ACKNOWLEDGMENTS

There are never adequate words to express all the thanks I have, but first and foremost, I must thank Esaul, Ciaran, Declan, and Fionn. You fine fellows are what keep me going and fill me with joy. You bring love to my world. A huge thank you to Elizabeth Pelletier for believing in my work, Lydia Sharp for always making it so much better, Alexander Te Pohe for helping me to hone my message into what I truly wanted, Curtis Svehlak for making it shine, Jill Marsal for being a guide, and the entire Entangled Amara production team.

Also, a huge thanks to Coochy, Kelly, and Matt for helping me to be myself.

And Elise, you human extraordinaire, thank you for being a sounding board and a light in the darkness.

AMARA

an imprint of Entangled Publishing LLC